MARBECK AND
THE PRIVATEERS

MARBECK AND THE PRIVATEERS

John Pilkington

This first world edition published 2014
in Great Britain and the USA by
SEVERN HOUSE PUBLISHERS LTD of
19 Cedar Road, Sutton, Surrey, England, SM2 5DA.

British Library Cataloguing in Publication Data

Pilkington, John, 1948 June 11- author.
   Marbeck and the privateers. – (A Martin Marbeck mystery ; 3)
   1. Marbeck, Martin (Fictitious character)–Fiction.
   2. Great Britain–History–James I, 1603-1625–Fiction.
   3. Spy stories.
   I. Title II. Series
   823.9'2-dc23

ISBN-13: 978-07278-8372-8 (cased)

All Severn House titles are printed on acid-free paper.

Severn House Publishers support the Forest Stewardship Council™ [FSC™],
the leading international forest certification organisation. All our titles that
are printed on FSC certified paper carry the FSC logo.

Typeset by Palimpsest Book Production Ltd.,
Falkirk, Stirlingshire, Scotland.
Printed and bound in Great Britain by
TJ International, Padstow, Cornwall.

PROLOGUE

I n the sweltering heat of Algiers, the prisoner was led through a dark passageway into a sun-drenched courtyard. He was bound, clad in a filthy loincloth, haggard and emaciated after weeks in the fetid, crowded bagnio that had been his prison. When the guards on either side of him halted he too stumbled to a halt, blinking in the harsh light, and found himself staring at a high wall: part of the battlements, of the city's defences. One of the guards grabbed his hair and pulled his head back, forcing him to look up . . . whereupon intense fear gripped him, like a cold hand on his stomach. In spite of the heat, he began to shiver.

Protruding from the wall were a number of large iron hooks, set firmly into the stonework, their points facing upwards. But it was the figures atop the wall that the prisoner stared at, for he saw what was about to happen. There were three men, ragged and bound as he was, surrounded by guards and shaking with fear as they contemplated their fate. Though his mouth was dry as dust and his tongue swollen with thirst, he swallowed, then started as a voice spoke from behind him.

'See what they do to pirates – to all infidels who transgress against the pasha's law.'

Breathing fast, he looked round into a face he had not seen before. The man was neither Turk nor Moor, but a native of southern Europe, perhaps one of the many renegades who thronged the notorious slave city: the most lawless of the Barbary states. One of the guards spoke a few words in the dialect of the *maghrib*, to which the European responded in his heavy accent. He was Spanish, the prisoner decided, trying hard to think of anything other than what he was about to witness – but the respite was all too brief.

There was a shout from above, whereupon he was seized by one of the guards and made to look up again. The other placed fingers about his eyes, forcing his eyelids apart. His throat tight, he watched as the first victim was thrown suddenly from the wall, to be impaled upon one of the hooks a dozen feet below, like a side of beef. The man's scream turned the prisoner's blood to ice, as in mingled horror and fascination he watched him writhe helplessly, his blood streaming onto the dust below. *Ganching*, it was called; he knew that much. As he knew it was only one of many grisly means of execution at the pasha's disposal. His stomach churned and bile rose in his gullet . . . then came a chuckle in his ear.

'How long you think he can stay like that?' the Spaniard asked. He took a step forward so that the prisoner could see him better: a heavily bearded man. 'It is surprising to me . . . sometimes they live an hour, even longer. It depends how they fall; many try to avoid the spike – they don't see that the hooks are placed in such a way that one cannot escape impalement.'

Had his hands been free the prisoner would have stopped his ears. The impaled man's blood-curdling screams rent the heat-laden air, causing the others atop the wall to cry out in terror and anguish at their imminent fate. Only now did he notice that there were other spectators too, standing some distance away. Some were even laughing at the victim . . . and it was then that, with a shock, he realized why he had been brought to witness the events from this vantage point.

'I . . . you want . . .' The words stuck in his throat. He coughed and gagged, trying not to listen to the cries of the man on the hook. He tried to swallow again, but could not.

'You wish to speak?' the Spaniard enquired. 'Why – you think to beg for your life?'

The prisoner turned to face him, and was not prevented. The guards even let go of him, though one held his tied wrists in a firm grip. Shakily, he nodded. 'You want something of me,' he said hoarsely. 'Or you wouldn't have brought me here . . . Whatever it is, you know I'll agree.'

'*Si*, I know it,' the Spaniard replied calmly, seemingly oblivious to the carnage a dozen yards away. A second victim was about to be thrown off the wall; the prisoner felt immense relief that, this time, he might not have to watch.

'The matter is . . .' The Spaniard paused as if thinking it over. He spoke good English, the prisoner thought. Perhaps he was one of those traders or ship-masters who enjoyed the pasha's favour. Though he hadn't the look of a sea captain or a merchant . . . he looked more like a soldier: one who had seen many battles, and was indifferent to suffering.

'I do have a use for you,' he went on. 'Though you're an Englishman and my enemy, yet the world is changing. Your government and mine will make peace soon. Already your king has ordered an end to hostile actions against our ships at sea. Though you, of course, know this.'

The prisoner drew a breath, but the next question was not unexpected. 'How much would you do?' the Spaniard enquired, suddenly leaning close to him. 'To escape a death like the one you see before you? I imagine you would do much – watch now.'

And at a glance from him, the guards forced the prisoner once more to look at the dangling figure, the sight of which made him gag a second time. The man had torn himself so much in his agony that he was almost disembowelled. His innards hung down, dripping gore; he would soon be but a carcass.

'Sweet Jesu – ask what you will,' the prisoner muttered. 'I'll not disappoint, I swear!'

There was a moment, while words passed between the guards and the Spaniard. Then came movement from the high wall, followed by a ghastly shriek: another condemned wretch had been despatched. Now two sets of screams rent the air; the prisoner gulped, but mercifully he was permitted to look away. Shaking and nauseous, he waited for it to be over.

'Of course you swear,' the Spaniard said. 'But that is of no import for us . . . I mean myself and my friends. We require a guarantee, since what we wish you to do will take place in another land. You understand?'

The prisoner understood perfectly. They wanted him to turn, to work for them against his own country. They'd known what he was from the moment he had been captured, passing himself off as a passenger on a Florentine galley, off the coast of Sicily. His mind was working fast, as he sensed the possibility of freedom. He exhaled deeply, and said: 'I'll serve your government in any way I can . . .'

He broke off then, for the Spaniard's smile had faded. 'I speak not for governments,' he said brusquely. 'All you need know is that whatever I order, you do it. If you betray me, you will find yourself on a ship back to Algiers – to the *beylik*, where your fate will be even worse than that of these men here. And more . . .' The man's smile returned, as he delivered his final blow. 'We know who your father is: that blind old man, in his house by the sea. His life rests in your hands – if you fail us, his death will be as terrible as yours. That, you see, is our guarantee.'

Dumbstruck, the prisoner gazed into the Spaniard's dark eyes, and saw that it was no bluff. He nodded weakly, while sweat ran down his neck in rivulets . . . The heat was stifling. The dreadful screams of the impaled men seemed to swell in volume . . . Suddenly his legs folded beneath him, while his vision blurred. His last memory of that terrible day was of being dragged by the guards, back to the passageway with his feet scraping its dusty floor, and into a welcoming blackness.

ONE

Marbeck woke up in a sweat, in semi-darkness. As had happened often of late, for a moment he forgot where he was . . . then he saw a sagging beam overhead and remembered. He tried to raise his head, and found that he could: the fever had lifted. He struggled to sit up, as a voice spoke out of the gloom.

'You've come to your senses. I'm glad.'

He blinked as a shape rose by the bedside, then recognition dawned. 'How long have you been here?' he asked.

'Three days. It's Monday, in case you wondered.' The woman's face was pale in the dim light. Marbeck looked to the window, saw that dawn had broken.

'So you've been my ministering angel, Meriel.'

She had turned aside to strike a flame from a tinderbox. There was a candle on a chest by the wall, which she lit before facing him again. 'For part of the time,' she replied. 'Another was here. He said he would return today. He called himself Roger Daunt . . .' She raised her eyebrows. 'But that's no more his name than yours is Thomas Fowler. That's the one you're using here, isn't it?'

He didn't reply, but glanced round the room: at his clothes on the floor, his basket-hilt rapier in a corner. His sick-bed was rank, the pillow and sheets stained with his sweat. He was unclothed but for a nightshirt, which stank. He had eaten nothing for days, he knew, though his memory was fuzzy. The sickness had come upon him suddenly, he recalled, though he barely remembered getting himself here. From the look of the poorly furnished chamber with its low ceiling, he could be in any one of a score of inns and taverns, though he recalled this one's name: the Three Cups in Botolph Lane, near to the Butcher's Hall. He thought he could smell offal, from the shambles across the street; the odour was nauseating to him.

'No matter.' Meriel was watching him. 'You know you've

naught to fear from me.' She indicated the chest. 'There's water here – will you take some?'

He nodded, whereupon she brought the cup to him. When he had drunk thirstily she set it aside and said: 'You're a deal better – until a day ago, you were vomiting everything up. What about food? The inn will be stirring soon, I could see what they have.'

'Later, perhaps . . .' He lay back, feeling the cool water swirling in his stomach. But a restlessness was already upon him, things undone crowding his mind. He had been sick for a while . . . had he been indiscreet, when the fever took hold?

'This man Daunt,' he said. 'What did he look like?'

'Like a schoolmaster,' Meriel replied. Stifling a yawn she sat down on a stool, spreading her skirts. 'Dry as dust, and a beak like a kite's. He had an accent – Dutch, I think.'

Levinus Monk, of course . . . Marbeck frowned. Sir Robert Cecil's new secretary, the man from Ghent, was handling a great deal of intelligence business these days. Then, England's chief spymaster was no longer Sir Robert, but must now be addressed as *my lord* – Baron Cecil of Essendon. And if rumours were true, he would soon be raised to the higher rank of viscount. Master Secretary, as Marbeck still thought of him, had become too lofty to deal with his own intelligencers. Sometimes he wondered whether the man gave him a thought.

'You should have payment,' he said suddenly. 'I don't expect you to nurse me for no reward. There are risks . . .'

'Save your breath, Marbeck.' Meriel's gentle manner was giving way to her brisker self. 'And if it sets your mind at rest, you've no tokens of infection. A physician came – for the landlord feared the worst – but he found no sign. You merely ate something your body disliked, he said, and you're fortunate in having a strong constitution. In short, he thought it likely you'd been poisoned.'

Marbeck stared at her. He recalled eating at an ordinary, on Fish Street Hill; then he'd been to a tavern . . .

'You've never been short of enemies,' Meriel said. And when he made no answer, she gave a sigh. 'Now I should go home . . . can you fadge for yourself?'

He indicated his assent, and managed a smile. She was the mistress of his fellow-intelligencer Joseph Gifford, and someone he trusted. 'Is our friend in London?' he enquired. 'I speak of your paramour . . .'

'My paramour?' She gave him a withering look. 'He ceased to be that weeks ago, did you not know?' Seeing that he didn't, she added: 'That could never have lasted . . . how long have any of his queans lasted? For that's all I was to him – you know it well enough.'

'What do you do now?' Marbeck asked, after a moment.

'I've been staying at my sister's house in Hart Lane,' she replied. 'Why – are you offering to keep me?'

She put on a wry smile, but it was more than a jest. He had known Meriel Walden for nearly a year: since last summer when England's new sovereign had been crowned at Westminster, and cheering crowds lined the streets. Gifford, drunk on Rhenish wine, had lurched up to Marbeck in the Strand and presented his new lover, whom he claimed to have rescued from a drab's life. Though this, like many of Gifford's tales, turned out to be a fiction: Meriel was the daughter of a lawyer, who despaired of her settling down and finding a husband. Though he always made light of the matter, Marbeck had enjoyed her company from the start.

'I could do worse,' he said. 'But you deserve better.'

She gave a snort and got to her feet. 'The potboy will run errands if you wish. I've done all I can for now . . .' She picked up a cloak from the stool and drew it about her shoulders. 'If you wish to repay me, you must think of some other means.'

She was moving to the door, but hesitated. 'I hear the King has a fear of violence – and no liking for people like you and Gifford,' she said. 'He fawns over his favourites, those perfumed coxcombs that flock about Whitehall . . . I can't help but wonder what the future will be, for men of your ilk.'

'You mean I should do something else?' Marbeck said. But without another word, she went out.

He turned away then, towards the window, and listened to the rising noise from the street. Like it or not, Meriel spoke the truth: things had changed a great deal over the past year, since he had risked his life to foil a plot against the new king. And though he had been rewarded for it, he felt a growing distance between himself and Lord Cecil, whose power under

the new monarch seemed to increase with each passing month.
Marbeck had found himself under-used, sent on missions of
small importance, which had made him edgy. He thought
briefly of Nicholas Prout, the grey-faced messenger, who had
incurred Cecil's displeasure and been pensioned off to live the
quiet life of a churchwarden in his home parish. What might
the future hold for others, Marbeck included? He'd even
thought of going abroad, trying his luck in some other land
. . . but then, wherever he went, he knew he would tire of it.

He yawned, and soon drifted back to sleep, to be woken
again by a loud creak of floorboards. The room was filled with
sunlight, and a stern-faced figure in black, hat in hand, was
standing over him. With an effort, Marbeck levered himself
up on his elbows.

'Monk . . .?'

'At last – are you well enough to rise?'

Levinus Monk was a man of sharp edges, it was said: sharp
elbows, hawk-like features and a sharpness of speech that
bordered on insult. He threw a distasteful glance about the
shabby room, saw the candle guttering by the bedside and
promptly snuffed it out. 'You need some air, Marbeck,' he
said, wiping his sooty fingers on the coverlet. 'And a set of
fresh linen. I'll await you out in the street.' He turned to go,
then added: 'You're ready to work, I assume?'

'I suppose.' Marbeck took a breath. 'Or I will be . . .'

'Good. It's almost one of the clock – the trumpet sounds
at two. Do you have a horse stabled here? It's too far to walk,
for a man in your condition.'

'There's no stable at the Three Cups,' Marbeck said. 'But
my horse is nearby . . .' He blinked. 'Trumpet? Where are we
going?'

'I'm taking you to the theatre,' Monk retorted. 'What do
you think I meant? Now, will you stir yourself?'

The Fortune in Golding Lane north of Cripplegate, the fine
new theatre built a few years back by the Lord Admiral's Men,
was busy that afternoon. It was almost the end of the season,
the start of summer when the theatres would close and players
would venture out on tour, away from the noisome city with
its ever-present risk of plague. Here, among the lively throng

about the doors, Marbeck dismounted stiffly from Cobb and paid a horse-holder to look after him.

It was an hour since his conversation with Levinus Monk. Having washed and put on clean clothing he felt somewhat better, if weak as a newborn foal. In silence he followed the man up the stairs to a private booth in the gallery, and sank down upon a padded bench. They were in one of the gentlemen's rooms that served various purposes, often having little connection to the performance taking place on the stage below. Just now, as one of the Crown's intelligencers, Marbeck was to be briefed by his spymaster.

'The play's a revival of *The Jew of Malta*, in case you're interested,' Monk said, taking his seat beside Marbeck. 'Penned by one of ours, you recall . . . before my time of course.'

Absently, Marbeck nodded. Everyone knew of the famous playmaker Christopher Marlowe, a Cambridge scholar as Marbeck had been. Few knew of his other life as an intelligencer: the product of an early phase of recruitment by Sir Francis Walsingham. But everyone knew how his career had ended: stabbed in a tussle, and dead at the age of twenty-nine.

'Though that has little bearing on why we're here,' Monk was saying. 'There's someone I want you to see . . .' He glanced round keenly, scanning the crowded galleries. From below, in the open pit before the stage, the noise of the groundlings rose: a cacophony of laughter and chatter punctuated by the cries of those selling nuts and bottled ale. While on the stage itself, prior to the performance some comedy was taking place, a clown in a parti-coloured suit struggling to be heard above the din.

'The man isn't here,' Monk said with a frown. 'But he will be, I believe . . .' He broke off with a disapproving look at Marbeck. 'What's the matter? I thought you said you were well enough for this.'

'I am,' Marbeck insisted, perspiring after his climb up the steep stairway. 'But I've a powerful thirst.'

'Why didn't you ask?' Impatiently Monk leaned over the railing, caught the eye of a vendor and beckoned him to come up. 'You must rebuild your strength quickly, Marbeck,' he added, sitting back. 'This is a crucial time in our affairs.

The rest of the Spanish delegation will come here within the week. Surely you haven't forgotten?'

The man's tone irked him: even during the hours of his delirium, he had thought at times about the peace talks. The conference had been a source of gossip for months, ever since last autumn when King Philip had sent an ambassador to King James. More representatives, and some from the Netherlands where war still raged, were due to arrive soon. After almost twenty years of conflict between England and Spain, the eyes of all Europe were now on London.

'I haven't forgotten,' he said. 'But I wonder what task you have in mind for me. Before I fell sick, I was watching a papist family in Crutched Friars – the Woodalls. It was a poorly kept secret that they held masses for half the neighbourhood—'

'Forget them,' the spymaster snapped. 'Others can snoop in your place. In any case the King's banned such practices, and in time they'll die out – especially as there's no chance of Spain attempting to restore Popery here. They agreed to that demand even before the treaty was planned. The days of Armadas and of desperate uprisings are over, thanks be to God.'

To that Marbeck said nothing: having mingled with dyed-in-the-wool Catholics of late, he didn't share Monk's optimism about their giving up the fight so easily. But his thoughts were interrupted by a knocking. Monk turned and called out, where-upon a boy entered the chamber with a tray around his neck. The purchase was completed in a moment, and the vendor waved away. Monk bought nothing for himself but handed Marbeck a bottle, from which he took a welcome gulp.

'Not that it's trivial – I mean, keeping a watch on malcontents like the Woodalls,' the spymaster resumed, as if to qualify what he'd said. 'But see now, the man I expected is here. Look at the end booth.'

Alert at once, Marbeck gazed across the theatre yard with its sea of bobbing heads to the gallery opposite, where several people were entering a private room like theirs. Prominent among them was a dignified, grey-bearded figure in a suit of fine silk and a wide ruff, his bald pate fringed with white hair. The other men, less grandly attired, fussed about him as he took his seat . . . and now, Marbeck recognized him.

'That's de Tassis, the Spanish ambassador . . . did you bring me here to see him?'

'Juan de Tassis y Acuña, Count of Villamediana, and King Philip's special *delegado*,' Monk said, with an attempt at correct pronunciation. 'No, I didn't bring you merely for that. Note his attendants too.'

Marbeck did so: four men beside the ambassador. All were Spaniards, dark of hair and beard, all of them dour-faced and watchful. Having observed them he half-turned to Monk, who said: 'At least one of his followers is a spy – the trouble is we're not sure which. He may not even be here . . . no matter.'

Marbeck sighed and took another pull from his ale-bottle. 'Then who do you want me to keep an eye on?'

'De Tassis himself,' Monk answered. 'I already have people watching Somerset House, where his delegation lodges. We know who comes and goes . . . and in any case, I don't want you to trail the ambassador from suspicion: I need you to watch his back.'

'Is he so vulnerable? Surely he'll be guarded on every side, day and night.'

'He is. And the King has provided him with a bodyguard whenever he ventures forth, which isn't often. We think an attempt on de Tassis's life unlikely, though there are many who hate Spaniards enough, and will do so to their dying day . . .' Monk paused, then: 'Besides – and keep this to yourself, Marbeck: the Count doesn't have plenary powers. It's not he who will ratify the treaty; that task falls to Philip's deputy, the Constable of Castile. He'll come when the ink's dry, and the paper's ready for our King's signature.'

To all of this Marbeck listened in silence, glad of the comfortable seat and the drink. Though a mutton pie would not go amiss, he thought . . . for a man who'd been poisoned not long since, his appetite was returning with some alacrity.

'And yet, we take no chances,' Monk went on. 'My lord Cecil and the rest of the Council have been adamant: nothing must threaten the treaty negotiations – too much is at stake.'

That much was obvious, Marbeck thought, to every man and woman in England, and no doubt in Spain too. In this summer of 1604, little else was being talked of. King James had been firm: his intention, he'd announced to his first parliament, was to be *Rex Pacificus* – the peacemaker king – and bring an end to a war that had left both countries exhausted and Spain bankrupt. Once Europe's foremost power, she was now desperate for a settlement. What fewer people knew was that England was almost bankrupt too, the King having inherited an enormous debt from his late cousin, Queen Elizabeth . . .

'So I'm relying on you, Marbeck,' Monk was saying. He peered across the yard to the ambassador's box, where the party was being served with wine and cakes. On the stage, the clown was departing, making way for the afternoon's performance of *The Jew of Malta*.

'Stay close to de Tassis, and report to me – be alert for anything amiss,' the spymaster added. 'There's a waterman hangs about by the Temple Stairs – a square-built fellow named Matthew Herle. He works for us, and will act as messenger. You'll need a new cover name, which I've already concocted. You're Giles Blunt, a scholar and bookman from Norwich – can you carry that?'

'I expect so,' Marbeck replied after a moment. 'So long as you're not proposing I attempt a Norfolk accent.'

'Don't be tiresome,' Monk retorted. 'You're a university man, employ a little imagination.'

'I'd better quit the Three Cups, find a lodging nearer to Somerset House . . .' Marbeck began, but was interrupted.

'I have a solution to that too. It was suggested, you'll be interested to hear, by my Lord Secretary himself. You will stay in his own mansion, Salisbury House. The place is still unfinished, but servants are in residence. They've been told to expect you – you've been charged with putting his papers in order. Such a task should permit you to move about as you please.'

Now Marbeck showed surprise. So Cecil was not only aware of his new mission: he had been involved in its planning. Suddenly, it seemed he was being entrusted with the most important task he'd had in a year. But he saw the reason for the placement: Salisbury House, the Secretary of State's palatial new residence, was two doors from Somerset House, where the Spaniards stayed. Moreover, a man could come and go by road or the river without drawing attention; it would serve him well.

He was distracted by a stir from below. There was a blast from a trumpet above the stage, and a robed figure stalked out to be greeted by applause. But as the player spoke his opening lines, it gave way at once to boos and jeering.

> Albeit the world thinks Machevil is dead,
> Yet was his soul but flown beyond the Alps . . .

Levinus Monk leaned forward then, wearing a rare expression: the closest thing to a smile, Marbeck thought, that the man was capable of. Yet he couldn't help a smile of his own. Only Kit Marlowe would have put the great cynic Machiavelli on stage as his Prologue: a fiendish comment on the way the world truly worked, born of his own experiences in the murky world of espionage.

'We're the shadow folk,' he said to himself.

Monk glanced at him. 'What?'

'Nothing . . . I was thinking of the role I'm about to assume.'

The spymaster grunted. 'I've said all I need to, I think. Now I have business elsewhere. Perhaps you should stay and see the play, rest while you can . . .' Then seeing Marbeck's expression, he frowned. 'What is it?'

Without answering, Marbeck kept his eyes on the stage a dozen feet below them. From the booth it was possible to see those at the front of the crowd, pressed up against the apron – and among them was a face he recognized. But what caught his eye was the fact that the man's gaze was directed not at the figure of Machiavelli, but upwards: towards the private box where the Spanish party sat. And the next moment, he realized who it was.

'Well?' Levinus Monk demanded.

'Solomon Tye . . .' Marbeck spoke a name he had not uttered in years. Turning, he added: 'He was one of our people . . . it was said he'd gone to France, even that he'd turned traitor. I thought he was dead. But if he's here it's not by chance, I'd wager – see the way he regards the ambassador.'

'Well then, he's suspect,' Monk said sharply. 'I want to know what the fellow's up to.'

With a nod Marbeck raised the ale-bottle and drained it.

Whereupon in silence the other went out, leaving him alone in the booth. From the stage, Machiavelli leered at the crowd:

Might first made kings, and laws were then most sure
When like the Draco's they were writ in blood . . .

TWO

That night was Marbeck's last in the shabby bed-chamber at the Three Cups. Having eaten a supper and taken a potion given him by his landlord, he slept soundly and awoke feeling stronger. By midmorning he had paid the reckoning, left the inn and the persona of Thomas Fowler with it, and was walking Cobb through the din of Candlewick Street and Budge Row into Watling Street. His belongings were in a saddle-bag, and he wore his old scholar's gown, his sword and poniard beneath it. Skirting St Paul's and its crowds, he passed by Bowyer Row through Ludgate and out into Fleet Street, fetching up at last in the Strand before the gates of Salisbury House. He gave his new name to the porter, and having seen his horse stabled, entered the great marbled hallway. Here, Giles Blunt presented himself to the steward.

'You'll be aware my master's not yet in residence,' the steward murmured, looking the newcomer up and down. He was aged, white-haired and clad in dusty black. 'But his private room is unlocked . . . I'll have one show you.' He paused, then: 'I trust you do not take tobacco – my lord forbids it.'

Politely Marbeck reassured him, and was soon following a liveried servant up an ornate staircase, into a small but pleasant chamber overlooking the river.

'So you're secretary to the Lord Secretary – *sir*,' the servant said. 'You'll have naught to do, will you? Some folk have it easy, right enough.'

Marbeck turned to the fellow, but in his new role as the scholarly Giles Blunt, merely put on a prim smile. 'My lord's papers will no doubt arrive in due course,' he said. 'And I have letters to write . . .'

The other sniffed and turned away. 'You're to sleep here too,' he muttered over his shoulder. 'They'll put a pallet down . . . aught else, ask in the kitchens.'

He went out, whereupon Marbeck closed the door on him and looked around. The room was empty save for a small table with writing materials on it, a stool and a chest which, when opened, proved to contain old books. Going to the window where there was an oak seat, he threw the casement wide to let in the sounds and smell of the Thames. The river was busy as always, craft of various sizes moving about while gulls flew above. He gazed across to Lambeth Marsh, and the distant towers of Lambeth House. The shouts of watermen rose in the still air: *Eastward Ho! Eastward for a penny!*

He glanced down at the waterfront with its wooden jetty, which looked newly built. The garden was yet to be landscaped: he recalled that Cecil's new house was unfinished. There was no boat tied up. Leaning out as far as he could, he looked downriver towards the city, but the great bulk of the Savoy blocked his view of Somerset House: one of the royal residences, destined for Queen Anne's use but now made ready as a venue for the treaty talks. He would, however, be able to see boats that came and went. Since he could hardly do both at once, he decided to watch the river rather than the entrance on the Strand. The Spaniards, he knew, generally used the water to get about rather than the streets, where hostile looks and even threats greeted them. The ambassador's visit to the Fortune, which had meant a coach ride through the crowded suburbs of Holborn and Clerkenwell, was a rare exception. Perhaps de Tassis had merely wanted to see *The Jew of Malta* . . .

At a sound from behind, he turned to see a boy stagger in bearing a stack of documents. Dropping them on the floor, he looked breathlessly at Marbeck. 'Master Langton ordered these sent up, sir. They were in the cellar . . . it's damp there – look at the mildew.'

'Langton . . . is that the steward's name?' Marbeck enquired.

'It is,' the boy answered. 'And you're Blunt?'

'On occasion,' he answered, but the jest fell flat.

'There's a stair in the turret, along the hallway,' the boy went on. 'You can get down to the gardens that way. The boatman will take you where you want – his name's Miller.'

'And what's yours, young man?' Marbeck enquired in an offhand tone. A pair of spectacles perched on his nose, he decided, might have helped him in his new role.

'I'm Miller too – Daniel,' the boy answered. 'The boatman's

my father . . .' He grinned. 'I'll fetch and carry for a halfpenny, sir – bring whatever you need. Even, you know . . .' He gave a broad wink that would have done justice to a player at the Fortune. 'Company of a night, if you wish?'

'I beg your pardon?' Marbeck assumed a frosty stare. 'I hope you're not referring to harlots, boy! I'm a scholar and a man of clean habits – you'd do well to remember that.'

'Ah . . . then 'tis I should beg pardon – *sir*.' Daniel Miller's grin disappeared. He hurried out, whereupon Marbeck set about examining the material he had brought. It didn't take him long to ascertain that it was of no substance: copies of old letters and out-of-date reports, some black with mould. Cecil, he realized, could have ordered any loose papers sent to him merely to give his role more credence. Straightening up, he moved back to the window and sat, musing on the boy's bold offer to provide women of the streets. The Secretary of State, he knew, would dismiss him in an instant if he learned of it.

A movement caught his eye from the waterfront: a skiff was pulling in. He saw the boatman ship oars, grasp the post and heave his little craft to the stairs. A slight figure, well dressed and hatted against the sunlight, got up and clambered onto the jetty. He stood there for a moment looking about, then walked up the path towards the house. As he did so he glanced upwards; there was something familiar about him, Marbeck thought . . . then instinctively, he ducked away from the window.

Simon Jewkes? With a frown, Marbeck stood up and moved across the room. Jewkes . . . *the merchant with three hands,* as he'd heard him described: two to do business with you, while the other rifled your pockets. What on earth could such a man be doing here?

He decided he had better find out.

At noon he took dinner in the kitchen with the servants, who paid him little attention. He was an outsider: a bookish fellow with a privileged position, and not one of their station. Daniel Miller avoided his eye, while Langton the steward, though an educated man, remained aloof. But after he had eaten, Marbeck made it his business to bump into him in the hallway. When he asked casually after the visitor who had arrived by boat, however, he was met by a blank stare.

'No such man has been here,' Langton said.

Meeting the other's watery gaze, Marbeck raised his eyebrows. 'Your pardon, master steward, but I saw him walk towards the house . . . He would have come in by those doors, I believe.' He pointed to the main entrance, twenty feet away.

'The riverfront doors are locked,' Langton said, with growing severity. 'And I hold the means of entry.' He indicated a ring of keys at his belt. 'Perhaps you'd care to confirm it for yourself?'

He gestured towards the doors, but Marbeck's mind was already busy. He had dealt with too many experienced deceivers, among them those who lied for a living. Langton was good, but his denial rang hollow. The question was, why should he lie? Yet now, Marbeck's instinct told him, was not the time for confrontation, and he must keep to his role. He knew the doors would be locked, but nevertheless went through the motions of going over and trying them. He even rattled the handles, then walked back to the steward with a sheepish expression.

'Perhaps I was mistaken,' he murmured.

Langton made no answer.

'And besides . . . it's none of my concern.'

'That is so.' The man cleared his throat and made as if to move away. Then as an afterthought, he said: 'My lord has made it known that you should have whatever you need – I trust all is to your liking?'

'It will serve. I thank you,' Marbeck said.

He watched the old man walk off . . . and a suspicion arose: that a little piece of theatre had just been played for his benefit. He had been allowed to see Simon Jewkes arrive, and to have his curiosity aroused. Was the Lord Secretary playing one of his games? And if so, to what end?

Thoughtfully he climbed the stairs and made his way towards the study, then remembered Daniel Miller telling him of the turret. He walked past his own door to another one at the end of the passage, which opened on to a spiral stairway. Descending quickly, Marbeck found himself emerging from a narrow doorway at the south-east corner of the house, with the Savoy towering above him to his left. He walked through the garden, which was cluttered with barrows and builders' rubble, to the waterfront. The skiff was still there, and sitting in it was the boatman, puffing on a blackened pipe. The tide was in, the boat rocking gently with the swell. When Marbeck suddenly appeared above him, the man almost jumped out of his skin.

'Mercy, master . . .' Removing his pipe, he touched his cap. 'Do you wish to go somewhere? I was, er . . .'

Adopting a brusque manner, Marbeck peered at him. 'You're Miller?' When the other gave a nod, he went on: 'I saw you land a visitor earlier today. As it happens he's one of my acquaintance – do you know if he's still here?'

A moment passed; he watched Miller carefully, and was not surprised when the other put on a puzzled look. 'Visitor?' he echoed. 'Nay, master, I've been here all morning – you must have been mistook . . .'

But he broke off, uncertain what to make of Marbeck's expression. For in that moment he had taken a decision: Daniel Miller's offer to provide him with women of the streets, he guessed, could only have been made with the connivance of his father, who no doubt provided the transport. Here was a man open to persuasion. Dropping to one knee so that he and the boatman were close, he put on a conspiratorial expression.

'Save your tale – you may speak freely with me,' he said. 'I know you brought that man here in your boat. He's a city dealer, the sort who'd skin his own mother and sell the flayed hide back to her. So – if I name a price, might we not do business?'

But Miller was uneasy. He trusted no one, Marbeck saw, and rapidly considered his options. The man hesitated, apparently considering his too. Finally he said: 'I may have brought a passenger, but I don't know who he was.'

'Your son Daniel,' Marbeck said. 'A bright lad, I think . . . most obliging.'

The other stiffened.

'Surprising what servants will get up to, when the master of the house is elsewhere, isn't it?' he went on. 'Though knowing Lord Cecil, I'll wager he'd take a dim view of anything untoward. Like running harlots – or even taking tobacco, for that matter.'

Miller caught his breath, but kept silent.

'The matter is . . .' Marbeck paused. Varying his role was providing a welcome extension to that of stuffy Giles Blunt, he realized. Glancing about, he put on a very un-Bluntlike smile. 'The matter is, I too have to watch my place here – I couldn't let your boy know my true feelings on the matter. But I see you're a man who knows what's what. I may yet be able to do business with you.'

The frown on the boatman's features eased, to be replaced by a wary look. Seeing that Marbeck would add nothing he lifted his pipe, upturned it and knocked the ashes out over the side of the boat. There was a tiny hiss as the embers hit the water, then: 'What did you have in mind – sir?'

'First tell me of Jewkes, the man you brought here,' Marbeck said gently. He fumbled for his purse, fished inside it and withdrew a coin. 'Here's a tester for your trouble.'

Miller blinked at the sixpenny piece, then a hard look appeared. 'What are you about?' he asked. 'I heard you were a Precisian sort of fellow, come to deal with my lord's papers . . . else why would he hire you?'

'Because he knows I'll do my work,' Marbeck replied. 'Whatever else I may do, would remain between ourselves.' He held the coin between thumb and forefinger and waited, then breathed a sigh of satisfaction as the man took it.

'I said I don't know the cove's name, and I spoke true,' Miller said. Ten yards away a skiff passed with its passengers, the boatman straining at his oars. The wash tilted Miller's boat, so that he had to grasp the jetty-post. With a glance out at the river, then another towards Salisbury House, he spoke low.

'Master Langton said the man was on secret business for my lord, and I should deny setting eyes on him. I picked him up at Queenhithe – the Salt Wharf, where I was told to. If he's not here he must have left by the street door . . .' Miller swallowed. 'See, I'm in your hands now,' he added. 'So you'd best deal plainly with me, or I can make trouble – mistake it not.'

'I hear you,' Marbeck said, without concern. 'The Salt Wharf, you say . . . was anyone else with him?'

The other shook his head. 'Nor did he say a word to me. He

was agitated – a man with much on his mind. And for a city dealer, as you say he is, he had the face of a clapper-dudgeon.'

'Had he indeed?' Marbeck replied absently, looking out across the water. Fearing that the conversation was coming to an end, Miller sought to stay him.

'The . . . the company you spoke of,' he said. 'I can row across to Bankside at sunset, fetch back a trull from the Paris Garden – one of Dame Holland's best. She'll slip in by the turret stair . . . what say you?'

'What, you mean you've done this before?' Marbeck asked in an innocent tone. The other blinked; then feeling he was being made a fool of, he scowled. 'Here . . . remember what I said,' he began, but was cut short.

'I've a different task for you,' Marbeck said. 'For I too have some private business on behalf of my lord.' He nodded downriver, past the Savoy's jetty to where another set of stairs could just be seen, lapped by the tide. 'Could you watch Somerset House for me, tell me when someone comes and goes?'

The question took Miller aback; nor did he like it. When he hesitated Marbeck reached for his purse again, but did not open it. 'There'll be a full fare for you, each time you bring me word,' he said. 'I speak of the Spanish nobleman who lodges there . . . Count de Tassis. Do you know what he looks like?'

After a moment the boatman gave a nod. 'As it happens, I rowed him myself once,' he said. 'To the Privy Stairs – him and a servant. He paid in foreign coin – ducats.'

'That's good . . .' Marbeck met his eye and held it. He needed to let the man know that he too could make trouble, if need be. Miller frowned, then said: 'See now, if you're planning something dark, I want no part in it.'

'If I were, would I be so bold as to involve you – a man I don't know?'

Another pause followed, until finally the other seemed to relax. 'Well, I'll be your watchman,' he said. 'But if I see the Spaniard set forth, how do I signal to you?'

'No need,' Marbeck replied. 'I'll come to you.'

'If you need me to follow his boat, I want double fare,' Miller said finally.

'We'll see,' Marbeck said. And he straightened up and left him.

Thus far things seemed to be working out, he thought as he mounted the turret stairway. But he was uneasy, and had been ever since he'd faced Langton and heard his bland denial of Simon Jewkes's visit. What the boatman had told him only deepened the mystery. The Lord Secretary would have nothing to do with a disreputable man like Jewkes, Marbeck knew: were the fellow ever to be brought to account for his underhand dealings, Cecil would be among the first to condemn him. Jewkes was a grubbing trader of middling stock, far outside the exalted circles of the wealthy and powerful in which the spymaster moved. Which only strengthened his conviction, that he had been allowed to witness his arrival for some purpose. What it might be, he did not know.

The next day, however, the matter was overshadowed by other events. For when he arose from his chamber and came downstairs, he found the house abuzz with news: several new peace delegates, it seemed, were arriving in London on the tide. A messenger had ridden up from Gravesend to bring word, the moment their ship from the Low Countries had docked. The Prince of Arenberg, the President of the Brussels Council and others were to join the Spaniards in their negotiations with the English.

So at last, the treaty talks would begin. And for Marbeck, the safety of Spain's chief delegate took on a new urgency from that moment forth.

THREE

That morning Marbeck absented himself from Salisbury House, saying he would take a stroll. Knowing Miller the boatman would be his eyes and ears for the present, he went out by the Strand door into the bustling street. He had put aside his old scholar's gown, and was clad in his customary black doublet. After walking a hundred yards, past the entrances of the Savoy, Somerset House, Arundel and Leicester Houses, he entered a lane to his right which led down to the Temple Stairs. There he asked among the handful of watermen who had gathered, and soon found the one he sought.

'Master Herle?'

A stocky man, whose thick shoulders bore testament to a life at the oars, came forward. 'Aye, master – do you wish to go east, or west?'

'Neither,' Marbeck said, speaking low. 'I'm Giles Blunt. My friend Roger Daunt thought I should make your acquaintance.'

The other did not react, but moved casually away from his fellows, down the stairs towards the water. Marbeck followed until they were out of earshot of the other men.

'Is there a message for me to carry?' Herle asked. He grinned, as if they were merely exchanging pleasantries. 'If not we'd best keep it short, or they'll wonder why you're not getting into the boat.' He indicated his skiff, tied up alongside several others.

'No message,' Marbeck said. 'But I'll ask how much you know about one called Miller . . . the boatman at Salisbury House.'

'John Miller?' The waterman gave a shrug. 'No real harm in the fellow – though I wouldn't wrangle with him when he's drunk.'

'He brought a visitor to the house yesterday morning. City trader by the name of Jewkes, picked him up at the Salt Wharf, he says. Does that chime with you at all?'

Herle thought for a moment. 'I've seen the man. He's some-times at the Quays . . . sly and tight-fisted as they come, I hear. You want me to keep my eyes open for him?'

'If you can.'

'Very well . . .' Herle glanced up the stairs, and added: 'We should part now, unless you want to hire me.'

With a nod, Marbeck touched him on the shoulder. 'I'll come tomorrow,' he said. And with a casual wave he turned and climbed the steps.

In the Strand, with the rumble of carts and the press of traffic to and fro, he paused, glancing towards Fleet Street. He would keep his sojourn short: for one who was supposed to be watching the Spanish ambassador, he thought, he'd had scant opportunity. Head down, he made his way back along the dusty street. But when he reached Somerset House, meaning to pass by quickly, he came to a halt. The doors were wide open, and several people stood about talking excitedly. Choosing a portly man on the edge of the group, Marbeck approached.

'What's the coil?' he enquired idly. 'Anything amiss?'

'You might say so,' the man replied, looking round. 'Someone fired a gun at the Spanish lord, I heard, by the river stairs, only it was a servant got hit instead. There's uproar within – they've sent for a surgeon.'

Straight-faced, Marbeck looked to the house and saw move-ment in the hallway. 'When did it happen?'

'A short while ago . . . look, here's the watch.'

Heavy footsteps sounded behind them. Marbeck stood back as an official-looking party stamped towards the doors: a sergeant and several guards. They were neither watchmen nor constables, he surmised, but the bodyguard Monk had spoken of, assigned to the ambassador. One of the household, a steward of some kind, hurried out to receive them. The onlookers watched them enter, until the doors were slammed shut. Marbeck walked off, quickening his pace to Salisbury House.

In the house however, all was calm: word of the event had yet to reach them. Cursing silently he made his way to the turret, down the stairway and into the garden. There he found Miller the boatman, standing on the jetty shading his eyes. As Marbeck came up he looked round sharply.

'There was a shot fired,' he said. 'From the water, I think . . . just as a party came out to the stairs.'

'Did you see anything?'

The other shook his head. 'I don't know what boat it came from—'

'You're certain it was fired from a boat?'

'Well . . . no, I can't be certain.'

'You must take me past the stairs,' Marbeck said abruptly.

'What, Somerset House?' Miller frowned. 'Sightseers aren't welcome there . . . they might be suspicious of us.'

'I'm requesting it, on my master's business,' Marbeck told him. 'I'll answer for the consequences.'

With a sigh, Miller bade him get into the skiff. Marbeck sat down, scanning the river. The traffic was heavy: if the shot had come from a boat, he reasoned, someone would have seen who fired it. Surely it came from elsewhere; but the neighbouring house on this side seemed an unlikely source: the old Savoy Palace, now a hospital. That suggested the far side – and at once Marbeck thought of the alley which skirted the gardens of Somerset House by its east wall; Strand Lane, which led down to another set of stairs.

They were out in the current now, the boatman bending to his oars. As they sculled past the broad front of the Savoy, Marbeck peered up at the windows. Unlike Salisbury House, the building gave directly on to the river, with no garden. It would be possible for a would-be assassin to get a clear view, he thought, from a corner window, though it seemed unlikely. Gazing ahead, he watched the Somerset House stairs draw closer until the great house itself appeared. He turned to Miller.

'Ship oars,' he ordered. 'Glide past, as slowly as you can.'

The other bristled, but complied. The skiff slowed, Miller giving his oars an expert touch from time to time. As they drifted past the house Marbeck saw several people in the gardens, though the Count de Tassis was not among them. He saw the sergeant and his men standing with two or three Spaniards, all wearing swords. Presumably the wounded servant had been taken into the house. He drew a breath: this was the worst possible start to the Anglo-Spanish negotiations – and now his suspicions arose, that it could be no coincidence.

'For pity's sake – don't stare at them.'

Miller's impatient growl broke his thoughts: the man was averting his eyes, his cap pulled low. Looking away from the house, Marbeck said: 'Row on, and stop at Strand Lane.' So in relief the boatman plied his oars, to send them scudding away from Somerset House towards the next landing. Turning the skiff, he brought it to the stairs where Marbeck at once stepped ashore. He produced a penny, saying, 'Don't wait . . . I'll make my own way back.'

Without a word Miller took his payment and pushed his boat out. Meanwhile Marbeck walked up the narrow lane, examining the thick hedge that separated it from Somerset House's gardens. And soon he found what he had suspected: broken foliage. An opening had been made recently, to allow a view of the jetty. It was a good spot for a man of average height to take a shot, with a caliver at his shoulder – and he realized something else: it was too close for a marksman of any ability to miss. The ambassador, he guessed, was not the target; perhaps it was a warning, or intended merely to cause alarm. And in that, he thought wryly, the perpetrator had succeeded.

He glanced about, but there was nothing to see in the lane. Whoever had fired had quickly made himself scarce, either in a waiting boat or by hurrying to the Strand, probably concealing his caliver under a cloak. Marbeck strode up to the busy street and looked in both directions, but nothing out of the commonplace met his eye. So, gambling on the ambassador's being unlikely to stir from his residence again today, he decided to do a little investigating. Retracing his steps down Strand Lane, he stood on the landing and after a short wait managed to hail a passing waterman. In minutes he was heading downriver in another boat, and within the quarter hour was stepping on to the stairs at Queenhithe.

The dock was noisy, barges and lighters being unloaded and men scurrying everywhere. After looking about the Salt Wharf, Marbeck made his way along the waterside, past the turnings into Stew Lane and Timber Street. He'd thought of looking for Simon Jewkes, even though the chances of running into him were slim. Then as he arrived at Broken Wharf he struck lucky, if not in the way he'd hoped. Standing idly at a corner was someone he had not seen in many months. The moment the fellow caught sight of Marbeck he turned away and sloped off . . . only to round another corner, and find him standing in his path.

'Good morrow, Peter,' Marbeck said.

Peter Mayne lurched to a halt, a curse on his lips. 'Sands . . . what the devil do you want?'

'I thought we'd exchange gossip.'

The other scowled. A former seaman, his body ruined by a life of hardship and disease, he picked up a meagre living on the wharves, begging and stealing when necessary. Marbeck had often found him useful, even if the man was not a natural informant. He knew Marbeck by the name he'd employed in the past: John Sands. And though he no longer used it, it would serve just now. 'There's a penny for you,' he said. 'Or would you prefer me to buy you a mug?'

Mayne's expression didn't alter. 'I'll not drink with you,' he grunted. 'But a penny would do, for charity's sake.'

'Soon,' Marbeck said. He gestured towards the Thames. 'Will you walk?'

So they moved to the riverside, and along it towards the opening of Trig Lane, Mayne with the shuffling gait by which he was known. After a while he said: 'What manner of gossip do you want? If it's about the Dutch lords, you'd best go down to the Tower Wharf. They're coming up from Gravesend . . .'

'So I've heard,' Marbeck said. 'I'm more curious about a man you'll know, a familiar sight about the Quays. Simon Jewkes, he of the three hands. Have you seen him about?'

A frown creased Mayne's brow. 'I might have,' he answered. When Marbeck slowed his pace, he added: 'I might even know where he can be found . . . did you say two pennies?'

'I might have,' Marbeck echoed drily. 'But if you mean the man's residence, I could find that easily enough.'

'Not now, you couldn't,' Mayne retorted. 'If you're thinking of the house near Tower Hill, he don't live there any more. He takes rooms when he's in London, does business other places.'

'So, which inn does he use at present?' Casually, Marbeck reached for his purse. But instead of answering him Mayne

said: 'I want my name kept out of it.' Marbeck peered at the
man, and saw a nervousness that was unlike him.

'Does something trouble you?' he enquired.

Mayne gave a start. 'Like what?'

'I know Jewkes is a varlet. But why would he object to
your pointing me to him, if it's on business?'

The *wharf weasel,* as Mayne was sometimes called, was
decidedly uneasy. He rubbed his unkempt beard and said:
'Mayhap he's changed his ways, grown suspicious, from
dealing in cargos he shouldn't. He has two fellows with him
now, as a rule: the sort who'd tap you on the head and roll
you off the quay's edge . . . You follow me?'

At this Marbeck's curiosity was aroused: his sight of Jewkes
the day before, on the jetty at Salisbury House, seemed to take
on a new significance. He opened his purse and drew coins
out. 'The place where he stays at present,' he said. 'Then we
part, and I'll forget I saw you.' Whereupon he opened his palm
to reveal two pennies.

Mayne sniffed, stuck out a grimy hand and spoke the
name.

It was downriver, by the Steelyard. Marbeck threaded his way
along the waterside, avoiding handcarts and porters with loads
on their backs. He passed the Three Cranes and Emperor's
Head Lane, but at Grantham Lane turned left and walked away
from the river as far as Thames Street. He mingled briefly
with the dense crowds, before crossing Dowgate and turning
right into Cosin Lane. Here, outside the Black Horse, he
stopped and thought.

He was puzzled that a man like Jewkes, who had always
made money and enjoyed the comforts it brought, should lodge
in an unsavoury tavern like the Black Horse. He was also
surprised to hear that the man had, as Peter Mayne claimed,
sold his townhouse. Jewkes was a Londoner to his bones and
lived by trade, dealing in goods which arrived by the river.
Having pondered the matter Marbeck pushed open the door,
his hand hovering by instinct near his sword-hilt. On entering,
however, he relaxed somewhat: the place was quiet, the only
customers a few men from the nearby yards. Despite the late
May sunshine outside, the interior of the tavern with its tiny

unwashed windows was gloomy. He glanced about, then as the drawer approached, put on a grin.

'Have you a pie, or a dish of pottage for a hungry man?'

But the other shook his head; as sour-faced tavern-keepers went, Marbeck thought, this one could win prizes. 'This is no ordinary,' he said. 'If you want to drink and smoke, you can drink and smoke. Aught else, there's the door.'

'Well, but you could have something sent in, could you not?' Marbeck asked innocently. 'I've done well at the tables . . . I could do with a wench to share in my luck, too.'

'You mean you want a private room?' The drawer shook his head again. 'We've chambers above, but they're taken.'

'By . . .?' Marbeck raised an eyebrow.

'By Master Goodenough, since you ask.' The man spread his hands and waited – then his face fell.

'Goodenough?' Marbeck beamed at him. 'How splendid! I'll go and surprise him . . . I haven't seen him in years.'

'Nay – he's not here.' In some confusion, the drawer moved to block Marbeck, who having seen the stairs in the corner, was starting towards them. 'I can't say when he'll return.'

'All the better,' Marbeck said brightly. Drinkers were looking curiously at him, perhaps taking him for a gallant who'd strayed somewhat out of his territory. 'I'll wait for him,' he added. 'You can send up a jug of Rhenish . . .'

'I don't have any Rhenish, and you can't go,' the other snapped. He made to seize Marbeck by the arm . . . then froze. From nowhere a poniard had appeared and was pressed lightly against his side, concealed by a fold of his apron. Still smiling, with his other hand Marbeck reached for his purse.

'Garnish for you, if you let me go up,' he said softly, leaning close. 'A cut below your ribs if you don't.'

A moment passed, in which the drawer wet his lips and looked around. Finding eyes upon him, he managed a nod. 'As you wish, sir,' he said loudly. 'I'll . . . see what I can find, send someone up with a tray . . .' And stepping aside, he gestured to the stairway. Marbeck found a coin and threw it up, forcing the man to catch it, then walked unhurriedly away. His poniard had disappeared, none but the drawer having been aware of its presence.

He climbed the stairs, glancing back once to see that no

one was paying him particular attention. On the upper floor he paused at the sight of two closed doors, then chose the nearer one and knocked. There was no answer; he knocked again and heard a noise, as if someone had got up abruptly from a bed – but it came from behind the other door. At once he moved to it and tried the handle. It opened, and he threw it wide but didn't enter – which proved to be wise. For the next second a figure sprang into view, sword in hand . . . only to stop dead on finding the point of Marbeck's rapier at his chest.

But it wasn't Simon Jewkes: it was Solomon Tye.

In surprise the two men stared at each other: Crown agents both, one on active service . . . the other, whom Marbeck had seen two days ago at the Fortune Theatre, apparently returned from the dead. For Tye, recognition took longer; when it came, he lowered his sword in surprise.

'Marbeck?'

'Tye . . . or is it Master Goodenough?' Marbeck kept his own sword levelled. 'Interesting name – but is that any way to greet a fellow?'

The other made no reply. His chest rose and fell, while Marbeck took a good look at him. It had been years, and in that time the man had changed: once handsome enough, his face was now gaunt, the crows' feet about his eyes streaked with lines of deep sunburn. Finally he drew a breath, and dropped his eyes to the rapier.

'Is that necessary?'

'It depends,' Marbeck said, but after a moment he lowered the blade. 'I came here seeking another . . . perhaps you'll serve instead. May I come in?'

FOUR

The conversation that followed was tense; and from the start, Marbeck felt as if he were facing a suspect rather than another intelligencer. Though sometimes, of course, the two were one and the same. He took the only seat, a rickety stool, while the other sat on the bed. Neither spoke for a while, until Marbeck decided to break the silence.

'Some thought you were dead,' he murmured. 'You crossed the Channel and vanished . . . when was it, five years back?'

He glanced round the squalid little chamber: compared with this place, his old room at the Three Cups would have appeared pleasant. Then he regarded Solomon Tye, who looked somewhat unkempt. His rust-red doublet, though of good quality, was second-hand and a poor fit, while his brown hair was lank and untidy . . .

'Why are you here?' Tye asked him abruptly.

'I would ask the same of you.'

'Does it matter? I've transgressed no laws, have I?'

'I came seeking a man named Jewkes,' Marbeck said. 'I was told he lodged here – hence my surprise, on finding you.'

'I don't know anyone of that name,' Tye said at once. He met Marbeck's eye, daring him to dispute it.

'I saw you at the Fortune, on Monday,' Marbeck said instead. 'Did you enjoy the play? One of his best, I've often thought.'

'I was there,' Tye admitted. 'I didn't enjoy it much.'

'I wonder if the Spanish ambassador did,' Marbeck said. 'Count Juan de Tassis, that is. You were staring up at him from the pit, as I recall.'

'Is that who it was?' The other raised his eyebrows. 'I saw a foreign lord, surrounded by lackeys. How times have changed, if Spaniards can walk about London without fear of arrest.'

'Or of being shot at,' Marbeck replied, watching him carefully. But there was no reaction. Tye looked away briefly, then said: 'I've no business with you, Marbeck, and no quarrel. I won't ask what you're about, and you know better than to ask me. We have our tasks—'

'And you know better than to treat me as a fool,' Marbeck broke in. 'I asked about Jewkes . . . what's he to you?'

They eyed each other. Tye threw a glance at his sword, which he had placed on the bed. Marbeck had sheathed his, but with a casual movement his right hand wandered across his lap, to rest near the scabbard. He barely knew the other man, but had heard of his ruthlessness, as well as his prowess with foil or rapier.

'I told you – I never heard of him,' Tye answered. 'As you said yourself, I've been away for a while.'

'I wonder where,' Marbeck mused. 'Somewhere warm? You look as if you've been in the sun.'

The other said nothing.

'I was with Levinus Monk at the Fortune,' Marbeck added in a conversational tone. 'He's everywhere these days, like a busy huswife – like the biblical Martha. Some even call him Martha behind his back, did you know? He was curious about you. I think he'd have mentioned it, had you been in his service.'

'Are you certain of that?' Tye enquired. 'Our masters have always told us what they need to, and no more.' Unexpectedly, a smile tugged at the man's mouth. 'Now I recall something else. I heard a rumour that you'd done a little outside business, last year . . . helped in the capture of one of our own people. Thomas Luce, wasn't it?'

Though he showed no emotion, Marbeck felt a stab of anger. The charge against him – a ruse by the Spanish to smear his name, and sow doubt within Cecil's intelligence service – had been false. But he hadn't forgotten how it felt to be under suspicion, shunned by his own spymaster. After a moment he said: 'I'm intrigued to know where you heard that. Surely not in Spain, whence the rumour came?'

The other's smile faded. 'I've never been there . . . and this conversation grows tedious. Shall we save our discourse for another day?'

Marbeck was about to speak, but all at once there came a noise from the passage outside: footsteps on the stairs. He glanced towards the door – which, it appeared, was the opportunity Tye had awaited.

Seizing his sword, he sprang up from the bed and lunged at Marbeck, who managed to avoid the thrust. He leaped aside, and the blade missed its target, but the momentum threw Tye off balance. Reaching for his own sword, Marbeck struck his assailant with his fist, the two of them lurching across the room. But as Tye recovered himself, the door flew open. Marbeck threw a quick glance, and saw the man he had come to seek, framed in the entrance. Simon Jewkes, in a fine doublet and feathered hat, stared at the two of them in surprise. Marbeck whirled to face his opponent again – too late.

Tye cracked him on the jaw, stunning him. Then with an unpleasant crunch, something thudded on his skull from behind. In a daze he fell to his knees, aware of someone brushing past him. There was a hasty, muttered exchange of voices above his head, before a savage kick to his side sent him sprawling. Then the door slammed and he was left alone, while two sets of footsteps thundered on the stairs and out of earshot.

Weakly, Marbeck got to his knees again. He tasted blood, while the back of his head throbbed and his ribs hurt . . . He breathed deeply, pressing a hand to his side, and retched.

But as he slumped to a sitting position, the question rose starkly in his mind: what connection could there be, between Solomon Tye and Simon Jewkes?

In the afternoon he returned to Salisbury House, trying to slip in unnoticed. He had tidied his appearance and fortified himself with a mug of spiced ale, though not at the Black Horse. His departure from that place had been awkward, if not embarrassing. When he'd descended the stairs, walking slowly, every eye was upon him. The surly drawer, for his part, merely watched him make his way to the door in silence. But the worst part was that he had let Tye get away – and instinct told him the man would not return to the Black Horse.

He was in the wide hallway, a foot on the bottom stair, when a voice sounded from behind. Groaning inwardly, he turned to face Langton's frosty stare. 'That was a long walk you took, Blunt,' the steward said. 'You should look in the study – more of my lord's papers have been sent over from Burleigh House. No doubt you'll wish to peruse them.'

'I will, of course . . .' Marbeck managed a prim expression, then seized the opportunity. 'I heard there was some mishap at Somerset House,' he said. 'Have you any news?'

'It seems an attempt was made on the life of one of the Spaniards,' Langton told him, with some distaste. 'A servant was hurt, but he will recover.'

'That's well . . .' Marbeck nodded sagely. 'History is being made on our doorstep, is it not?' he ventured. 'This time may prove to be my Lord Secretary's finest hour. I speak of the peace negotiations, with the Spaniards and Hollanders.'

The steward raised his brows. 'My master's a great man. The King himself has admitted how much he owes him, for preparing the way to a peaceful accession to the throne.'

'And has rewarded him handsomely for it,' Marbeck muttered under his breath, but Langton had already turned away. Stiffly he mounted the stairs and walked to the study, where he stopped in his tracks. Papers were stacked everywhere, in towering columns. He stared . . . was Cecil having a joke with him?

He closed the door, went to the casement and threw it wide, then slumped on the window seat. Perhaps it was well, he thought: none of the household would disturb him, with all the work he was presumed to be doing. In fact most wouldn't know, or care, whether he was in the house or not . . .

From somewhere, an unwelcome thought sprang up. All at once, the mission that Monk had charged him with looked odd. How could he watch the Spanish ambassador's back, as the spymaster had put it, from two doors away? Others were keeping an eye on Somerset House, Monk had said . . . what then was Marbeck supposed to do? He could no more prevent an attempt on the Count de Tassis's life than he could have prevented the shot being fired from Strand Lane this morning . . . He frowned, as a suspicion formed. Was he simply being under-used again – given something trivial to do, to keep him occupied? In which case, he wondered, why take him away from the undemanding task of watching a Papist family in Crutched Friars?

Staring out at the Thames, he reviewed the events of the past days, sifting them rapidly. Something, he thought, lay just beyond his knowledge. There was the sighting of Tye at the theatre, and that of Simon Jewkes arriving at the house, only for Langton to deny knowledge of it. Then had come the shot into the garden of Somerset House, and finally the presence of both Tye and Jewkes at the Black Horse . . .

He stood up and paced the room, wandering around the stacks of mouldering documents. What should he do? He could send a message to Monk via Matthew Herle, but there was little to say. Tye had fled, and was unlikely to be found. Which left Jewkes . . . at least Peter Mayne's information had been true. But would the man return to the tavern, after what happened? There was the drawer, who could perhaps be made to talk . . .

He stopped, and made his decision. For the moment he saw only one course of action: go back to Cosin Lane that same evening and try to get some answers. So a few hours later, having rested and eaten a light supper, he made his way outside, found John Miller and asked to be taken downriver to the Steelyard. And though the man glowered at him, he could not refuse. A half-hour later, on an outgoing tide, he was drawing his skiff up to the stairs, and Marbeck was clambering ashore. His determined look made even the boatman uneasy.

The tavern was rowdy now, lit by candles, the air thick with smoke and beer fumes. He pushed his way through the drinkers, and the trulls who had wandered in looking for business. The drawer was busy serving customers, helped by a blowsy, perspiring wench. Glancing at the stairway in the corner, Marbeck thought he could reach it before they noticed him . . . whereupon another possibility presented itself.

At the back of the room was a door, ajar to let in the evening breeze. Marbeck moved towards it, waiting for the moment – then as the drawer passed by with a jug of foaming ale he seized his elbow, causing the man to jerk round in alarm. 'You! What do you—' But the words stuck in his throat, as for the second time that day something sharp was pressed to his side.

'A word, if you please,' Marbeck said, smiling, and placed his other arm around the man's shoulder in comradely fashion. 'We'll take some air – I won't keep you long.' And with that he steered his captive outside, into a tiny yard filled with refuse.

'Put that on the ground, if you like.' He indicated the jug, which the other still gripped as if for comfort. With a baleful look the drawer complied, then straightened up, sweat sheening his brow. 'By the Christ,' he breathed, 'I should have floored you when I had the chance—'

'Your tenant – Master Goodenough,' Marbeck broke in. 'I mean the well-dressed fellow, not the other . . . though I'm now uncertain which one you meant. Is he here?'

'He's not,' the other threw back. 'He paid up and left – thanks to you! Not safe here, he said. If he owes you money, why don't you swear out a warrant? Your fight's naught to me . . .'

'Where did he go?'

'How would I know?' The drawer's anger was rising. 'And you won't dare use that whoreson blade . . .'

'What, this?' With an innocent expression, Marbeck showed him the tailor's bodkin he had employed instead of his dagger. 'The matter is,' he went on, 'I think you know his name's Jewkes. He's no stranger to the waterfront. And I wonder why he uses a shambles like this for a bolthole, when he could afford a room in a proper inn. I'm a curious man, you see.'

The other was breathing hard, his neck swelling like a bullock's. He threw a glance at the door: he would be missed at any moment, they both knew; he had only to call, and help would be forthcoming . . . it was time to increase the pressure.

'Aid me, and none shall know you did so.' Stowing the bodkin away, Marbeck patted his purse. 'I paid you before, did I not?'

The drawer remained silent, but he was debating with himself. Marbeck paused, then: 'Shall we say another tester . . .'

'Limehouse,' the man snapped. 'Try the Grapes.'

He glared and held out his hand, but Marbeck hesitated. He knew of the waterfront tavern by Limehouse Reach, the seamen's haunt . . . With a glance at the inn door, he leaned closer.

'You mean I'll find Jewkes there?' he said in a sceptical tone. 'That's somewhat hard to believe . . .'

'Did I say so?' the other retorted. 'I merely said ask at the

Grapes. Some might know where he can be found – that's all I'll say.' Defiantly he waited, and would tell no more; digging in his purse, Marbeck found the promised coin.

'And don't come here again,' the drawer growled, snatching his payment. 'Else you might find yourself cracking your pate on the quay, and fetching up in the river!' The man was not only giving vent to his anger, but salvaging his dignity. Backing away, he picked up the jug, then gestured to the door; but Marbeck was already leaving.

At the Steelyard stairs he found Miller sitting in his boat, smoking. When Marbeck appeared the man seized an oar impatiently . . . but on receiving the instruction his mouth fell open, releasing his pipe. With difficulty he caught it, a look of annoyance on his features.

'Limehouse, at this hour? It's almost dark – and I'd have to shoot the Bridge. You can go to Hades!'

'Limehouse Reach,' Marbeck told him, clambering into the skiff. 'You'll be paid . . . and I won't mention your whoring sideline to Langton. I doubt he'd approve of it any more than Lord Cecil would.'

'The devil take you, Blunt,' Miller snarled. 'I wish I'd never set eyes on you!'

But he shoved the oar against the stair and launched his boat. It turned with the current, and soon they were making headway: past Coldharbour, then the Old Swan Stairs, with the Bridge looming ahead. Finally, calling to Marbeck to hold on tight, the boatman steered his boat under one of the arches, drew in his oars and let it glide between the starlings. With the echoing roar of the Thames around them they shot through, dropping several feet to the water below. They were in the calmer reaches of the Pool of London, and Miller was plying his oars again. Marbeck set his face to the gathering dusk and stared ahead.

On his left Billingsgate passed by, then the great forbidding mass of the Tower, torchlight showing at some of the windows. He glanced at the ominous opening to Traitor's Gate, half of it below water level. Soon they were past the Iron Gate Stair, and beyond the city's border. The crowded tenements of St Katherine's followed, then riverside cottages, thinning the further east they went. To Marbeck's right, on the south bank, the lights of Southwark had fallen behind, and those of Bermondsey were visible. Ahead, the view darkened. Muttering under his breath, Miller stopped to light his stern lantern. Then they were moving downriver again, further into open countryside.

A quarter of an hour later, lights appeared on the northern bank: the Town of Ramsgate Inn, named for the Kent fishermen who gathered there. Then a grimmer sight followed: the gallows of Execution Dock, where those unlucky enough to be condemned for piracy were hanged at low water, and left until three tides had washed over their bodies. Beyond it a few dim lights showed from the hamlet of Wapping, and further off Shadwell by the marsh. But Stepney, which they now approached, was busier and livelier. Buildings crowded the water's edge: the shops of chandlers and victuallers, the cottages of seafaring men. The long ferry to Gravesend would call here on its way downriver: the gateway to the open sea beyond.

'See the old stone stairs? I'll drop you there. You'll find yourself in Narrow Street at Ratcliff. Limehouse is beyond.' Miller was eying Marbeck grimly from under his cap. 'Though why you want to go there at night, I can't fathom,' he added. 'Best keep your sword-arm free.'

'Is that the Grapes tavern?' Marbeck pointed to a light some hundred yards further. The river was wider here, a sweep to the left which gave on to the shingle of Limehouse Reach, before it took its great southward bend. Beyond that, there was only the desolate marsh of the Isle of Dogs.

'It is,' Miller grunted. 'I'll go to the stone stairs and no further . . . it's but a short walk.' He hesitated, then added: 'I'll wait a half-hour for you – after that you're alone.' And with a look that brooked no argument, he guided the skiff to the bank, where several boats were already moored.

So a short time later Marbeck stepped on to a set of well-worn stairs, dark and slippery with weed, and grasped a hand-rail that shook alarmingly. He climbed to the narrow roadway above, which was lined with tumbledown tenements. Then he was walking unmade streets, with sounds of revelry floating from a nearby tavern. There were people about, though in the poor light he could barely see them. He quickened his pace, crossed a wider street, then quite soon he was in Limehouse, gazing up at the sign: a bunch of grapes, lit faintly by a glow from the windows below. Cautiously he entered the tavern – and caused a lull in the conversation.

Those within regarded the stranger with frank curiosity. Most were sailors, of many nations: Scots, Frenchmen and Dutch, and others from far further off: dark-skinned, keen-eyed men in dyed toques and canvas shirts. There was room at a table by the wall, so he moved over and took it. Those sitting near eyed him . . . whereupon a hand suddenly appeared, to be placed on Marbeck's. He looked round sharply, into the face of a wizened, brown-skinned man with a blotched, hairless skull.

'Are you come to have your fortune told, master?' he croaked. 'Then you're at the right berth. I'm Fahz, the Three-fingered.' For evidence he held up a mangled hand, which lacked both thumb and forefinger.

Marbeck blinked, but when the other favoured him with a toothless smile, he could only return it. He signalled to the drawer, and asked the three-fingered man his pleasure.

FIVE

Fahz claimed to be Portuguese, but Marbeck knew that he wasn't. He formed that opinion quite quickly, after the two of them had sat for a while. His shabbily dressed companion drank a mixture of strong water thickened with sugar, which the drawer brought without comment. Marbeck drank ale, watered but passable. Having accepted his presence, the tavern's customers turned aside and left the two to their business.

'I see a quest before you,' Fahz said. He had peered into Marbeck's face and looked at his palm. 'You're seeking someone . . . do I hit the mark?'

In silence Marbeck waited. This man could not know that he had been acquainted with several mountebanks in his time, all of them skilled at drawing information from customers before telling them what they wanted to hear.

'And more . . .' Fahz gazed past him, seemingly into the distance. 'There are several paths . . . you are uncertain which one to take.' When Marbeck did not react he hesitated, then said: 'You've no cause to think ill of me, master. You bought me a drink of your free will, and that is enough.'

But Marbeck leaned forward, causing him to blink. 'It's true I came here seeking someone,' he said gently. 'His name is Simon Jewkes – do you know him?'

To his surprise, the other nodded at once. 'I know of him. He's a man with many interests on the river . . .' A puzzled look appeared. 'Why do you look for him here?'

Marbeck gave a shrug. 'You're the soothsayer, master Fahz. Can you not tell?'

Fahz appeared uncertain. He took a gulp from his mug, wiped his mouth with a frayed sleeve, then lowered his eyes. But when he looked up again, he wore an expression Marbeck found difficult to read. 'I fear I cannot aid you, master,' he said suddenly. 'Other than to bid you go carefully. I offer this counsel as to a friend . . . as any man who sees danger on the road ahead would warn a fellow-traveller.'

In spite of himself, Marbeck's curiosity was aroused. He sipped his own drink and said: 'Then will you not converse with me as a fellow-traveller, instead of a dupe? I speak of your trade, if such it is. I've had my future foretold a dozen times, and it's yet to fall out as predicted.'

The brown-skinned man's eyes widened. 'Then you have not yet encountered one with true powers.'

'Perhaps . . .' Marbeck held his gaze. 'And I'm prepared to listen, if you're willing to speak the truth.' Deliberately he looked at Fahz's damaged hand, the three remaining fingers curled like a claw.

'Where did you get the wound?' he asked. 'Indeed, why not tell me where you come from? For you're no Portugee.'

A moment passed. The other looked uneasy; perhaps he had judged his questioner as a man of courage and resources, skilled with the sword he wore. But his words came as a surprise.

'There's a *djinn* following you, master,' he said, speaking low. 'That's all I meant, about danger on the road ahead.'

'A *djinn*?' Marbeck blinked. 'Why, you're a Turk . . .'

'Please.' With a rapid movement, Fahz put out his good hand and gripped Marbeck's wrist. 'If I once was, I am no longer. I'm as loyal to the King as any man here. And my past can be of no interest to you . . .' He paused, then lifted his hand and pointed. 'You too have fought, and risked your life,' he muttered in his throaty voice. 'I see burns: the scar that will never heal.'

He meant the powder burn on Marbeck's arm, got in a house in Flanders when he had escaped from the Spanish . . . Marbeck stared. 'You see them?' he echoed. 'Through my sleeve?'

The other nodded. 'In here,' he replied, tapping his head. 'As I see your companion, that you were forced to leave behind . . .' He smiled, displaying once again the absence of teeth. 'We all have our *djinns*, master . . . though yours are hard to shake off, I think.'

He fell silent. Marbeck was startled, more than he liked to admit to himself. He glanced about, saw other men at their tables, none of them looking his way. He sipped his ale and faced the soothsayer again.

'Will you aid me, then? You divine correctly: I'm in a fog, looking for the path. I promise you I've no evil purpose in mind, only to serve, and protect those I'm charged to protect.'

'I believe that,' Fahz said, after a pause. 'But I fear I can tell you little.'

'Then at least tell me of the merchant Jewkes,' Marbeck countered. 'Does he come here? If so, I'd be curious to know why.'

'He has not done so, to my knowledge,' Fahz replied. 'I merely said I knew of him. He trades in many commodities: wines and silks, dyes and spices. Unlike me, he has many fingers.' With a fleeting smile, he raised his mug and drank.

'There's a man named Solomon Tye,' Marbeck said, after a pause. 'I think he works for Jewkes too – do you know him?' But to that, the other shook his head.

'The name means nothing.'

He had come to the end of the information he would give. Thinking fast, Marbeck was about to frame another question, when the other frowned suddenly. 'This quest of yours leads into darkness,' he said. 'I perceive wicked men, doing wicked deeds . . . You should step aside from the path, let others walk it.' He let out a sigh. 'Believe it or do not, as you will . . .'

'I believe it,' Marbeck said. 'And perhaps I should go now. Take this for your trouble.' He reached into his purse, found a silver coin and laid it down. Then raising an eyebrow he added: 'If we were in another land, isn't this where you'd say, *Peace be upon you*?'

But Fahz didn't smile, nor did he pick up the coin. He merely regarded it and said: 'I won't take it, master. I mean no offence to you, but I fear it would go ill with me if I did.' When Marbeck showed surprise, he added: 'I fought Christians, many years ago . . . I think you know that. I was but a boy, learning gunnery skills. I had much to learn. Now I'll die here by the cold Thames, without seeing the waters of my homeland again.'

'What waters would those be?' Marbeck ventured . . . then in a moment, something fell into place. 'You were at Lepanto?'

Fahz merely lifted his mug and drank.

'That's how you lost your fingers.' In amazement Marbeck looked down at the ruined hand: the ugly, blackened stumps of the missing thumb and forefinger. Could this man be a veteran of that terrible sea battle, more than thirty years back? Off Lepanto, while all Europe held its breath, the massed navies of the Holy League had destroyed the Ottoman fleet, ending their dominance of the Mediterranean. There had been prisoners, Marbeck knew, some sold as slaves, or forced to work on the ships of the victors. Had Fahz somehow ended up in England?

But the wizened man was shaking his head. 'You're mistaken. I came out of that battle with nothing worse than broken ribs.' He looked away and grimaced.

'You needn't speak of it,' Marbeck said.

'Nor will I,' the other answered quickly. 'But you reason well . . . you're a clever man.' He eyed Marbeck for a moment, then added: 'I wasn't always a gunner. I was put to the oars, after I was captured. There are accidents sometimes, with the chains . . .'

A galley-slave.

Marbeck peered into the man's leathery face, then lowered his eyes. The silence between them grew. Finally he took up his mug and drained it. 'I leave the coin,' he said. 'If you won't take it, give it to another . . .' But he broke off as Fahz caught his sleeve.

'The place you should look is to the west,' he said, leaning close. 'I know not the name, but there's a fortress that is cracked and falling into the sea. Seek there for the ones they call in my tongue the *chekirge*, in Spanish *langostas* – locusts, it means. But these are not creatures of the hot lands: they are the *langostas del Mar* – locusts of the seas.'

Deliberately he lifted his mug and turned aside; their business was done. Without a word Marbeck got up and left him, stepping out into the pitch darkness.

In the morning he woke early, having spent the night in a lice-ridden bed in a seamen's lodging-house. He dressed quickly and made his way down to the riverside, and after waiting on the stairs, took the first skiff going west to the Legal Quays. From there he walked round the Bridge by Thames Street to the Three Cranes by the Vintry. Then it was a case of tedious hours wandering the waterfront in search of the man who was as likely as anyone to tell him what he wanted to know: who, or what, were the Sea Locusts?

The name both intrigued and troubled him; and having pondered it since the previous night, he was impatient to know more. Meanwhile, he knew he was neglecting his appointed task back at Salisbury House; he would have to write a report for Monk explaining his actions. Having taken a late breakfast he was back at Queenhithe, on the verge of giving up and hailing a boat, when at last he saw the shambling figure of Peter Mayne emerging from an alley. He was in the company of another unsavoury-looking fellow, who took one look at Marbeck walking towards them, turned on his heel and vanished. Mayne had barely time to register his absence before he was collared.

'By the Christ!' the wharf-weasel snarled at Marbeck. 'You've scared my friend off – you act like a whoreson constable, coming up like that!'

'I need to talk to you, Peter,' Marbeck said. 'The quicker you aid me the quicker I'll be gone. There's payment for you.'

'No doubt,' the other grumbled. 'But it don't do me any good, being seen with you. Some will think I'm a louse – I could get a poniard in my back . . .'

'Indeed . . .' Marbeck nodded gravely. 'You told me of Jewkes's whereabouts. That alone could get you killed, I imagine.'

'You vile cunny . . .' Mayne stepped back. 'You wouldn't finger me . . .'

'Can you be sure?' Idly, Marbeck glanced around. The wharf was busy as always, so as he'd done the day before, he gestured upriver. 'Shall we walk a while?'

The other sniffed, rubbed his rough beard, then said: 'Damn you, Sands – this is the last time. If I see you again, I'll point you out as a snooper for the Admiralty Men . . . for I think that's what you are! You'd be unwise to show your face hereabouts, after that.'

He shuffled off. With a sigh Marbeck followed, until at a quieter spot on the Broken Wharf they stopped. 'Well, what do you want?' Mayne demanded.

'I need to know about the Sea Locusts,' Marbeck said.

His informant looked blank. 'The what?'

After repeating the words Marbeck watched him, but soon realized the man's ignorance was genuine. Mayne merely shook his head. 'I don't know what you speak of.'

'You're certain? It could be a nickname, or . . .'

'I never heard it,' the other insisted.

His disappointment rising, Marbeck considered; then something else Fahz had told him sprang to mind. 'Have you heard of a castle somewhere in the west, that's cracked and falling into the sea?'

The wharf-weasel frowned, scratched his head, then his face cleared. 'It could be Weymouth. There's two castles there . . . Portland Castle's well armed and well manned. The other one's smaller; decaying now, or so I've heard.' He gave a nod. 'Could be that one.'

'Very well.' Marbeck reached for his purse. 'One last thing: has Jewkes an interest in more than mere imports? I wonder if he had a hand in seafaring ventures . . . maybe held letters of reprisal?' He spoke of the old practice, whereby licences were granted to attack Spanish ships at sea and seize their cargos.

Mayne grunted. 'Likely enough: him and a hundred others,' he replied. 'It's no secret – but that's over since the King outlawed it.'

It was true enough: one of King James's first acts had been to revoke letters of marque and reprisal. The days of state-approved piracy were finished.

'And you'd be a fool to start prying into that kind of venture, Sands.' Mayne gave him a dark look. 'There were too many men had a hand in that . . . men with too much to lose, and who'd swat you like a fly!'

Whereupon he held out his hand; and when the payment was handed over, he slouched away without a word.

Within the hour Marbeck was back at Salisbury House, and soon realized that there was a new air of bustle about the place. When he saw Daniel Miller hurrying along an upstairs passage, he waylaid him and asked for news.

'You don't know?' The boy looked surprised. 'The master's here . . . he'll be staying from today. The peace talks will start, with the Spaniards.'

Marbeck eyed him sternly. 'I'm aware of the negotiations planned at Somerset House,' he said, adopting Giles Blunt's officious tone. Seeing the look on Daniel's face, he frowned. 'What are you smirking about?'

'You weren't here last night, were you?' the boy said. 'My father knew it . . .' He put on a crafty look. 'But you're a scholar and a man of clean habits, is't not so?'

'It is,' Marbeck answered. 'And whatever reasons I may have for being elsewhere are no concern of yours.' With that he turned and stalked off. But as soon as the boy had gone, he made his way out via the turret stair, and walked out to the riverfront. Today was fair again, the Thames sparkling in the sunlight. And there was John Miller, basking on the jetty with his shirt unbuttoned. When Marbeck appeared, he barely looked round.

'I'm engaged today,' he said sourly. 'I won't be able to do your bidding.'

'I don't need you to,' Marbeck said. 'But you'll remember our arrangement: have you observed any goings-on at Somerset House?'

The man gave a shrug. 'Nothing untoward. My Lord Secretary will go there each day, they say. No doubt the Spanish bastards will start their wrangling, now the Hollanders have come.' He jerked his thumb upriver. 'They're lodged at Durham House. Mayhap you should hire another to keep watch on them. I'd go cross-eyed, looking both ways at once.'

In silence Marbeck took in the news. At last the treaty talks had begun in earnest. He looked away to his right, towards the great mansion of Durham House fronting the river. Boats would be plying to and fro each day from now on – and Miller was right: it would be hard, if not impossible, to keep a watch on all the delegates. Then, Marbeck had been charged with watching only the Spanish ambassador . . . The oddness of that task troubled him once again.

'Good night in Limehouse, was it?' Miller's voice, heavy with sarcasm, broke into his thoughts. 'The whores there are all poxed, they say. Then what can you expect, when they go with Scots, Danes, Lord knows what . . .'

'Is the Lord Secretary in conference already?' Marbeck broke in, giving his voice an edge.

'He is. I ferried him down to Somerset House this morning
. . . after a poor night's sleep, I could add. Having had a long
journey back.' As a thought struck him, Miller put on a smug
grin. 'But see now, you won't have heard. There was another
coil there last night. A servant stabbed.'

His face blank, Marbeck eyed him. 'Stabbed?'

'With a needle, or some such.' Miller was fumbling for his
pipe. 'Then, there's many folk with long memories who wish
the Spaniards ill . . . mayhap you should have a poke about.
That's what you do, isn't it?' With a leisurely air, he stuck the
pipe in his mouth and brought out his tinderbox.

With thoughts whirling, Marbeck left the man and returned
to his room. There among the untouched stacks of documents
he pondered the situation, but not for long. His immediate
course was clear: he should contact Levinus Monk. Sitting at
the table, he found ink and quill and penned a hasty report.
Then having changed his clothes and tucked the paper into
his sleeve, he left the house by the street entrance.

Once again he walked the length of the Strand, past Somerset
House, which was now guarded by armed men. Without
slowing his pace he looked about, saw a coach drawn up by
the entrance. A few curious bystanders stood near; but then,
what was taking place behind those doors was no secret.
Moving on, Marbeck turned into Strand Lane and made his
way down to the Temple Stairs where the watermen gathered.
Today they were all out on the river, it seemed – save one: to
Marbeck's relief, it was Matthew Herle. But as he approached
and saw the look on the man's face, he stopped abruptly.

'I waited all morning for you,' Herle said. 'You'd best get
in.' He indicated his skiff, then seeing Marbeck's questioning
look, he added: 'Monk wants to see you – at once.'

SIX

The journey didn't take long. Skilfully Matthew Herle rowed Marbeck downriver, past Whitefriars and Bridewell, then veered towards the shore. With the tower of St Paul's looming behind, they neared the busy waterfront of Blackfriars and hove to. The two of them had barely spoken, but it seemed there was little the messenger could tell. No doubt Monk would have more to say . . . with an air of resignation, Marbeck stepped on to the stairs where people were waiting for boats. Having paid Herle a penny, he paused and leaned close.

'He's on the corner, by the Blackfriars Theatre,' the messenger murmured, before turning away to do business.

Marbeck walked up Castle Lane to where Thames Street opened on his right. There was a tumbledown corner house, which he remembered had once been used as a letter-drop. Having knocked on the door, he waited. Nearby was the indoor playhouse leased by the King's Men, but not yet in use. Perhaps the new spymaster had a weakness for theatres, he mused . . .

The door opened to reveal a dark passageway. Marbeck looked, but made out only a figure in shadow. When the person stepped aside he entered, and the door was closed. Seeing a light to the rear, he made his way into a candlelit chamber with the windows covered. There was a single occupant, seated at a table.

'I wonder what kept you?' Levinus Monk said drily. He waited, elbows on the table, while Marbeck reached in his doublet for his report. As he fished it out he looked round at the man who'd showed him in . . . and paused in surprise.

'Oxenham?'

The other inclined his head. 'It is, Marbeck.'

They exchanged looks. Marbeck had not set eyes on Thomas Oxenham for a year, perhaps longer. A florid-faced fellow with a penchant for garish clothes, as Crown intelligencers went he was not one of the brightest. He had been given few tasks in recent times, Cecil having decided he was unreliable.

'This man's one of my party just now,' Monk said, from which Marbeck inferred he was one of those watching Somerset House. He handed over the paper, which Monk took and unfolded quickly. There was nowhere to sit, so he stood by the table as Oxenham did. Both intelligencers waited as the spymaster read the report, then dropped it on the table in irritation.

'Is that all you have to tell me?' When Marbeck made no reply, he went on: 'You don't think I might have learned already about the wicked device that went off?'

'Device?' Marbeck echoed. 'I heard a servant was stabbed . . .'

'No, not stabbed.' Monk frowned at him. 'If anything it's more serious, even though the only victim was the ambassador's clerk. He had the task of opening despatches yesterday evening, it appears, and unfortunately for him, the first letter he chanced upon was the one containing the needles. They had been placed inside in such a cunning, mathematical order that the moment the seal was broken the package sprang apart, launching a salvo of barbs into the man's face. As forcibly as if they'd been shot from a crossbow, I gather. He's been blinded in one eye.'

Having delivered his account, the spymaster sat back and allowed Marbeck to take in the grim news. 'Coming on top of the shot fired at the house yesterday, the picture grows uncomfortably clear,' he added. 'Someone's trying to disrupt the talks – or at least to cause unrest among the delegates.'

'My Lord Secretary always feared that possibility,' Marbeck observed, after a moment. He glanced at Oxenham, who remained impassive.

'Of course he did,' the spymaster snorted. 'He leaves nothing to chance, which is why you were charged with keeping watch on the Count de Tassis: a task in which you appear to have failed, I might add. Not surprisingly, both the Spanish and Netherlands delegations are angered by these events. They've threatened to postpone the talks; fortunately Lord Cecil's assurances of good will have prevailed – for the moment.'

'Speaking of my own task,' Marbeck ventured. 'It's somewhat difficult to carry out, from two houses away.'

'What do you mean?' Monk looked sharply at him. 'Have you not had every assistance? Besides, from what I see you've paid a boatman to be your watchman. Yet two attempts have been made on the ambassador's life—'

'Not on the ambassador's,' Marbeck broke in, keeping a level tone. 'I believe the shot was fired deliberately at a servant – any good marksman could have hit his target from that range. And everyone knows that ambassadors don't open their own letters.'

'Agreed . . . but there are other matters, that alarm me equally.' Monk glanced at the papers on his table, before eying Marbeck again. 'We received a coded despatch some days ago. It accuses de Tassis himself of intending to press for a restoration of Papistry in England, something the man would never do. Such matters were agreed long before dates for the treaty were even set. The missive was designed to arouse suspicion and unease – as were the acts of sabotage.'

'Then what would you have me do?' Marbeck asked, struggling to hide his impatience.

'That fellow Solomon something . . . the one we saw at the Fortune. You managed to get in a fight with him, then lose him – do you think he's involved in this?'

'I don't know,' Marbeck admitted. 'I'd like to find out what Tye was doing in the company of Simon Jewkes, who's aroused my suspicion from the start . . .'

But impatient himself, Monk dismissed that matter. 'Jewkes has no relevance in this matter. He has much to gain from a successful conclusion to the treaty, when trade with Spain and Portugal opens up again. Men of business like him have an eye to the future.'

'Then can we speak plainly?' Marbeck said, after a moment. 'Do you have an idea who—'

'Who might stand to gain by wrecking the talks?' Monk gave a hollow laugh. 'Well, where shall I begin? I fear the list would be long. And I don't simply mean Puritan fanatics, and others who hate the Spanish. There are always people who profit from war, and have been throughout eternity. Do you follow me?'

Marbeck followed well enough. Perhaps the King's intention to be *Rex Pacificus* was not universally popular . . . the picture was widening. He frowned, hearing Oxenham say: 'The one who escaped – that rogue Solomon Tye. He appears to be a renegade, and should be found.'

'That's obvious,' Monk snapped. But he was looking at Marbeck, who said: 'There are other trails I might pursue, if you'll allow.'

'Such as?'

'This letter filled with needles . . .' He thought for a moment. 'It's a rare skill, to fashion such a device. I've a notion who might have done it.'

'Very well.' Quickly Monk came to a decision. 'Make your enquiries then, and if they bear fruit, inform me at once. I don't mean here . . .' He indicated the room. 'It's temporary – you may send a message through Herle. Whereas you . . .' He turned to Oxenham. 'Find that devil Tye, take him to the Counter on a pretext and inform me.'

Taken aback, Oxenham blinked, and Marbeck almost sympathized with him: since Tye might be anywhere, it was a tall order.

'Now, I think we're finished.' Monk put his hands on the table and waited. And though there were other things he would have liked to air, Marbeck decided to hold his tongue.

Once outside he was eager to be gone, but Oxenham stayed him. 'I . . . I thought perhaps we might pool our resources, you and I,' he said, somewhat haltingly.

'In what way do you mean?'

'Well . . .' The man appeared embarrassed. 'To tell truth, I've been at a loose end of late. Cecil's all but disowned me. Monk throws a few scraps my way: following people of small importance, searching boats at Dover or Gravesend . . . you know what I speak of.'

'Perhaps . . .' Marbeck found himself frowning; how much did Oxenham know of his own recent affairs? But it seemed the man's thoughts ran on a different tack.

'They treat us like whores,' he said, with sudden bitterness. 'Only we're paid a deal less.' He forced a smile. 'That's why I thought . . .'

'I work better alone,' Marbeck said, after a moment.

'That's not what I've heard.' The other eyed him. 'You and Edward Porter were close companions, were you not?'

He used Gifford's codename, though Marbeck suspected he knew his real one. 'In the past,' he replied. 'Though I haven't seen him in months . . .' Suddenly he thought of Meriel, who had nursed him through his sickness. He'd meant to seek her out . . .

'Even so,' Oxenham was saying. 'Yet can we not strike a bargain? I let you know of anything I uncover, and you do the same for me . . . I mean, before you take it to Monk?'

At that Marbeck frowned. 'Why so?'

'Well, only . . .' The other hesitated as people passed by, then lowered his eyes. 'No – it's naught,' he said, as if suddenly changing his mind. 'I'm fretting like a fool. You have your work, and I have mine.' And abruptly he left, walking briskly towards Blackfriars Stairs.

After a pause Marbeck too turned, to walk in the other direction. Oxenham's manner was strange, but he had neither the time nor inclination to ponder it. Instead he set his mind to a new purpose: that of finding a rogue named Elias Fitch.

A short distance along Castle Lane, he turned left down a narrow street which led directly to the city wall. There was a postern gate here, which opened on to Bridewell Bridge. He crossed the foul-smelling Fleet Ditch, and having skirted Bridewell itself, was soon in a different world: the warren of ruined buildings and noisome alleys commonly known as Alsatia, which claimed old rights of sanctuary. The law held little sway here . . . One hand on his sword-hilt, he moved through ever-narrowing ways, sagging jetties closing above him so that sunlight was almost blocked out. Finally, with the noise of Fleet Street away to his right, he stopped outside a low doorway. Dogs barked, and though the closed yard was deserted, he felt eyes upon him.

Drawing a breath he knocked, and at once there was a muffled sound within. He stepped back and looked about, but there could be no other egress from the hovel. Then he glanced up and sighed: at the upper storey a casement had opened, and a face peeped over the sill.

'There's sickness in the house – get you gone!'

'Fitch?' Marbeck shaded his eyes and peered upwards. 'John Sands . . . I'm here on business.'

The face had disappeared. A moment passed, then a voice called down: 'I will not open. Depart, for this is a plague-house!'

'I don't see any painted cross,' Marbeck called back. 'Might I come in?' And before the other could reply he lifted the latch. The door was locked, but a single kick broke the fastening. He made his way inside, into a foul-smelling room with one small window and a ladder-stair in the corner. He pushed the door to, allowing his eyes to grow accustomed to the poor light. Above him was a thump of footsteps, then at last with much creaking and cursing a figure appeared, clambering downwards. As he reached the floor he turned jerkily, an old poniard in his hand . . . and faced Marbeck, who stifled a laugh.

'In God's name, Fitch, what's the matter?'

Elias Fitch glared at him. Four feet tall and bald as an egg, he was dressed in a hand-me-down coat that reached to his knees. 'Breaking in is construed as a felony!' he cried. 'I'll call a constable!'

'Can we cease this tomfoolery?' Marbeck said. 'You know I'm not an enemy . . . I may even have work for you.'

'Indeed? Well, I think not,' the other retorted. 'You promise much, Sands – but you always leave having done little but ask questions. There's nothing for you here.'

With a sigh, Marbeck reached for his purse and tugged it open; a generous payment was called for this time. Finding a shilling, he placed it on the windowsill and stepped aside.

'That's for the door – as a mark of my good will,' he said.

Slowly Fitch lowered his dagger, though his look of suspicion remained. Marbeck took in the details of the grim little chamber: a straw pallet in one corner, a broken press in another. But beneath the window was a cluttered work-bench . . . the man was still in business.

'Well then, what is it you want?' Keeping his eye on Marbeck, he moved to the sill and scooped up the coin. 'I'm a busy man . . . a scrivener. People hereabouts need me to write letters.'

'You're a cunning man, who makes things to order,' Marbeck broke in. 'Trickster's props, say . . . I won't forget that dagger you made for the theatre folk. The blade disappeared inside

the handle when a man was stabbed, squirted pig's blood . . .
very effective at the Globe, I remember.'

The other said nothing. Despite his ways – for Fitch had
been a party to many crimes – Marbeck rather liked him. He
had been a blacksmith, a spurrier and a dozen other things in
his time. If it could be made, the word went throughout
London's underworld, Fitch was the man who could make it.

'That was a while back.' He had relaxed a little, and was
looking Marbeck up and down. 'Why do you seek me out
now?'

Before answering Marbeck glanced at the window, saw
shadows flicker past. Fitch was a valuable asset here, and if
he called for aid it would follow. Facing him, he said: 'I heard
from a friend that you made a wondrous weapon recently. I'd
like you to make me one too . . . Its purpose must be a secret.
The shilling is but a part-payment. My people would reward
you well, after the success of the first device.'

'Your people?' Fitch eyed him uneasily, but the greedy look
in his eyes gave Marbeck encouragement. Pressing his advantage, he said: 'I needn't spell out the nature of this cunning
machine, save to say that it was made with a mathematical
precision that only you, I think, could have accomplished.
The one who opened it has learned that to his cost.' When the
other made no reply he added: 'I speak of needles, cleverly
placed so that—'

'No, don't!' Fitch shook his head quickly. 'It's not part of
my craft – to make such a thing would risk the gallows.'

But he wore another expression now: one of disappointment.
Marbeck had expected the man to deny knowledge of the
needle-bomb, but now doubts arose. Was Fitch regretting the
loss of potential business? 'Then you couldn't contrive such
a device?' he asked. 'Or you could, but you didn't make the
one I speak of?' When the other hesitated, he added: 'Well
. . . perhaps we might do business anyway.'

The other's greedy look returned at once. 'How so?'

'I mean, if you knew of another who might have constructed
such a weapon,' Marbeck replied. 'And if you were to point
me to him, another shilling could be yours.'

At that Fitch began a struggle with himself, of a sort not
unfamiliar. Fear and greed did battle: fear of informing on

another rogue like himself, which might have grave consequences, vied with the risk of losing a shilling – a day's wage for a craftsman. Finally, to Marbeck's silent relief, greed won the day.

'You leave here without having seen me,' Fitch said.

Marbeck's silence served for assent.

'And were you to tell anyone I'd named the man – one I know only by reputation, you understand – I'd deny it on oath.'

A further assent.

'More, you don't return here. And the price is not shillings, but a half-angel.'

Slowly, Marbeck reached in his purse. But having found the coin, he kept it in his fist until the other stepped closer, and with the air of a stage conspirator, said: 'Seek out Richard Gurran – a needle-maker, turned joiner.'

But the name was unknown to him; and frowning, he withheld the coin. 'Where might he be found, this Gurran?' he demanded. 'For in a city of two hundred thousand souls, one might speak of other needles . . .'

'I cannot say with certainty,' Fitch said quickly. 'I spoke the name truthfully, and you must seek him for yourself.'

'Where?' Marbeck demanded. 'I need more than that.' He moved towards Fitch, who shrank away.

'Well . . . he's probably at sea by now.'

'You mean he's fled the country already?' Marbeck loomed over his informant, who took a step back. His old poniard reappeared – then he gave a yelp. With a rapid movement Marbeck seized his wrist and twisted it, forcing him to drop the weapon. As it clattered to the floor, he pulled the man close.

'By the Christ, let go of me!' Fitch cried. 'I spoke truly: he's a seaman, the sort you'd do well to steer clear of. If 'twas he made the device, he'll have gone back to his ship. It's called the *Amity* . . . that's all I know. Now release me!'

Frowning, Marbeck let go of him. A seaman . . . With a curse on his lips, he thought suddenly of Limehouse. He might even have been close to the man, only the day before. Absently, he held out the coin. Fitch snatched it, then scuttled past him to the doorway.

'We're finished!' he said angrily. 'Now get you gone, before I call for a friend who'll break both your legs!'

But Marbeck barely heard him. Without looking back he went to the door and stepped outside.

Two hours later however, after he had made his way back into the city, and walked most of the length of Thames Street and back again, his mood had changed. For it took only a few casual enquiries on the quays to learn of the vessel the *Amity*.

She was a fast merchantman of a hundred tons, he was told, with a crew of about fifty men. She carried ten guns, and often sailed the Channel – and further, to the Bay of Biscay and beyond; she rarely came to London. In the days of licensed sea-plunder she had made many voyages under her master: a man of bad reputation, who went by the name of Reuben Beck. But it was one last piece of news that struck Marbeck most forcibly, and sent him hurrying to the nearest stairs to hail a boat.

The *Amity*, he discovered, had sailed that very morning from Gravesend bound for her home port: Weymouth.

SEVEN

Back in his cluttered chamber at Salisbury House, Marbeck made up his pack. A restlessness was upon him: a desire to follow a trail, and hang the consequences. And though it was based on little more than instinct, and the testimony of a toothless man in a Limehouse tavern, he meant to pursue it. Let Oxenham hunt for Solomon Tye, and others watch Somerset House: Marbeck had found a reason to leave Cecil's mansion, with its oppressive atmosphere. He was about ready to depart when the door opened, and there stood Langton the steward wearing a look that would sour fresh milk.

'I sought you earlier, Blunt, but you seem to be everywhere except at your duties,' he droned, with a glance at the untouched piles of papers. 'It's come to my attention that you've been using Miller for private purposes – purposes of pleasure, I might say.'

'Might you, master steward?' Marbeck buckled the straps on his pack and straightened up. 'I thought your place was to see that I was well bestowed, then leave me to my own devices.'

The other frowned. 'My place?' he echoed. 'You wouldn't dare presume to tell me that.'

'I presume nothing,' Marbeck said. 'And I have to leave again, on business for the Lord Secretary.'

'That's odd,' Langton sniffed. 'In fact my lord exchanged a few words with me about you this morning, before he left for Somerset House.' Seeing that he had Marbeck's attention, he added: 'You'll be aware that he's now in residence here, in his private rooms. But he has issued orders he's not to be disturbed at this crucial time, while the talks are in process with the Spanish delegation – not for any reason. He was particular about including you in that instruction – almost as if he thought you might try to seek an audience with him. Though that would be highly presumptuous, in any case.'

'It would,' Marbeck agreed, with relief. He had no intention of asking to see Cecil; in fact just now he preferred to avoid him. He was summoning some words to get rid of the steward, when another thought occurred. 'By the way: I stumbled across that fellow I saw by the stairs two days ago,' he said brightly. 'The one you claimed had never been here – name of Jewkes.'

Langton stiffened.

'He gets about a good deal, I gather,' Marbeck persisted, enjoying the other's discomfort. 'Yet I confess it has troubled me, your denying all knowledge of him. Then, you're a man who obeys orders to the letter, I see. Loyal to the last.'

'In that you are correct,' the steward said after a moment. But he spoke low, the phrase almost catching in his throat. Marbeck pressed on.

'So if you were told to invite the man here, on the very day I arrived – on some pretext of business, perhaps . . . and then send him away again, saying your master was too busy to see him, you would of course carry out that instruction. You understand that this is mere speculation on my part.'

The other said nothing, though his unease increased.

'You dislike telling lies, don't you, Master Langton?' Marbeck said, in a different tone. And when the other blanched, he went on: 'Even for our Lord Secretary, who in turn is often obliged to lie himself, on the King's behalf. We're all deceivers, aren't we?'

'Yet I am a Langton of Hertford, who has served the Cecils faithfully all his life, as my father did before me,' the steward replied, puffing himself up. 'Whereas you are . . .' He hesitated. 'Well – were I a gambler, I'd lay odds your name's not Blunt, for one thing.'

'I *am* a gambler,' Marbeck said. 'And I'd lay similar odds you know very well who Simon Jewkes is: a double-dealing cockroach who appears to be hiding himself much of the time. Why the man would believe Lord Cecil wanted to see him, I can't imagine.'

But Langton was recovering. 'How dare you question me!' he snapped, with sudden anger. 'I'm a gentleman chamberlain, who commands respect all over London! You're insolent . . . unfit to be in my lord's service. I could have you thrown out onto the street!'

'There's no need,' Marbeck told him. 'I'm taking my leave

anyway . . . I'd express gratitude for your hospitality, but I'd be lying.'

And picking up his pack, he moved to the door. For a brief moment Langton blocked his path, then with a snort of indignation stood aside. Without looking at him Marbeck stepped out into the passage and walked towards the stairs.

An hour later, having crossed the Thames by ferry, he was mounted and on the road to Wandsworth. From there he would travel west to Kingston, and should make Cobham by evening. After that a long ride stretched ahead: Woking, Basingstoke, Andover and Salisbury. He was uncertain of his way beyond Salisbury, but he would find it; he thought it led through Blandford and Dorchester. With a fresh breeze in his face he spurred Cobb through the Surrey fields, as London fell far behind.

The next morning he awoke in unfamiliar surroundings, then remembered he was not in Cobham, but in Woking. The road was good, and the horse had run well after several days in the Salisbury House stable, taking him further than he'd hoped. After a breakfast of hard bread, bacon and peas he left the inn and was soon on the road again, crossing the border from Surrey into Hampshire. It was twenty miles to Basingstoke, where he halted to water Cobb. Then he was back in the saddle, with the Marlborough Downs rising to the north and west. By late afternoon he was in the old town of Andover: roughly halfway. Here he decided to rest himself and his mount, and to take stock of what lay ahead.

He was bound for Weymouth, and with luck and a good road would arrive there by the end of the next day. Then he intended to await the *Amity*, and seek out a crewman by the name of Richard Gurran. By riding, he was well ahead of the ship, which might take a week to reach the Dorset port. Meanwhile he would wander the town, and see if the castle was indeed falling into the sea as he had been told. Not that it seemed to have any bearing on his investigation, despite Fahz's words. Having found an inn in Andover, he installed himself in the taproom and took a mug . . . and only now did he face up to the flimsiness of his quest.

As long shots went, he thought wryly, this had to be one

of the longest he'd taken. More, by taking off like this he would incur the wrath of Monk, and probably that of Lord Cecil too. But then, he had matters to delve into: the Sea Locusts for one. In this quiet Hampshire inn, he pondered the name once again.

Weymouth, like other south-coast ports, was a departure point for many places. In Queen Elizabeth's time merchantmen, armed and refitted, had sailed out to waylay Spanish treasure ships and rob them. It was a lucrative wartime activity, licensed and carried out with the monarch's blessing: after all, she received a handsome share of the plunder. Many high-ranking lords, including some of the Privy Council themselves, had invested in ships of reprisal. But now everything had changed, with King James's banning of such practices to appease the Spanish – to the chagrin of those who'd reaped good returns from the business. So it was unsurprising that some were suspected of defying the ban, at the risk of being condemned as common pirates; the grim sight of Execution Dock at Wapping came to mind, as Marbeck had seen it from Miller's boat. So, was that it? Were the Sea Locusts simply a crew of pirates?

He was yawning; it would have to wait. Putting the matter aside he finished his drink and went to order a supper. Once again, stiff and saddle-sore from his long ride, he slept soundly and rose to another warm day.

May was almost over, and the countryside hummed with life as he rode across the Wiltshire plain towards Salisbury. Back in London, he reflected, some of the most important men in England, men like Lord Cecil and the Earl of Nottingham, and the Lord Treasurer too, were sat in a chamber in Somerset House hung with fine tapestries. Facing them across a table spread with a rich Turkey carpet would be the Spaniards and their allies, including Count Juan de Tassis. Each day they would wrangle over terms and demands, conditions and concessions. For many people, the outcome was in little doubt: neither side wanted the talks to fail. But there were others, perhaps, who hoped they would.

Marbeck turned the matter over again on his journey from Andover to Salisbury. Later he passed near Cranborne, one of Cecil's own manors, which his lordship never visited. From there it was a long ride up the Stour valley to Dorchester, until he found himself on a windswept southward route – an old Roman road – with the scent of the sea in his nostrils. With evening drawing in, he topped the rise called the Ridgeway and descended via the villages of Upwey and Broadwey. Then it was a further three miles, until finally he reined in. Before him, clinging to the curve of Weymouth Bay, was the town of Melcombe Regis. And beyond, joined to it by a bridge across the River Wey, was Weymouth itself.

So as twilight fell, he dismounted and led his tired mount through cobbled streets to the wooden bridge that separated the two towns. The bridge was but a few years old, having replaced a ferry on a rope: a sign of the division between these communities that had at times erupted into bitter rivalry. Marbeck had heard of old feuds and trade disputes that had led an impatient Queen Elizabeth to issue a charter making them one town. And as he left the bridge and stepped on to the stones of Weymouth quay, an odd feeling came over him: of passing through a kind of barrier . . . or even crossing a border.

When he stopped and looked about however, he saw only a small but thriving seaport. The masts of ships riding at anchor towered above him; taller ones were visible towards the harbour mouth. Children ran about in the fading light, while fishwives gossiped and men walked the quayside, their voices drowned by the din of seabirds wheeling overhead. Small houses and shops crowded the narrow strip between the water and the steep hill behind: sail-makers, ships' victuallers, cook-houses . . . and a tavern, the King's Arms, where lights burned. Turning from the waterside, he led Cobb by the reins through an archway into a stable-yard, where an ostler took charge of him. Then he made his way into the inn.

The place was busy enough: sailors and harbour folk mingled, their heavy Dorset accents strange to Marbeck's ears. A black-bearded drawer worked the barrels by the far wall. Since there weren't enough benches men stood about, some in rough fishermen's garb. After attracting a few glances, he made his way to the drawer and asked about a chamber for hire; but the man's reply was disappointing.

'There's naught here, master. We live above, and have no

spare room.' Then having taken Marbeck's measure swiftly, he added: 'Yet there are folk who might have. Walk along to Hope Cove, ask for Mistress Buck.'

Marbeck thanked him and was about to leave, when an odd sight caught his eye. Dangling from a beam, along with other curios brought back by sailors, was what looked like a human finger, black and shrivelled with age. He gazed at it, then turned as the drawer said: ''Twas took off a corsair by Sallee, sir. One of the captains who used to come here, he wore it round his neck for a while . . . We keep it for luck.'

'And has it proved lucky?'

'Well now, that's hard to tell.' The man finished filling a mug, turned off the tap and eyed him. 'Some say luck departed last year, when the reprisal booty stopped coming in. While others say it's but moved further away . . . I for one have no complaint. Now, will you drink before you go?'

'Later, perhaps.' With a nod Marbeck left him and went out, occasioning more curious glances. He walked along the quayside shiny with fish scales, the air laden with the smell of tar and hempen rope. Unwittingly he found himself slowing down, taking a closer look. He'd seen hard-faced men in the King's Arms, not unlike some of those in the Grapes in Limehouse: men with few scruples. He stopped, gazing across the estuary to the lights of Melcombe Regis. There, he decided, was the respectable town, with its royal name and its church spires. Here was its rougher underbelly, which had thrived on sea-plunder. He could almost smell the whiff of riches looted from ships off the coasts of France and the Azores, even from the Spanish Main . . . The words of the inn-keeper struck him again. Luck had flown when the King outlawed corsair practices, and thereby ruined a lot of people; but it was more than likely they continued, out of sight. Weymouth, he mused, was as likely a place to find them as any in England.

He picked up his pace again, until quite suddenly an inlet opened to his right, lined with tiny houses; the homes of sailors and their families. Baskets and nets lay about, boats were moored to rings set in the worn stones. Marbeck asked for the house of Mistress Buck and was directed to the last one, set against the steep hillside. On arriving he found the door open, and stepped inside to the aroma of smoked mackerel. He called out, and a middle-aged woman in a workaday gown appeared.

'Mistress Buck?'

'John's not here,' the woman said at once. 'Likely he'll return tomorrow.' She surveyed him swiftly, with an air of wariness. When Marbeck explained his needs however, her expression changed.

'Lodging? Oh indeed, I can aid you there . . . Mary!' In a voice that would have stopped a horse and dray, Mistress Buck shouted over her shoulder. Soon a spindle-thin girl appeared. At sight of Marbeck she stopped dead, and a look appeared that he could not mistake: one of fear, almost of dread.

'This gentleman will take the front chamber. See it's aired, take fresh linen up and strew some rushes.'

The girl vanished, and clearly making an effort, the woman of the house smiled at Marbeck. 'It's the best we have, sir. Will you take supper? There's a fish pie, and cider . . .' She began to speak quickly. 'I'm Sarah, wife to John Buck. My husband and I sleep at the back, you wouldn't be disturbed. I've hired out rooms for many years – there's been no complaint. Were you intending to stay long? I'll ask for a shilling a day – that's with your meals and cider or ale. Or wine if you prefer, I can get it easily . . .'

She trailed off as Marbeck managed a smile. 'It will serve well,' he said. And since he hadn't thought of a new one, he gave his name as Giles Blunt.

'You're welcome, Master Blunt.' His hostess beamed, but it was false. She was a nervous woman, he saw; perhaps one who was used to keeping secrets. The terrified look on the face of the servant-girl had stuck with him . . .

'Don't you mind Mary Kellett,' Mistress Buck said, as if divining his thoughts. 'She's simple-minded but willing. She'll fetch and carry for you . . . Be firm with her, that's the only way. Has been ever since she came to us.'

'She's not your daughter, then?' Marbeck said, whereupon the woman shook her head quickly.

'By heavens, no. She's but a waif we took in. John's a soft hearted-man, whatever folk say . . .' A suspicious look appeared. 'See now, might I ask what business you have in

Weymouth, sir? You must forgive my nosy ways, but we get few men of your station stopping by now.'

She waited, so Marbeck summoned a few answers and picked one at random. 'I'm a trader, mistress,' he answered. 'I thought to hire a vessel – only for coastal work, you understand. I've heard rates are cheaper hereabouts than in Portsmouth. That's where I was last . . .' but he too broke off as realization struck him: Sarah Buck did not believe a word of it. Brazenly she returned his gaze – whereupon he decided to gamble.

'Or at least, that's what I tell folk,' he said, and raised an eyebrow. But there was no inkling of understanding.

'Then that's what I shall tell folk, too,' the mistress of the house said coolly. 'Will you come up and see the room?'

EIGHT

That night Marbeck lay awake in his chamber, while a sea breeze rattled the casement. The noise of the port had died away, and the only sounds were those of night birds from the hill behind the house. He'd learned that there was a pathway over the hill leading to Newton's Cove, which looked to the open sea and out to the Isle of Portland. And he had learned something else: there were indeed two castles, device forts built long ago by Henry the Eighth as part of the South Coast defences. Portland Castle was well maintained, but the other one, known as Sandsfoot, was in a poor state of repair. It seemed frost had made cracks in the walls, which were no longer safe; in short, they had begun to slide into the sea.

He had garnered these scraps at supper, which he took in the small parlour with Sarah Buck. Apart from her absent husband there were no others in the household. The only servant was Mary Kellett, who went about her duties without a word. Having observed the girl discreetly, Marbeck found his curiosity aroused: despite what her mistress had said, he didn't believe Mary was simple-minded at all. Instead he saw a fearful girl, constantly on watch. More than once he found her eyeing him when she thought he wasn't looking, and formed the opinion that her initial fear of him had dissipated. What she now thought, however, was impossible to know.

Over a middling supper – Mistress Buck, it seemed, was an indifferent hostess – he strove to put the woman at her ease. She asked nothing further about him, and answered his own questions in perfunctory fashion. Things had changed a good deal here over the past year, she admitted, and from her tone he gathered that the King's new laws, and the impending peace with the Spanish, were unpopular with some. At this point Marbeck hinted that he'd no love for the new monarch either, and had even lost money because of his actions. But Sarah Buck had merely changed the subject.

Turning matters over, he thought about how to spend the time while he awaited the arrival of the *Amity*. He'd been relieved to learn that the vessel was indeed expected, having been on a coastal voyage to London. She was one of a score of ships based in Weymouth; apart from that, he learned little. And though he was keen to know of her crew, and of her master Reuben Beck, he held his tongue. Tomorrow, he decided, he would cross the bridge to Melcombe and make enquiries on the other side of the river. That settled, he was drifting off to sleep – but in an instant, he was fully alert.

There was a soft click from the latch, and the door opened, wide enough to admit a slim shape. It closed swiftly, and the figure was beside his bed . . . by which time Marbeck had sat up and whipped his tailor's bodkin from under the pillow. But when the person spoke, he froze.

'Master Blunt – I mean no ill. It's Mary Kellett.'

He let out a breath. 'What do you want?'

'Please hear me. Or whether you will or not, promise you'll not speak of this, or else I will be beaten.'

He put away the weapon, threw the coverlet aside and stood up in his night-shirt. In the near-darkness he couldn't see her face, but felt her eyes upon him. Finding his tinderbox he struck a flame and lit a stub of candle. But when he straightened up he received a shock: there was an ugly bruise on the girl's cheek. She shivered, drawing the edges of her shift together.

'Get into the bed and warm yourself,' Marbeck said, more sharply than he intended. 'I'll stay here.'

After a moment she complied, sitting hunched against the wall with the coverlet pulled to her neck. It may have been the light, but when he glimpsed another mark on her wrist he frowned. 'It looks to me as if you've been beaten already.'

But she dismissed the matter quickly. 'Hear me now, for I dare not stay long. This may be the only chance I have, before the master returns tomorrow. He's only at Abbotsbury.'

'Where?'

'A village above Chesil Beach . . . eight miles to the west.'

Having got over his surprise, Marbeck was uneasy. When the girl paused as if gathering her words, he said: 'I see you're troubled, but I ask again: what do you want of me?'

'First, promise me something,' she said.

He hesitated. 'If I can . . .'

'Say that when John Buck invites you to take me to bed, you'll not refuse him. Then we may speak again, in private.'

'What?' Marbeck gazed at her in the flickering candlelight. 'You mean he panders you – offers you to guests?'

Her silence was answer enough. Whereupon several thoughts sprang up, among them a memory of Sarah Buck telling him her husband was a soft-hearted man. Suddenly his anger rose: he had a feeling he had been assessed, and grossly misjudged.

'Does she know you're here?' he asked. 'Mistress Buck, I mean—'

'No.' Mary shook her head quickly. 'She's asleep . . . She's little to do with it, save for keeping me indoors. John Buck's the one . . .' She shivered again. 'I've borne it as long as I can, and now I must get free of them. I thought you might help me.'

All at once Marbeck felt a weight settle on his heart. The girl was frightened and desperate; she knew nothing of him, but was trusting him on a whim. 'Have you tried to run away before now?' he asked.

'Once,' Mary replied. She lowered her gaze, hugging her knees, then looked up again. 'He caught me with ease. And what happened after was my worst time. Ever since then, they've watched me closely.' Then almost to herself she whispered: 'Keep her well fucked and poorly shod. Those were his orders.'

Marbeck drew a long breath. 'Did you not come here of your own will?' He asked, after a moment. 'Your mistress said you were a stray.'

'That's a lie, but leave it aside. I came to ask you to aid me. To get me away as far as you can, or soon it may be too late. Once on the roads, I can beg for myself . . .'

'Wait . . . please wait.' Marbeck took a step back, and sat heavily on the end of the bed. Just now, this was the last thing he needed. He looked at the floor, fresh strewn with rushes by Mary herself, then raised his eyes again and saw her gazing at him.

'I ask too much,' she said, with sudden disappointment. 'Mayhap my heart overruled me . . . I've known many men here: sea traders, ships' masters, even gentlemen. But you seemed different.' Then in a harsher tone, she added: 'I'll pay if you wish it, in the only way I can . . .'

'No!'

At once he was on his feet: she had lowered the sheet, and was reaching down to raise her shift. 'Cover yourself,' he hissed, lowering his voice. 'Yes – I'm different, if you like. Not that I'm a saint, but using someone like you in that manner is not one of my vices.'

A pause followed, until in relief the girl let out a sigh. 'Then you will help me?'

'I'll try,' Marbeck answered. 'But has no one offered to help you before? To pay off the Bucks, for instance, and set you free?'

Mary shook her head. 'If they have, I know nothing of it. In any case, many are afraid.'

'Of John Buck?'

'Not him, in the final turn. He's but a servant.' She hesitated, then: 'As for offering to buy me, they would be too late. Such a bargain was struck even before I came here . . . last year, when I was ten.'

He blinked. 'You're eleven years old?'

She nodded, and as the import of her words sank in, added: 'I can tell you things, Master Blunt. Testimony that you may use to your advantage, even to getting a reward. Wickedness abounds here. Can you not sense it?'

'Perhaps.' In sympathy, and with a deep anger at her plight, Marbeck met her gaze. He saw her pinched face and slatternly appearance, but there was no deceit in the girl's eyes. And though he wanted to know more, his questions must wait. On impulse he reached out to take her hand, then thought better of it. 'Can you sit a horse?' he said finally. 'And can you be ready to fly from here at a moment's notice, with only the clothes you wear?'

'Gladly,' she replied, and a wan smile appeared. 'I weigh little . . . your horse wouldn't even notice me.'

He looked away and listened: the house was quiet. 'Go to your bed now,' he said. 'Leave me to think. I can't say how soon it will be. I have some business here.'

She got up, padded to the door and lifted the latch. 'I'll wait for a sign,' she said, and was gone.

*   *   *

The next day was the Sabbath. Weymouth people, Marbeck discovered, climbed the hill above the harbour to a little chapel of ease, or went further off to the village of Wyke. Others crossed the bridge into Melcombe, however; so letting Mistress Buck think he had gone to find a church, he left her house as soon as he could. A breakfast had been set for him, but to his relief his hostess did not share the table. Just now, he thought, he would have found it difficult to maintain his calm. Instead the woman hovered about with one eye on Mary Kellett, who served Marbeck in her usual downcast manner. None would have suspected that anything had passed between them, let alone revelations that had set Marbeck's teeth on edge.

Soon he was outside, standing by the inlet which he now knew as Hope Cove. Seabirds screeched, and across the river a church bell tolled. All looked peaceful . . . but what Marbeck saw now was a veneer of tranquillity, masking a darker subsurface. And suddenly his own quest looked somewhat lame, if not futile: how could what went on here have any bearing on the supposed scheme afoot in London, to damage the peace negotiations with the Spanish?

Restlessly he walked the quayside. He needed an informant, he thought. But he knew no one here, and must tread with caution. As for confronting Richard Gurran and demanding to know whether he had fashioned a needle-bomb in London: the notion now seemed preposterous. He decided to make for Sandsfoot Castle. There, if nothing else, he could see the walls for himself.

He walked over the hill to Newton's Cove, a sandy beach with boats drawn up. Then for almost a mile he followed the rough coastal path, and soon found the castle: little more than a two-storey blockhouse facing the bay. It had been a gun emplacement in a time when invasion was feared – not from the Spanish, but from the French. And it was crumbling: Marbeck climbed a stairway and stood on the top, which was windy and deserted. Below him were walls faced with the hewn stone called ashlar, which, as Fahz had told him and Peter Mayne had confirmed, presented a sorry sight. Whole sections were falling away, and some stones had indeed slipped into the sea.

He stayed a while, gazing southward to the Isle of Portland,

and made out the distant shape of the larger castle. This coast-line had a watchful air about it: French raiding parties, Spanish invasion fleets and pirates had sailed by, and no doubt come ashore too. Out in the Channel, Dunkirkers still prowled, seeking ships to plunder. No cancelling of letters of marque and reprisal hindered them, Marbeck thought, while farther away in the Mediterranean, nations like Spain, Malta and Florence still permitted their galleys to attack and plunder enemy ships. Disgruntled English corsairs, it was said, now talked of leaving their home waters and seeking prizes in warmer climes . . .

He turned away from the sea, and walked briskly back to the town. This time he went on as far as the bridge, crossed over to Melcombe and walked the quayside as far as the Custom House. It was open, despite today being the Sabbath, and there was movement within. He hesitated, then on impulse walked inside. Two or three men stood about, and one important-looking fellow was sat beside a small table. Having greeted him politely, Marbeck introduced himself as a gentleman seeking a vessel for hire. He had a cargo over in France – in Le Havre, he said – and would be interested to hear of owners he might approach.

The customs master, if such he was, looked him over. He was white-haired, his skin deeply tanned. His gaze wandered past Marbeck, to the other men who were taking their leave. A murmur of farewells followed, and the two were left alone.

'There are several owners hereabouts, and ships' masters who are part-owners too,' the old man said. 'I could mention names like Coker or Randall . . . What size cargo do you speak of, sir?'

'Fifty tons or so,' Marbeck replied, realizing he had better move away from the subject. Seizing the opportunity, he added: 'In London I heard mention of a ship called the *Amity* . . . A hundred tonner, commanded by a man named Beck?'

'Not in port,' the customs master said, somewhat blandly. 'And in any case, I understand that vessel is not for hire.'

'Ah . . . a pity.' Marbeck eyed him, saw that here was a man who would let nothing slip. The face was blank, the eyes watchful. He nodded politely and made as if to go, then with a casual air said: 'I heard a curious thing when I was last in

London – perhaps mere hearsay. Do the words *Sea Locusts* mean anything to you?'

There was a moment, then to his surprise the older man threw back his head and laughed loudly. 'There's no such thing,' he said. 'I fear you've been spun a fable.'

'Is it so?' Marbeck smiled ruefully, while watching him closely. He saw the deep-lined cheeks, the brown blotches on the skin that spoke of a life at sea. And he saw a small vein that throbbed on the man's temple . . .

'It is!' Tugging a kerchief from his coat, the other made a show of wiping his eyes. 'Old tales, sir . . . Were you a Dorset man, you'd have heard them already. The Sea Locusts were said to blow in off the Channel, pick the land clean and then vanish again. Nobody ever saw them, but it was a handy way to explain things gone missing. A sword, a cloak or a bit of jewellery – blame the Sea Locusts, for they must have taken them.'

'Well, I confess I've always had a weakness for old tales,' Marbeck said, keeping his smile. 'Though perhaps I should be more circumspect in future.'

'That's wise,' the other said. His laughter had ceased, and raising his eyebrows he put on a familiar look: that of a man who feels he has spared enough time already.

'One last question then, if you'll permit,' Marbeck said. 'Who owns the *Amity*?'

'I forget,' came the reply; far too neatly, Marbeck thought. With a brief nod he went out; but the moment he was on the quayside he regretted his impulsiveness. He had shown his hand, way too soon.

Gathering pace, he walked beside the water into the town, which was now bustling with people coming out of the churches. The man in the Customs House had lied: he was certain of it. But whatever the reasons, he knew he had been rash to speak of the Sea Locusts. Further enquiries would bring only more ridicule, he suspected. But why would the fellow deny knowing who owned the *Amity*? He should have asked that question back in London, he decided. Surely such information was common knowledge?

Still pondering the matter, he crossed the bridge back to Weymouth, but this time did not turn left to the harbour. Instead he took the path to the right, which led to a steep climb up a stone stair. At the top he paused to get his breath, and found himself on a pathway leading south-west. He was above the little town, and there were people coming back from the church at Wyke. It took but a brief enquiry to find out that he was on his way to Portland, a walk of some three miles. It would suit him well, he decided; he had a deal of energy to work off, and not a little anger.

Soon he was striding purposefully through fields, with a fine view of the sea beyond. It was but a mile to the hamlet of Wyke, where he stopped and changed his plan. He would not follow the narrow way towards Portland; instead he took a path directly ahead, which soon dipped. Finally it petered out, and facing him was a vast bank of shingle, with an expanse of water before it stretching to left and right. But there was a rough bridge of planks on wooden piles, which he crossed. Then he was climbing the ridge of pebbles with some difficulty – until he reached the summit and stopped.

Ahead of him a broad beach opened out, stretching westwards as far as he could see. This was Chesil, he realized; and it wasn't empty. Thirty yards away a longboat was drawn up on the shingle, with several figures around it. And instinctively Marbeck stiffened: for the moment they saw him there was a shout, and two of them started towards him.

NINE

With a hand on his sword-hilt, Marbeck stood his ground and waited. The figures became young men in seamen's clothing, their heavy shoes crunching on the shingle. The first one drew close, then stopped suddenly. 'Your pardon . . .' He half-turned as the other came up. He too halted, and Marbeck heard him curse under his breath.

'We mistook you for another.' The first youth threw him a glance, noting his clothes and his sword. The pair exchanged looks, as if suddenly eager to be gone.

'Who were you expecting?' Marbeck asked.

'No one,' the second youth said shortly. Both turned away, but on impulse he stayed them. 'I'm a stranger here,' he said. 'I had mind to purchase a boat . . . might yours be for sale?'

The first youth, little more than sixteen or seventeen years old, kept his eyes down. But the older one, a hard-faced fellow, shook his head. 'She isn't ours,' he said. 'She belongs to Buck – and he wouldn't sell.'

Marbeck raised his brow. 'You mean John Buck, of Hope Cove?'

But the younger one remained silent, while the other merely shrugged. They started back down the beach towards their companions, who were looking their way. After a moment Marbeck followed, which as he'd expected caused some alarm. Some yards from the shore the young men stopped and turned. Waves crashed and rolled, rattling the shingle.

'Why do you follow us?' The older one demanded.

'I needed a walk,' Marbeck said.

They were distracted by a shout from those by the boat. The older of the two threw a sour look at Marbeck and started off again, but the younger hesitated. 'You know John Buck?'

'I know his wife,' Marbeck said. Then as an afterthought he added: 'And I know Mary Kellett.'

He'd hoped for a reaction – but not the one he received.

For the boy scowled, and his fists clenched. 'The devil with you, then!' he cried, and hurried off.

Marbeck watched them join their fellows. A brief conversation took place, before the group took positions about the boat and pushed it into the waves. Oars appeared, and soon all had climbed aboard. Then they were moving, rowing hard away from the beach. Still Marbeck watched until the boat was some distance from the shore, whereupon it veered to westward. Only then did he turn and start to retrace his steps.

Something nagged at him. As far as he could tell, the boat had been empty. The men were not fishermen, nor was there any sign of nets or tackle. How long had they been there, he wondered, and who had they taken him for? He paused, turned about and walked down to the surging waves, to the spot where the boat had been beached. He looked in all directions, but saw only brownish pebbles, some tinged with other colours. Slowly he began to pace the beach, back towards the shingle bank. He thought about the younger seaman's reaction on hearing Mary Kellett's name . . . and then he understood. Perhaps it was no secret that John Buck pandered the girl; and Marbeck, a well-dressed stranger, had just been identified as the sort of man who might have paid to use her. He stopped walking, cursing his own carelessness . . . then with a frown, found himself peering down at the shingle.

What he saw was a faint line of pebbles, whiter than those around them, stretching away at an angle to the shore. They had been placed deliberately, two or three abreast. The row was barely visible, and could easily be missed; it was pure chance that had made him stop where he had. His curiosity rising, he began to follow the line, having looked round to see there was no one observing him. He walked for twenty yards or so until, for no apparent reason, the row ended.

He reached down and picked up one of the stones, about the size of a peach, and turned it over. The underside was amber: like the others, it had been selected for its partial whiteness. Was the row a signal, or a marker of some kind – and if so, for what?

He dropped the pebble and looked along the line, all the way to the sea. The tide was coming in, he judged, so perhaps it extended further out beneath the waves. Then he looked

back in the direction he had walked, but there was nothing:
no mark on the horizon, not even a tree on the distant hills.
He knelt and searched the spot where the row ended, but there
was nothing there either. Finally he straightened up – and then
he saw it: the end of an iron bar, protruding from the shingle
beside the last pebble in the row.

He'd almost missed it; indeed, had it not been for the pebble
markers he would have done so. From a few feet away it was
unnoticeable: a blunt, brownish rod sticking up no more than
four or five inches. He looked for others, but saw none. He
bent down and tugged at it, but it would not yield. So having
unbuckled his sword and laid it aside, he knelt again and began
removing pebbles, throwing them aside as he dug. He found
that the iron bar was fixed to something larger . . . and soon
after that, a barrelhead appeared. It was then but a few minutes'
work to expose the cask, buried some two feet below the
surface of the shingle. When he tried to move it, he found it
was heavy.

He sat back on his heels, saw crude letters burned into the
side of the barrel: *MADEIRA,* along with some numbers that
meant nothing. But all was now clear: the beach was a pick-up
point for contraband goods.

In some disappointment, he glanced out to sea. The boat
– John Buck's boat, he'd learned – was out of sight. Marbeck
had heard of how cargoes of wines, tobacco and other bonded
goods were put ashore by night, cached in places known only
to local folk. No doubt if he walked the length of the vast
beach, he would find other places of concealment too. By
torchlight, or by daylight, it was possible to follow the trail
of pebbles . . . and now the young men's nervousness made
sense. If they knew the barrel was there, had they feared
Marbeck would stumble on it? And more, if John Buck owned
the boat, it seemed likely that he was involved in the business.
Then, that was of small surprise: Marbeck had already formed
a far worse opinion of the man.

After a moment he began scooping pebbles back in place
to cover the barrel. Finally only the end of the iron rod
protruded as before, whereupon he stood up and dusted off
his hands. With a last look at the deserted beach, he began
the walk back to Weymouth.

It was past noon by the time he returned. Having no wish to go to the Bucks' house, he went to the King's Arms stable to see that Cobb was well cared for. Then he walked into the inn, which was as busy as before. Having found the drawer he gave his order, then lingered as the man worked the spigot. He exchanged a few words with him, and described the two young seamen he had just met at Chesil, to be rewarded by a nod.

'It sounds like the Swann brothers. They're the sons of Gideon Swann, sea captain.' The drawer topped up the mug and handed it to him. 'I hear you're looking for a vessel to hire, master, is that so?'

Marbeck paused, realizing that by now he had probably been observed and assessed by half the town. With a rueful smile he sipped his ale and nodded. 'I had a mind to look about here, that's all.'

The drawer gave a shrug. 'Well, some hereabouts would be glad of any sort of work,' he said. 'They tell us trade will open up with the Spaniards again after peace is made, but nobody expects a windfall any time soon.'

'This man Gideon Swann, is he someone I should seek out?' Marbeck asked casually. He kept his voice low, but two men close by heard him. One looked round; the other peered at Marbeck over his friend's shoulder, then dropped his gaze.

'I wouldn't know about that.' All at once there was a look of unease on the drawer's face, as if he regretted what he'd said. But it was only to be expected, if the Swanns were involved in contraband; and it was of no interest to Marbeck.

He walked away to drink alone, standing by the doorway. Men came and left, some throwing glances his way. Then he grew aware of a stir outside: people were moving past, heading towards the harbour mouth. Setting his mug down, he left the inn and stepped out to the quayside. It seemed busy . . . He stopped a boy who was following the general surge.

'What's the coil?' he asked.

''Tis the *Amity*'s longboat coming in,' the lad answered. 'Seems they've a dead man on board . . . fell sick on the way here, and died within sight of home. What evil luck, eh?'

He started off again, and Marbeck fell into pace with him. 'Evil luck indeed,' he said. 'Who is the poor fellow, do you know?' Whereupon the lad spoke briefly, causing him to stop.

'Ship's carpenter – Gurran,' he called, and hurried off.

A small crowd was gathering. After a moment, Marbeck walked up to stand at the rear and looked out towards the harbour mouth. Soon he saw a boat approaching, with several seamen aboard. In a few minutes it was alongside, and a rope was thrown down. People gathered around a ladder-head, where a burly sailor appeared and was at once surrounded. But the talk was subdued, and soon ceased altogether. A short while later, an unmistakable shape appeared: that of a body wrapped in sailcloth and bound with rope, being hauled onto the quay.

His face expressionless, Marbeck stood aside, as with a rumble of wheels a handcart was rolled up. The body was placed on it, and a few people formed up behind. He watched with others as the party moved off towards the bridge. Soon the little crowd dispersed, and he found himself alone but for two sailors from the longboat, who were about to descend the ladder. Seeing this might be his only chance, he walked over to them.

'Your pardon, but I'm dismayed by the news,' he said. When they looked to him he added: 'Is the dead man truly Richard Gurran, carpenter of the *Amity*?'

After a moment one of them nodded. 'Aye . . . fell sick some days back. By the time we rounded St Aldhelm's Head he was fading . . .' A frown appeared. 'Were you acquainted with him?'

'Briefly,' Marbeck answered. 'I knew him as a skilled fellow, mighty clever . . .' Then casually he added: 'Your vessel moves fast, does she not? Is she lying offshore? I was told you only left Gravesend three days ago.'

'She's a flyboat,' the other sailor said shortly. 'With a wind she makes good speed. What's your interest, friend?'

Both men were regarding him with hostility. It was unwise to ask questions, he knew, even if his only chance of learning more about the needle-bomb sent to Somerset House seemed to have vanished. 'Just a passing interest,' he answered. 'I've a cargo in France . . . been looking about for a vessel.'

'Ours isn't for hire,' the first man said, in a tone that brooked no argument. And with that the two turned from him and descended the ladder. There was a plash of oars, and soon their boat was moving out towards the harbour mouth.

Head down, Marbeck walked along Hope Cove as far as the Bucks' house, but at the door he halted. He had no desire to enter; instead he would take Cobb out for exercise, he told himself. But he knew perfectly well that he simply wanted to ride far away from this town and think.

He did ride far: back up the Dorchester road, then along the high Downs as far as a village called Long Bredy. Letting Cobb have his head he cantered further, until finding himself on the road for Bridport he stopped. The day was fair, the air fresh and sweet, but in the end the ride did him little good; there was no denying his long journey to Weymouth appeared to have been for nothing. Finally, with the light fading, he rode Cobb back down the Roman road through Upwey and Broadwey and into Melcombe. Once again he dismounted, crossed the bridge and delivered his horse to the ostler at the King's Arms. Low in spirits, he tipped the man to give him a rub-down and a good supper and started for his lodging. It was growing late, and he was hungry. This would be his last night there, he decided . . . then he remembered Mary Kellett.

He had all but promised the girl he would get her away; leaving her in the clutches of John and Sarah Buck, he realized, was not something he could do. But his horse was weary from today's ride; it would have to be the following night. He would pass the day somehow, and get word to Mary to be ready. Then by some means, with Cobb saddled nearby, he must get her out of the house.

A soft footfall sounded behind . . . and in an instant he was on his guard, reaching for his sword. But when he span round he saw only a young couple, walking arm in arm. With a surprised look they passed him, then gave him good-night. Exhaling, he nodded in reply, then turned into Hope Cove and walked towards the Buck house. Dusk was falling, and the inlet was quiet. Night seemed to fall more quickly here, he mused. He was almost at the house when there was another footfall. This time he barely glanced round – which was a mistake.

Figures loomed: two or three of them, at least. A blade glimmered . . . He reached for his poniard, but something swung towards him. He ducked aside, and it struck his shoulder. His arm was seized, while a fist slammed into his stomach. Winded, he threw a punch into a face, heard a grunt, but already he knew he was undone. Struggling desperately, he was forced down onto the hard stones, while blows rained on his chest . . . finally, pinned to the ground, he could only pant as someone leaned close.

'Leave, and don't return – or the next cut will be to your throat.'

There was a sharp pain at his ear, and warm blood welled. He gasped as the figures rose and drew back, leaving him in a heap on the quayside. Somewhere a dog was howling; the men melted away, and a door was opening, spilling light. Then came a squeal of alarm.

'Mercy, Master Blunt. Look at you!'

Sarah Buck was gazing down at him. Behind her the slight figure of Mary Kellett appeared. Another shape emerged from the house, and a man's voice boomed.

'What . . . is he drunk?'

Weakly Marbeck sat up, feeling a trickle of blood at his neck. Out of breath, sore in half a dozen places, he peered up as they gathered round him. But both Sarah Buck and Mary were pushed roughly aside by the stocky man who now bent over him.

'I'm not drunk,' Marbeck muttered. 'I was detained, you might say . . .' He put a hand to his left ear and groaned.

'They've pinked it,' the man said in a matter-of-fact tone. He was holding a lantern aloft. 'Can you stand up?'

He straightened himself, but did not offer a hand. So with an effort Marbeck heaved himself to his feet to stand before the fellow – who had to be his host, John Buck.

And the moment he looked into his face, he knew that he would probably have to kill him.

TEN

In more than fifteen years' service as a Crown intelligencer, Marbeck had dealt with rogues of every stamp and stripe, and of many nationalities. But John Buck was a home-grown villain of a sort peculiar, he believed, to the sea ports. The man may have had salt water in his veins, but he was no mariner. His features reminded Marbeck of one of the mastiffs that could be seen any afternoon at the Bankside bear-pit. The lives of such creatures tended to be short, and to end but one way.

'You should rest . . . my wife will bring a supper. You want me to find a barber-surgeon, get your ear sewn up?'

Buck was standing in Marbeck's chamber with the door half-open, clearly wishing he were elsewhere. Marbeck sat on the bed, pressing a wad of linen to his ear; the worst of the bleeding had stopped. He looked at his host's swarthy face, covered by a thick beard to the cheekbones, and shook his head.

'I'll attend to it myself.'

'Did you see who attacked you?' Buck asked, though the question was half-hearted at best.

'Not enough to identify any of them.' Marbeck met his eye . . . and a suspicion arose. 'Did you not see them?'

'I?' Buck frowned. 'Nay – they were gone by the time I came out.' Then rather quickly, he added: 'Sarah didn't see 'em either.'

'Well, it shouldn't be too hard to find other witnesses – were I inclined to do so.' Marbeck spoke deliberately, watching the other man – and saw that his instincts were correct. Buck barely reacted, but it was enough.

'An odd thing: it's as if they were waiting . . . as if they knew where I lodged,' he went on. 'Then, in a town this size, I should have known I'd attract attention. I'm a nosy sort of fellow . . . always have been.'

Buck made no reply.

'Like today, on Chesil Beach. I took a walk and came upon two brothers – named Swann, I'm told. They thought I was snooping about . . . it rattled them somewhat. Do you think they could have anything to do with me getting my ear slit?' Marbeck paused, then when the other still said nothing, delivered his final thrust. 'I ask because they had a boat . . . said it belonged to you. Looked to me like they were up to some roguishness. I wonder what it might be?'

A moment passed; then John Buck pushed the door closed, allowing the latch to click. He took a step towards Marbeck, his broad shoulders tense. 'What game do you play, Blunt?' he asked softly.

'Game?' Marbeck echoed. 'Why, are you a gambler?'

'Not I . . .' Buck was frowning now. 'I'm a careful man. Weigh my chances, then act as and when I have to.'

'That's very astute.' Marbeck lowered the bloodstained cloth and made a deliberate show of inspecting it, while weighing his own chances. Here was a man who had a lot to lose, he decided. He looked up, saw the glint in Buck's eyes.

'Is there something you want?' He asked.

'Perhaps . . .' Marbeck held the wad to his ear again. 'I see you're one who knows a good deal . . . where the barrels are buried, so to speak.'

The other caught his breath, but showed no fear. Marbeck read the danger in his gaze, and allowed himself a smile. 'Does that alarm you? It was but a conceit . . .'

'Enough!' Buck stood over him: a brutal man, with hands like shovels. Marbeck had already noted that he carried no weapon; perhaps the hands were enough. 'Lay out your demands, Blunt,' he went on. 'It's your choice . . . you can leave here richer than you came, or you can wash up with the tide somewhere along the coast. It's of no import to me.'

'You waste no time,' Marbeck said, after a moment.

The other merely glowered.

'Mary Kellett . . . what is she to you?'

As he had hoped, the question threw Buck off balance. For a moment he wavered, then a different expression appeared.

'Is that what you want? By the Christ, why didn't you say.' The man rubbed his sweaty face, and almost smiled. 'Well, if that's all, I'll send her to your bed tonight . . .'

'No – that's not what I want.'

The change in Marbeck's tone was so abrupt, Buck blinked. For a second he wavered, then his hard look was back. On impulse, Marbeck snapped out a question.

'The Sea Locusts – who are they?'

Buck went rigid, and his mouth shut like a trap.

'Pirates, plunderers . . . contrabanders?' Marbeck eyed him coldly. 'I'm curious to know.'

There was no answer.

'I heard the name in London,' Marbeck went on, 'only no one here wants to tell me anything. Fellow in Melcombe said I'd been spun a fable . . . but you know better, do you not?'

Buck lowered his gaze, seemingly in consternation; but when he looked up again, there was merely a vacant look. 'You've just written your own death warrant, Blunt,' he said.

He turned away, wrenched the door aside and went out. Marbeck heard him stamping down the stairs, then let out a long breath and lay back on the bed.

Early the next morning Sarah Buck came to his room and told him things had changed, and he would have to seek lodgings elsewhere. She would take a shilling, even though he had spent two nights in the house. Mary would bring a breakfast, then he must vacate the chamber. Seeing he wasn't about to argue, she left him. Her manner was brisk and businesslike, but there was a cut on her mouth which she tried to conceal: a testament, Marbeck guessed, to her husband's displeasure.

He rose, bruised and sore, and began to dress. He had slept fitfully, but had not been disturbed. As he finished, Mary appeared with his breakfast – and at once he saw that, for her too, matters had changed. When she placed the tray down without looking at him and turned to go, he stepped close.

'I haven't forgotten,' he murmured. 'I'll get word . . .'

'Please – it's no use.' She drew away, one hand on the latch. 'I shouldn't have spoken . . .'

'Yes – you should.' Frowning, he took her arm, but released it when she flinched away. 'What's happened?' he demanded. 'Has he threatened you, or . . .'

'Why did you come here?' She turned suddenly, her eyes

full of suspicion. 'You're no trader, or aught to do with the sea. What is it you wanted?'

'You said you could tell me things,' he said after a moment. 'Can you give me an inkling—'

'No . . . not now.' But she wavered, seeing that his concern for her was real. 'You must go – get far away, and quickly. I know John and his ways, and I know the others . . .'

'The Sea Locusts?'

But Mary simply shook her head and went.

He let her go out, hearing her soft steps on the stair. She was always barefoot, he thought; then he turned to look at the tray she had left, and realized he had no appetite.

Within the hour he left the Buck's house, retrieved Cobb from the King's Arms and walked him across the bridge out of Weymouth. Suspecting he was watched, he made no effort to hurry, leading the horse by the reins. Once in Melcombe he walked up St Thomas Street, among housewives and servants with baskets. Without pausing he continued to the northern edge of the town, where the road began to rise through sandy hills, then halted and turned round.

He was alone; rabbits bounded away, while larks sang above. To his left Weymouth Bay stretched eastwards, the sea a brilliant blue-green. While he'd been here, May had ended and June had begun; briefly he wondered how the peace talks progressed in London . . . then unbidden, a wave of anger swept over him. There by the dusty road he sat down, let Cobb's reins dangle and gave in to it.

The journey down here had not merely been a failure: it had been a disaster. He had blundered in, thinking he could ask questions with impunity, and now his life was in danger. He had alarmed people who feared he was at best a paid rummager, at worst a rival of some kind. Buck's words the night before had been no idle threat: he knew the man was capable of anything. And whether he'd arranged the beating for Marbeck the night before or not, it made little difference: the warning was stark. While he had ridden the Downs the previous afternoon, he reasoned, the Swann brothers had reported his appearance on the beach; likely that was enough. And again he had shown his hand, naming the Sea Locusts . . .

He looked down: the knuckles of his right hand were red, where he had connected with the jaw of one of his attackers. His ribs hurt in several places, including one where he had received a kick, back in the Black Horse in Cosin Lane. Meanwhile his ear lobe hung half-off; he muttered a curse – and the next moment was laughing at the absurdity of it. 'Written my own death-warrant, have I?' Since there was no one else about, he said it to Cobb. 'But it's not signed yet . . . so it's worthless.'

He drew a breath, touched his ear and saw fresh blood on his fingers. In one respect he had to agree with John Buck: he needed a surgeon. A ride would only hasten the bleeding, and hence he was obliged to retrace his steps into Melcombe. So after some enquiries in the town he presented himself at a house in Maiden Street, and was admitted.

'Don't trouble yourself to say it – you slipped on the quay,' the barber-surgeon said brusquely. 'If I had a crown for every man who told me that, I'd buy a coach and four horses. As if one like me doesn't know a knife-cut when he sees it.'

Marbeck didn't speak: he was concentrating on bearing the pain as the man sewed up his wound. He sat on a low stool, his teeth clenched. When the other at last stood back and signalled that he was done, he threw him a wry look.

'And yet, you know not to ask how it was earned,' he said. 'Best to keep a closed mouth hereabouts, I think.'

'Not only hereabouts, but everywhere else I've been, for that matter,' the surgeon replied, raising his brows. 'Discretion has been my watchword, sir. That's how I've lived beyond fifty years.' He turned to his table, put aside needle and suture and rinsed his hands in a basin. Then, when he offered a piece of linen to wipe the blood from his ear, Marbeck sensed an opportunity.

'Would it be indiscreet to enquire about a dead man who was brought ashore yesterday?' he asked casually. 'Carpenter of the *Amity*, I heard . . . a man called Gurran. I was in Weymouth when the body arrived.'

The barber-surgeon regarded him for a moment. 'I know little of it,' he replied. 'Likely some sickness he picked up, or poison from vile food. There are a hundred ways a seaman can perish – that one was lucky, in a way.'

'Lucky?'

'Indeed – for if he hadn't been close to home when he expired, they'd merely have thrown his body into the sea.'

'Well, I suppose that's true.' Marbeck stood up, examined the cloth and found only a little blood. 'You're a skilful man, master,' he said. 'I thank you for your pains.'

'The pain was all yours, sir,' the other said drily. 'Shall we say one shilling?'

Marbeck dug out the coin . . . then paused. 'Odd that the sickness only affected one man, in the close confines of a ship,' he said, almost to himself.

'Well, it depends on many things.' A frown creased the surgeon's brow. 'The *Amity*'s a vessel that rarely comes here. Sails far, even to the Americas they say. There are many strange diseases in distant lands – and besides, the crew changes. They're a shiftless lot.'

With interest Marbeck absorbed the information: and all at once, he realized he wasn't inclined to ride back to London. There was something here, in the invisible fog that seemed to hang over the twin towns, that he wanted to uncover. And there was Mary Kellett too . . . He drew a breath, and took a chance.

'Do you happen to know who owns the *Amity*?'

The barber-surgeon hesitated, and an expression appeared that Marbeck thought he recognized. For a moment they eyed each other, then the man gave a sigh.

'Does the name Roger Daunt mean anything to you?' he asked.

Slowly, Marbeck relaxed. 'By heaven . . . I might have known.'

'As should I . . .' The older man surveyed him, then glanced towards the closed door. But when he faced Marbeck again, there was strain about his eyes. 'I knew the look,' he said. 'Though it's been a long time . . . you're one of Cecil's men?'

'I'm Giles Blunt, just now,' Marbeck told him.

'I'm Thomas Woollard. I was one of Walsingham's brood . . .' The other wore a look of resignation. 'I put it all behind me, after the Armada year. Came down here, and . . .'

'Became Thomas Woollard.'

'It serves well enough.'

A moment passed. Marbeck waited, until finally the other said: 'Well, Giles Blunt – is there some way I can help you further?'

'I need somewhere to stay for a day or so . . . somewhere I won't attract the sort of attention I did in Weymouth.' Marbeck raised an eyebrow and waited, until Woollard heaved a sigh.

'Then you may as well stay here – I live alone but for a servant, and she's almost deaf.' Before Marbeck could speak, he half-raised a hand. 'I ask that you tell me nothing of what you do – and that you don't speak of me after you leave. This is just between us . . . you understand?'

'I do,' Marbeck replied, with relief. 'Anything you say is mere gossip betwixt myself and another, whose name I'll forget. Though your local knowledge would be invaluable . . .'

But at that, Woollard's brusque manner returned. 'Perhaps we may talk at suppertime,' he said. 'Now, I have patients.'

That evening however, Marbeck talked long with him – longer, it seemed, than his new host had intended. As they shared a supper and a pint of claret, the man thawed somewhat. Though unwilling to recall past times when he had served Sir Francis Walsingham as an intelligencer, he was amused to learn that Marbeck had been a Cambridge scholar too.

'So you're a St John's man. I was at St Benet's . . . a long while before you, of course.'

'I was a raw recruit in eighty-eight,' Marbeck said with a smile. 'The same year you put it all behind you . . .' He raised an eyebrow. 'I confess I'm surprised they let you leave.'

'Once and for always, eh?' Woollard gave a shrug. 'Well, my case was somewhat particular . . .' He lowered his gaze, as if the memory troubled him. 'In short, dour Sir Francis was relieved to see the back of me.'

'There are times when I believe my lord Cecil – for by such a title he's now addressed – feels the same about me,' Marbeck said. But the other looked up sharply.

'You misunderstand. I was a danger to the service, if through no fault of my own. It's delicate . . .' He searched for the words, until Marbeck thought he understood.

'They imprisoned you?'

'Not exactly . . .' Woollard took a breath, then: 'They locked me up in Bedlam.'

He looked away, but had no need to tell more. This man had seen – and probably done – terrible things, Marbeck sensed. And if his nerve had failed him at the last, he was not alone in that. A current of understanding passed between them.

'So . . . now you heal people instead,' Marbeck said quietly. 'Your atonement, perhaps?'

'My penance.' The older man threw him a bleak look, then added: 'What's done is done. We make our own destinies . . .' Seeming to shrug off his melancholy, he took a drink. 'Well now, what can I tell you of these warring little towns, Melcombe and Weymouth? If it's tales of plain roguery you want, we'll be here all night. But if it's a matter of probing murkier waters, I fear I'll be small help. In short, I try to close my ears to anything that might be treasonous.'

'Can you tell me of John Buck?' Marbeck asked.

A frown creased Woollard's brow. 'You've encountered him, have you? A very devil, up to his neck in all manner of things. Thievery, running illegal cargoes . . . he isn't particular. Beats his wife and servant as fancy takes him.'

'I gathered as much,' Marbeck said. 'And it's the servant who troubles me. A mere eleven years old, yet . . .' He fell silent: Woollard was staring down at the table. Finally he looked up, his face grave.

'I know of the girl, though I've not seen her. She's kept indoors for her own good – or that's what John Buck tells people.' When Marbeck stiffened, his host eyed him and added: 'She was given to Buck, to deal with her as he pleased: a payment for services rendered, I believe. Her tale is no doubt familiar enough to you: she was got on a servant, by a man who didn't want the trouble of raising her.'

So that was it; Marbeck drew a breath. 'The girl needs help,' he said, with some anger. 'They use her cruelly, as a—'

'I can imagine it well enough.' Abruptly Woollard cut him off. 'But if you'll take my advice, you should leave it alone – Master Giles Blunt.' He used the cover name deliberately. 'Whatever your business here, it's unlikely to have much to do with Buck. He's as bad as they come, yet he's, well . . .'

But a servant . . . Mary Kellett's phrase sprang to Marbeck's mind. Woollard had trailed off, as if letting him know he had said enough. But in spite of the warning look on his face, Marbeck had to ask.

'The Sea Locusts,' he said. 'Will you tell me of them, or not? I need to know.'

Woollard looked away, and was silent.

ELEVEN

The silence grew longer. Darkness was falling, and through the casement the distant sound of waves drifted in; the house was close to the bay. Finally Woollard rose to light candles, and when he returned to the table his expression was severe.

'I'll tell you what I know,' he said at last. 'Though it's precious little . . .' He eyed Marbeck grimly. 'And you didn't learn it from me. I hope to live a little longer, to set bones and stitch wounds.'

Though his pulse had quickened, Marbeck fell into his habit of appearing unconcerned; but his host sensed his eagerness. 'When you first appeared at my door I saw you walk stiffly, from hurts you carry,' he said with a frown. 'Was the cut to your ear a part of it – a warning, not to meddle?' When Marbeck said nothing, he went on: 'In which case, my advice to you is to heed the warning and leave. Concoct a story for your masters, say the trail went cold. Whatever Cecil pays you nowadays, it isn't worth a violent death, for a man of your years.'

'Very well . . .' Marbeck lifted his cup and took a fortifying drink. 'Your advice is noted. Let this be the only conversation we have on the matter, for I'll not put you in danger. Tomorrow I'll leave, and none shall know I was here . . .'

'Oh, they know – be clear about that.'

Woollard gazed steadily at him. 'Likely you were followed all the way – they have eyes in every street. But as for putting me in danger . . .' A tight smile appeared. 'I can bluff well enough – and besides, I've been useful to them at times. They can buy my compliance whenever they like.'

Marbeck considered his words, gazing at the candle on the table. It flickered in the draught . . . and suddenly he was in the Grapes in Limehouse, and a wizened man with three fingers was telling him of danger ahead, and of a *djinn* following him. He met his host's eye. 'Perhaps you shouldn't say more,' he said finally. 'For when I return to London, I must report anything that threatens the peace of our nation. And I'll not be the cause of your arrest.'

But his answer was a short laugh. 'Arrest? There are worse things, believe me . . .' Woollard took a drink too, and set his cup down carefully. 'What have you discovered thus far?'

'Not a great deal,' Marbeck replied, and told him of the man in the Customs House who'd said the Sea Locusts were a fable.

'Yes, that's how the tale goes,' Woollard said. 'But it's no myth. Your informant is probably one of those in their pay . . .' He gave a snort. 'In brief, Giles Blunt, the Sea Locusts are two ships that sail together: a tight – and dangerous – pairing. One of them you've already heard of: the *Amity*, captained by a murderous fellow named Reuben Beck. The other is the *Lion's Whelp*, and her master's a local man named Swann.'

'Gideon Swann?' Marbeck sat up. 'I encountered his sons on Chesil Beach, up to something unlawful, I'm certain.'

'Then you're already in more danger than you know,' Woollard said. 'And fortunate to have earned nothing worse than a cut to your ear.'

'But what is it they do?' Marbeck demanded. 'Are they pirates, or . . .?'

'Pirates now, who were once seen as patriots,' Woollard said drily. 'Since the King stopped the licensed plundering that's made so many men wealthy, they've simply widened their activities. And who knows what happens out at sea? If they still attack Spanish ships in defiance of the law, you may be certain they leave no witnesses behind to make a complaint.'

'I see that,' Marbeck said, thinking fast. 'But I sense there's more to this than sea-plunder. You told me they voyage far . . .' Then he caught his breath and looked at Woollard, who merely nodded.

'Yes – they are slavers too.'

It was obvious: so obvious he should have seen it sooner. And yet his reaction was disappointment rather than outrage. The practice, though wicked enough, would be of little concern to the King or his Privy Council. And it had little bearing on the Spanish, who carried out such activities themselves.

'A lucrative trade, in captured Africans,' Woollard went on. 'Yet hardly one that, as you put it, threatens the peace of our nation.'

'Then why are they so bent on secrecy?' Marbeck wondered, thinking of Buck's words of the night before. Suddenly he thought of Richard Gurran: the man had been a member of the *Amity*'s crew.

'It's the way of such people,' Woollard was saying. 'And hence there's nothing for you to do here. The Sea Locusts are contrabanders, slave-traders and no doubt more besides, but . . .' He made a dismissive gesture.

Marbeck let out a long breath. 'Well, I'll not impose on you further,' he said finally. 'In the morning we'll part, and I owe you my thanks.'

'Just guard yourself,' Woollard said. 'Now I'll go to my books, while my servant lights you to the spare chamber.'

'With your forbearance, I need some air first,' Marbeck said. 'The bay beach will be deserted at this hour, will it not?'

'I suppose so,' Woollard answered, after some hesitation. 'The Shelf, it's called here. You may encounter a pair of lovers making sport, but . . .'

'Discretion shall be my watchword – as it is yours,' Marbeck said, and rose from the table.

Outside, there was a little moonlight to see by. Breathing deeply of the salt air, he turned his back to the town and began to walk. He was irritated, as well as disappointed: in the end, he had learned nothing of value. Meeting Woollard had been fortunate, he'd thought, but now it merely threw his wasted efforts into sharper relief. A long ride back to London loomed ahead, followed by a gloomy session with Levinus Monk . . . and perhaps more dallying at Salisbury House, staring at the Thames. Head down, he walked through a narrow street, then along a path that led to the bay. Soon loose stones crunched beneath his feet; there were no lights anywhere, though far out to sea he thought he saw a glimmer. Nearing the shoreline, where waves hissed and rattled on the shingle, he made out the faint whiteness of the surf and began to walk parallel to it. He strode faster, working off his frustration as he went. But after a while, having turned everything about, he began to retrace his steps.

He had resolved one thing, at least: he would keep his word, and take Mary Kellett away from John Buck. He would do it the following night, though getting a message to the girl posed a difficulty. He was pondering this when, alarmingly close, there came a crunch of footsteps on the shingle.

He stopped, determined not to be caught out again. Sweeping his sword from his scabbard he swung round, crouching low . . . whereupon something whistled above his head and landed with a loud *clack!* on the pebbles. A curse rang out in the near-darkness. He glimpsed a silhouette, and levelled his blade.

'Stand still, or I'll strike!'

But his answer was the sound of another sword being drawn. Whoever it was stumbled on the shingle, cursed again and righted himself.

'This is foolishness,' Marbeck said harshly. 'We cannot fence in the dark. And the moon's behind you – I can hardly miss.'

Another curse flew from the lips of his opponent, followed by another rasp of pebbles as the man stepped forward. He was as clumsy as a carthorse, Marbeck thought . . . then he stiffened, and threw himself backwards as the other's sword arced across in front of him. 'Enough!' he breathed. 'I've no wish to fight someone I can't see – lower your blade!'

But his answer was a cry – more of desperation than anything else, it seemed. He was puzzled: this blundering figure was not one of those who had waylaid him the previous night. Such a man would know the terrain, and could have killed him by now had he wished to . . . but sensing another thrust coming his way, he ceased to think of that. His fighting skills taking over, he merely parried the blow. Swords clashed, sparks leaping in the dark . . . then Marbeck drew back, lunged and felt his blade penetrate flesh. There was a yelp, and a clatter as his assailant dropped his own sword. With a moan he sank to his knees . . . whereupon a doleful voice floated out of the night.

'By the Christ, Marbeck . . . what have you done?'

In Woollard's candlelit surgery, the man lay sprawled in a chair, his chest smeared with blood. The barber-surgeon had cut his shirt away to expose the wound: a deep gash between the ribs. He worked to stem the blood-flow, his face set in a grimace; but there was little doubt what would happen.

'The lung is badly pierced,' he said, without looking up. 'I'll have a corpse on my hands by morning.'

But Marbeck could only stare at the man he had last seen in Castle Lane by St Paul's, asking him if they might strike a bargain. Their eyes met, yet there was no anger in Thomas Oxenham's gaze: merely a look of helplessness.

'Well then, why not hasten it?' the wounded man said hoarsely, his eyes on Woollard. 'Pour a vial of something down my throat, and spare yourself the wait . . .'

'Be quiet!' Woollard snapped. 'Save your breath for sweeter words . . .' He sighed. 'Must I fetch a parson?'

'No . . .' Slowly, Oxenham shook his head. 'No parson or priest . . . but I need some time alone with my friend here.'

At that Woollard stiffened, then faced Marbeck. 'I wish you'd never set foot in my house,' he said angrily. 'And I wish to know nothing of what's between you and this man. There's just one thing you can do, to make amends—'

'Dispose of my body?'

It was Oxenham who spoke. A wheezing laugh followed, then a cough which brought a bubble of blood to his lips. With a muttered oath, Woollard bent over him and dabbed at his mouth.

'Aye, he may do it,' the dying man said. 'Take me out in a boat, weight me with stones and heave me over the side . . . a watery grave will serve as well as any other.'

Nobody spoke for a while after that. The surgeon patched the wound, drew a length of cloth about Oxenham's body and bound it, while the man's breath soughed in his windpipe. Marbeck stood by, until finally Woollard straightened up.

'There's nothing more to be done,' he said. 'I've dulled the wound with clove oil, but when air invades the chest cavity the heart will likely fail. And that, Giles Blunt, will be the end of my part in this.'

The intelligencers eyed him: a man who had once been in the same service as they, though only Marbeck knew it. Finally, it was Oxenham who broke the silence again. 'There's a purse at my belt, master surgeon,' he said. 'Take what you will, and give the rest to this man. He'll find a use for it.'

Woollard drew a breath, but made no reply.

'And it was no jest . . . about burying me at sea,' Oxenham went on. 'I meant to disappear when my task was done; this one last act of idiocy . . .' He turned to Marbeck. 'You were right, about it being foolish. I was never made for such sport.'

His voice was weak, his skin a deathly grey beneath what Marbeck now saw was not floridness, but deep sunburn. He turned to Woollard, but the surgeon was already moving away.

'I'll leave you,' he murmured. 'Call me when . . . when you must.'

He went out, closing the door. Outside the window a breeze had got up, carrying the noise of the surf with it. As soon as they were alone, Marbeck slumped down on the stool where he'd sat that morning to have his ear mended. 'So – instead of hunting Solomon Tye, you followed me all the way here,' he said at last. 'Why did you so? Or rather, who ordered you—'

'Not Monk,' Oxenham broke in. 'You may set your mind at rest there.' He wheezed again, a feeble attempt at laughter. 'You've never had any difficulty making enemies, Marbeck, but he's not one of them. Even though it's often our own kind we fear most, is it not?'

Marbeck made no reply.

'And yet . . .' The dying man paused, wincing in pain. 'By the Christ, it hurts. Despite our friend's clove oil . . .' He exhaled slowly. 'Not long ago, if any man had told me I'd perish within the sound of the sea, I'd have called him a liar. For after I returned to England, I swore I'd never go near it again.'

'Which sea was that?' Marbeck asked, for want of anything else to say.

'It's a fair question, for I've seen several,' Oxenham answered. 'The Mediterranean and the Ionian, to name but two . . . but it was in the Tyrrhenian Sea I met my nemesis . . .' He groaned; speaking was becoming a strain. 'Then, I fear I've no time for traveller's tales. You should hear of the man who's sworn to have you killed, or kill you himself.'

Marbeck frowned. 'What man . . .?' he began – then a notion sprang up, that made him draw a sharp breath.

'He calls himself El Roble,' the other answered. 'In Spanish it means "the Oak" . . . but his true name is—'

'Juan Roble.'

Oxenham saw the look on his face, and fell silent. But for Marbeck the name hung in the air, and years rolled away.

Juan Roble: the Spanish spymaster whose circle of agents he had broken four years ago, after the man's beautiful lover, the Comtesse de Paiva, had cried out his name in a French château; Roble, who had despatched forged letters only last year, designed to fall into Cecil's hands and brand Marbeck a traitor. And now, in a house in Dorset, he heard the name again from the mouth of a man who would die by his own hand . . .

'I see you know of him . . . you'd best come closer.' There was urgency in Oxenham's voice; Marbeck stood up and moved nearer to him.

'There are things I'll tell,' he said. 'They matter not to me now, but I ask something in return. Do you swear you will do it for me?'

His face taut, Marbeck nodded briefly.

'Go to my father, Richard Oxenham. He's a shoemaker in Dover . . . almost blind, lives near the quays. Make sure he's safe – for he's the reason I had to kill you – among others. You see, I first thought I'd despatched you back in London, when I doctored your drink.'

Marbeck stared. 'It was you who tried to poison me . . .?'

His answer was a feeble nod. 'Your pardon for that,' Oxenham sighed, with an attempt at a smile. 'But had I refused the order, they said my father would die the same vile death I faced. And that's a death I wouldn't wish on any man . . . save perhaps those who mete it out to others.'

'*They* said?' Marbeck echoed. 'You mean Roble?'

'I never set eyes on him – but one of his captains had me at his mercy, in Algiers . . .' Oxenham screwed his eyes up, as if at some terrible memory. 'Listen to me, Marbeck. There's a fleet – a force of pirates and raiders that spreads terror before it, and anguish in its wake. Their reach stretches from the Azores to the Levant: and behind it are a group of wicked men: Spaniards, all-powerful. Roble is one of them – El Roble, I should say. I know nothing of the others, but their name is feared across the Mediterranean: Las Langostas – it means—'

'Locusts – the Sea Locusts.'

'Yes . . .' Oxenham's eyes narrowed. 'You've already heard this?'

Slowly, Marbeck nodded, trying to order his feelings: remorse tempered with amazement – and despite everything, a grim sense of satisfaction. Weighing every word, he leaned close. 'Tell me all you can,' he murmured. 'I must know this.'

'Las Langostas despise their own king,' Oxenham went on, after a moment. 'They think Philip a pious fool, and a traitor to his father's wishes. They hate the peace he now makes with our king. They've broken loose, made their base on islands where there's no law . . . like Formentera, where the salt-fields lie. They're renegades like others in Barbary – and can you believe that some of them are Englishmen?'

He coughed, and his hand shook; all Marbeck could do was nod. 'I think I can,' he answered.

'Well, there now . . . I've made amends,' the other sighed. 'And so can you, Marbeck. I've a horse nearby, stabled in the White Hart Inn. Sell it, and my pack too; everything I own is inside it. Then go to my father and tell him of my death . . . only embroider it, won't you? So that he may go to his grave in peace . . . he'd given up all hope of my being aught but a disappointment. A city dandy and a spendthrift . . . if only he'd known.' He smiled feebly, and his eyelids fluttered. '*Ecce Aurora*, eh?'

'*Ecce Aurora*,' Marbeck repeated.

Suddenly he felt exhausted: a tiredness in his bones, that no sleep would assuage. He looked into Oxenham's face, saw his approaching end – then gave a start.

'You said you had to kill me, among others? Who . . .?'

But it was no use; he looked into his fellow-intelligencer's face, and saw his approaching end.

'Oxenham, listen to me,' he said urgently. 'You've done much – given me tidings we can use. I'll carry them to Cecil . . . then I'll ride to Dover and find your father. He'll hear news of you that will gladden his heart . . . this I swear. You can rest – take heart, and rest.'

But the other barely heard him. His breath came in rasps,

and another crimson bubble appeared at his mouth. Finally his eyes closed, and his chest rose and fell, ever more slowly.

Marbeck sat down heavily, and waited for Thomas Oxenham to die.

TWELVE

L ate the following night, Marbeck was back in Weymouth. He had slipped into the town after dark, and tethered Cobb to a ring on the quayside. Now, with the streets empty, he walked to the corner of Hope Cove and readied himself.

It had been a long day, of regret and remorse, but he'd been spared one grim task: that of disposing of the body of Thomas Oxenham. In the morning, after Marbeck had stayed up half the night and watched his fellow-intelligencer die, Woollard had changed his mind and said he would deal with the matter. The surgeon wished to be rid of both his unwanted guests, the living and the dead, but Marbeck's departure seemed to him the more urgent. Having handed Oxenham's purse to him, he said he would dispose of the man's horse and belongings. So with few words the two of them had parted at dawn, Marbeck riding swiftly out of Melcombe and concealing himself in a copse on the road to Broadwey. There, he'd formed his plan to free Mary Kellett from her dreadful captivity.

Oxenham's death, as well as his testimony, had shaken him; but now he saw it differently. Juan Roble, the man he had thwarted in the past, wished him dead and had forced Oxenham to carry out the task – though his people, it seemed, had misjudged the man's capabilities: someone like Levinus Monk, perhaps, could have advised them differently. As for Roble's corsair activity: it took Marbeck's breath away. It revealed a link between the Langostas of the Mediterranean and their fellows in the northern seas: the Sea Locusts. And after all that Oxenham had said, was it not likely that this network of renegades was behind attempts to spoil the peace talks in London?

He had turned the matter about, and the more he looked the darker the whole business appeared. There were people on both sides who disliked the planned treaty – even if both their nations had much to gain from its successful conclusion.

But in the end he felt helpless in the face of these wider events, and after hiding out all day, he'd grown weary of it. Two things he could and would do, because he had given his word: one was to go to Oxenham's father, but the first was to rescue Mary Kellett from John Buck. And for that task only a bold approach would serve: in short, he would go to the house and take her away by force.

Now, with the town quiet and most folk abed, he steeled himself to the task. In the evening clouds had scudded in; as a result the place was almost pitch dark, with only a couple of lanterns on the quays. After a final look round, he walked the short distance to the Buck house and rapped on the door.

For a moment nothing happened; then came a creak overhead as a casement opened. Drawing his poniard, he pressed himself against the doorway. From above he couldn't be seen; and when a voice called out he made no answer. The voice was Sarah's; he waited, but no further sound came. If John Buck was in the house it would be he who came to the door, and for that Marbeck was prepared; he heard the window close, and tensed in every muscle. There was no back entrance to the building, he believed . . . and at last, he heard the sound of a bolt sliding back. The door opened only inches, but it was enough.

With all his strength he shoved it inwards, heard a cry and the thud of someone falling. Then he was in, kicking the door shut behind him . . . and against the wall, eyes wide with fright, lay Sarah Buck tangled in a voluminous night-shift. When he bent and showed her the dagger-point, she gasped.

'God's mercy . . . you won't use that!'

'Where's Buck?' Marbeck snapped.

'He's upstairs – he'll have heard!' Sarah threw back. 'Go while you can, or he'll kill you . . .' But seeing Marbeck knew she was lying, she faltered.

'Get up,' he ordered, with mixed feelings of relief and disappointment. Reaching down, he grasped Sarah's bony arm and dragged her to her feet. There was light, from a candle she'd placed on the stairs. Glancing round, he steered her towards the parlour doorway. But at that moment there came a soft footfall . . . He looked up, and there stood Mary Kellett in her thin shift.

'It's time,' he said. 'Will you get ready?'

In amazement Mary stared at him . . . then her eyes flew to Sarah Buck, but Marbeck was quicker. The woman's mouth was open: a split second later, and her shout would have woken the whole street. Instead she found Marbeck's hand clamped over her jaws, and the dagger's point an inch from her nose.

'One sound,' he hissed, 'and I'll end your life here.'

As bluffs went it was not one of his best, but on this occasion it worked: having no cause to doubt him, Sarah nodded quickly. Marbeck looked at Mary, who was still on the stairs.

'Bring me something to gag her,' he said.

The girl hesitated; only now, it seemed, had she grasped the reality: that freedom was within her reach. She turned on her heel and ran upstairs. A moment later she was back with a pair of woollen stockings, which she handed to Marbeck before disappearing again. There was a spring in her step, which in spite of everything eased his heart.

And in a matter of minutes, it was done. Mistress Buck was seated in a corner of the parlour, gagged and trussed: first with her own stockings, then with a rope Marbeck found in a closet. Meanwhile Mary Kellett, dressed in her workaday clothes and a tattered gown, was in the hall trembling visibly. Marbeck sheathed his poniard, and lifted the door-latch.

'I never thought you'd come back,' she said at last.

He drew breath, calming himself. 'Where's John Buck?'

'Abbotsbury,' Mary answered. 'He goes there often . . .' She cocked an ear towards the door. 'Are you sure it's safe? Someone might have seen you, when you entered Weymouth . . .'

'Perhaps. Which is why you must follow a few steps behind. When I get to the corner I'll whistle. My horse is nearby.'

A frown puckered her brow. 'You're leaving Sarah like that?' Her eyes strayed towards the parlour. 'It's dangerous . . .'

'Nevertheless, that's how it must be,' Marbeck said. 'By the time she frees herself we'll be clear, and Cobb will outrun any horse Buck can lay hands on.'

'You don't understand,' Mary said. 'It's not Buck who'll come after you . . .' But he shook his head.

'I go now – whatever happens, run to me.' He opened the door, then glanced down. 'You've no shoes still . . .'

'Everything I have is here,' she whispered, and indicated a

bundle tied about her waist. So with a nod, he stepped out into the street.

He listened, heard nothing but the distant wash of the sea, and hurried to the corner. Here he crouched, peering round at the quayside, but it was clear. There was a sound from further off – from the King's Arms, perhaps; but Cobb was between himself and the inn. He could see the silhouette in the gloom. Sensing his presence, the horse snickered. Having judged the distance, Marbeck half-turned and gave a low whistle. Then came the pad of feet, and Mary was beside him.

'I'll make a stirrup, hoist you into the saddle,' he said. 'You must grasp the reins tightly – is that clear?'

For answer she merely gripped his arm. So he straightened up and walked swiftly to Cobb, who was stamping restlessly. It was the work of a moment to loosen the reins, and when he looked round Mary was already hurrying to him. As she placed her foot in his cupped hands he found she was light, as she'd told him, three nights ago. Then she was in the saddle, Marbeck's foot was in the stirrup, and he was up behind her . . . and with a clack of hooves, they were moving along the quay. Somewhere a door opened, but it no longer mattered. Breaking into a trot they clattered across the bridge and were soon riding through Melcombe, the ground rising beneath Cobb's hooves.

As they passed the last house and rode out onto the northward road, Marbeck heard a sound from the figure who sat before him, her bony back pressed to his body. She muttered a few words, which were indistinct; but then he understood, and concentrated on guiding Cobb in the dark.

Mary was weeping, and her shoulders shook against his chest.

Dorchester was a bare eight miles away; but as he'd planned to do, Marbeck stopped at the copse three miles north, near Broadwey. He set Mary down and led Cobb away to graze, then returned to find the girl muffled in her hand-me-down gown, hunched against a tree. He handed her his leather flask, from which she drank thirstily. Though he could barely see her face, he sensed how frightened she was.

'We can't stay here,' she said. 'It isn't far enough. They'll come for me – I know they will.'

'As soon as dawn comes we'll ride on,' Marbeck said. 'They can't follow in the dark, and we have a few miles' start. In Dorchester I'll get you some better clothes. None will recognize you, I promise.'

She hesitated, then: 'Isn't it best that I go a different way – take the road to Wareham, or to Winterborne Abbas? They'll follow the horse, and by the time they find out . . .' But when he squatted beside her, she broke off.

'I'm not leaving you on foot, within their reach. You told me you tried to run before – how far did you get?'

At that she sighed. 'Only to the rabbit warrens above Melcombe.'

'Well – this is your chance, and you must seize it. In Dorchester you can decide where you want to go . . .' He paused, recalling what Woollard had told him. 'Is there any family . . .?'

But she made no answer, and he too fell silent. In truth he was uncertain what to do with her. He had to make his way back to London, but it was a very long ride for two people on one horse. He sat on the grass and drew his cloak about him. 'You should try and get some sleep,' he began – but gave a start as her hand clutched his arm.

'Why did you come back?'

'Because I told you I would.'

'But your life was threatened . . . you knew the danger, yet—'

'Let's say I've taken a strong dislike to John Buck, shall we?' In the darkness, Marbeck wore a wry smile. 'And had he been at home, it would have given me satisfaction to stick a poniard under his nose, and hear him beg for his life.'

She paused, then: 'Sarah's life will be torture, when Buck finds out what's happened. He'll blame her like he always does – I daren't think what he'll do.' And when Marbeck said nothing, she added: 'There's much I could tell you about Buck. You should know what manner of danger you face . . .'

'Tomorrow – when you've rested, and we're in Dorchester. I'll find an inn . . .'

'And where do you mean to go, after that?'

'To London,' Marbeck answered after a moment. 'But I cannot take you all the way there.'

She sighed. 'I know that . . . I would not ask so much.'

She was silent after that, and to allay her fears he added: 'But I'll take you wherever you wish. I know a few people . . . there might be a place for you, as—'

'A servant in a trugging-house?'

The bitterness in her voice was stark as it was sudden. He sighed, for it rang true: the girl's future looked bleak. He was seeking some words of comfort, when she spoke again.

'You asked me about the Sea Locusts.'

In the dark, he turned to her.

'How much do you know about them?' Mary asked.

'I know of two ships called the *Amity* and the *Lion's Whelp* . . . and that they're slave-traders,' Marbeck said.

'But do you know what kind of slaves they carry?'

'Those poor wretches taken from the coasts of Africa and elsewhere, I imagine.' He broke off: her voice was taut. Suddenly, an ugly thought occurred to him – and her next words confirmed his suspicion.

'I was to be one of them,' Mary said flatly.

He started, and let out a long breath.

'The bargain is already made, and Buck meant to turn me to good profit,' she went on. 'English girls, and those of other fair-skinned races – Irish or Danes, say – fetch high prices in the Barbary states. Though it's better if they're virgins, of course . . .' She gave a hollow laugh. 'But there are ways to fake that, Buck said. I would be instructed how, in the Bedestan – that's the slave market in Algiers. If I was lucky, he used to say, I might even end up in the pasha's *harem*. Then he'd laugh, and say I wasn't pretty enough. And he'd send me upstairs again to earn my keep, as he put it . . .'

She stopped talking; somehow, in the dark, she sensed Marbeck's anger. He knew little of the slave trade, though he'd heard tales of people being snatched from many countries, even northern Europe: men, women – and it seemed, children too . . .

He got up suddenly, startling Mary, and walked away. It fitted: Woollard's telling how the girl had been passed to Buck, to dispose of as he pleased; why secrecy surrounded the Sea

Locust ships, and why people were afraid to speak about them. Breathing hard, he gazed into the dark, wishing John Buck had been there when he'd forced his way into the house. Finally he turned, and made his way back to Mary.

'You said there were things you could tell me,' he said finally.

'I can still,' she said at once. 'For I know who owns those ships – who pays for their fitting out, to send them to sea again and again. And who takes the biggest share, when they return.'

He froze. There was a scrap of intelligence here at last: something that might have a bearing on his stalled investigation. Again he heard the voice of Fahz in the Limehouse tavern: *wicked men, doing wicked deeds* . . . with an effort, he sat down beside her again.

'I want to know more . . . indeed, I want to know all of it,' he said, somewhat harshly. 'But it must wait until tomorrow, when you've rested. I have to write it down . . .'

'Why would you?' she broke in sharply. And when he made no answer, she seemed to shrink from him. 'Are you one of the Admiralty men? That's what Buck told me. He told me you'd have me arrested as a whore, and sent to Bridewell to be whipped . . .'

'He lied.' Marbeck broke in. 'I'm not from the Admiralty court, nor any other court . . . you've nothing to fear from me. And there are men – decent men – who might help someone like you . . .'

'Oh, indeed?' The change in her tone was stark, but he understood. What cause had she to trust any man, after what she'd suffered? 'But . . . I will go with you,' she said finally. 'You've been my saviour – and what other choice have I?'

'Then try to rest now, and I'll wake you when it's light,' Marbeck said. A weariness had come upon him, yet he doubted he would sleep. He wrapped himself in his cloak and lay back. When he heard Mary stretch herself out, he assumed tiredness would get the better of her. But instead, she suddenly turned to him.

'I'll tell you his name now. I may speak it in my sleep anyway . . . I sometimes do, for it's a name I knew before any other. He's the man in whose house I was born . . . it's but seven or eight miles from where we are now.'

After a moment, Marbeck sat up again.

'It's a fine manor house, on the hills above Abbotsbury,' Mary went on. 'It's where Buck goes, sometimes. I might have lived there still, had I been born of another woman . . . but I was an embarrassment, and a trial to the master's wife. And now, I know he had other plans from me from the beginning. The man who lives in that house, I mean . . . a knight, one of the richest in the county they say. He claims acquaintance with the highest . . . owns more land even than they . . .' She yawned; for a moment he thought she was drifting into sleep – until she spoke the name.

'He is Sir Edward Quiney,' Mary said. 'He owns the Sea Locusts, as he owns their captains and much else besides . . . and he is my true father.'

THIRTEEN

The inn at Dorchester was named the Ship, and it was both well situated and busy, which troubled Marbeck. They could be noticed, here in the centre of the town. But since Mary was weary and he had no wish to search further afield, he hired a small chamber. When she fell asleep within minutes of crawling into the narrow bed, he left her and went out.

It was still early but the town was stirring, and finding an ordinary he ate hungrily. Then, having seen Cobb stabled and fed, he walked into the square where the shambles stood, with stallholders setting out their wares. From there he followed a street to the northern edge of the town, and found himself on the banks of the River Frome. Here, with swans gliding on the water and larks calling from above, he sat down to make his decision. For the choice was plain: he was being pulled in two opposite directions. One led to Salisbury and then to London, and his spymaster. The other, dangerous as it was, lay westward: to Abbotsbury, and the seat of Sir Edward Quiney.

The name was known to him, as it was to many. Quiney, the rake who had spent time at Queen Elizabeth's court; Quiney who had outlived two wives, and being yet in his forties, had married for a third time. Yet he was a man who was not born into wealth, but had acquired it by other means . . . and much was now explained. Here was one of those who, thwarted by the King's cancelling of letters of reprisal, had been swift to turn his attention to other kinds of seafaring. And there were few more profitable trades, Marbeck thought, than that of abducting people and selling them into slavery.

But it was not unknown: reports sometimes reached London of individuals disappearing from boats out at sea, or from beaches and isolated farms. Seamen spoke with dread of the slave-markets of Tangier, Tunis and Algiers, and of the great Ottoman galleys rowed by slaves. Some female captives were sent eastward, across the Mediterranean to the palace of the Grand Sultan in Constantinople. Marbeck had heard tales of women from as far north as Scandinavia ending up in the harem – though he hadn't known that English sea captains were among the slavers. Again he thought of the *Amity* . . . and of Gurran, who may or may not have set a needle-bomb to frighten the Spanish . . .

He got up, stiff from riding, and began to walk downriver through sunlit fields. Cattle grazed and sheep stood on the distant hills; but on the Dorset coast, an evil trade was being practised. The Swann brothers, whose father captained one of the ships; Reuben Beck too, and those in their pay, like John Buck – all were party to it. And behind them was the one who financed the voyages and reaped the lion's share of profit: one of the wealthiest noblemen in the county – who was likely in league with Spanish renegades: ruthless men on both sides, who had become a law to no one but themselves.

A splash startled him, breaking his thoughts. He glanced at the water, saw the circle of ripples where a large fish had leaped to take a fly. Across the river a boy was sitting, fishing pole in hand. He saw Marbeck, took off his straw hat and waved it cheerfully. The lad was about Mary's age. He returned the greeting, and drew a breath.

He wasn't going back to London; he'd known it already. Let Monk berate him all he liked – surely there was something he could do here? Events that took place in foreign lands, even slavery, were outside the reach of English law – but if nothing else, the Sea Locusts might be arraigned as pirates. The *Amity* still came at times to its old port of Weymouth: couldn't a strategy be devised? He wondered what the vessel had been doing in Gravesend . . . then remembered Elias Fitch's tale. Of course Gurran had set the needle-bomb: a carpenter who sailed on a slave ship would have few scruples about turning his skills to darker use, if the price was high enough . . . or if he'd been ordered to do it.

Head down in thought, he walked for a mile or so, then turned back towards the town. A scheme was forming, but it was risky, and might involve his finding a new role. He thought of personas he'd employed in recent times – Richard Strang the jobbing lute-player, say, or Thomas Wilders, dealer in ordnance – but rejected them both. For this task he had to be bold, since what he had in mind was nothing less than riding to Sir Edward Quiney's seat and somehow gathering enough evidence to take to Monk, or better still to Lord Cecil. It would give meaning to his journey here . . . and besides, ever since hearing Mary Kellett's tale he'd been angry. Yet for now, he must rein it in: one slip, and his life would be ended.

Dorchester was bustling by the time he walked through its streets again. Thinking of his promise to Mary, he roamed the shops and the fripperers' stalls and picked out clothes of about the right size: a plain kirtle, skirts and petticoat, stockings and shoes; she would not go barefoot again. Finally he found her a wide-brimmed hat to keep the sun off, and laden with purchases, made his way back to the inn. But when he entered the chamber he stopped dead: the bed was empty, and Mary was gone.

Cursing roundly, Marbeck dropped the clothing and went to the window, but the casement was shut fast. He stepped outside and glanced along the passage; chamber doors were open, and a maid was at her work. Standing in the doorway, he asked if she had seen anything of his younger sister, having decided on their relationship there and then; but the woman knew nothing.

Still cursing under his breath, he hurried downstairs and, after a hasty look about the inn, went out into the street. People moved to and fro, and horses clopped by. On a whim he turned left and began walking towards the Guildhall. He passed the turning to South Street, the cross and the water-trough. The town was at its busiest here; he neared the hall . . . and halted.

There stood Mary Kellett in her tattered gown, her hand outstretched in the manner of beggars the world over. When she saw Marbeck she gave a start, then came towards him with an air of resignation. 'You can leave me here,' she said, drawing close. 'I would have gone and . . .' But she trailed off, for in his relief Marbeck had allowed his anger to surface.

'So – you ran away from me too.'

'Please . . . it's best.' In the daylight she wouldn't meet his eye, but kept hers on the ground. 'I was going to beg until I made enough to pay a carter to take me somewhere. I owe you much, but you cannot carry me far . . . and besides, it may already be too late.'

'What do you mean?' Taking her by the shoulders, he forced her to face him. 'Have you seen someone?'

She nodded. 'But not Buck, nor his fellows. It's a man I've not seen in many months. He was here by the Guildhall a while ago, but I don't think he saw me.'

'Who is he?' Marbeck demanded.

'I don't know his name. He's a friend of Sir Edward. He came to Abbotsbury sometimes, though he's no Dorset man.'

'Very well . . .' Marbeck hesitated, then made his decision. 'I ask you to go back to the inn. There are clothes for you in the chamber – at least you can dress yourself better. You may ask for water to wash: say your brother ordered it. Then you can choose to wait for me, or to leave. I can't force you, nor will I try . . .' He paused, as a notion occurred. 'I've a mind to get you to Cranborne . . . it's a manor, where I might find a place for you as a kitchen maid. If that doesn't suit—'

'But it would.' Her hopes rising, Mary's face cleared. 'It's far away, is it – Cranborne?'

'Not very far,' Marbeck told her. 'But you'd be safe there.'

'Then I'll await you . . .' She threw a grateful look at him and would have started off, but he stayed her. 'Wait – this man you saw. Where was he, and what does he look like?'

With a shrug, she told him: he had been talking with others, near the Guildhall. He was somewhat slight, and wore a fine silk doublet; his beard was fair, trimmed to a point . . . But she faltered then, as Marbeck stared over her head.

'I see him,' he said, almost to himself. And he started past Mary, pausing only to grip her shoulder. 'Wait for me, and don't leave the chamber.' Then he was gone.

Mary blinked, then began walking. Once she glanced back, but Marbeck had disappeared. She could not know, of course, that he too had recognized the gaudily dressed man from London, who stood out in this country town like a peacock in a hen-house. Or that Marbeck had last seen him in a tavern in Cosin Lane, where he fought swords with Solomon Tye . . . and that this same man had struck him on the head before making a hasty retreat.

His name was Simon Jewkes.

*   *   *

The Guildhall was busy, a hubbub of male voices with merchants thronging on all sides. Servants dogged their heels, officials came and went and even a few beggars ventured inside, only to be thrown out. Through it all Marbeck moved, alert and watchful; he had lost sight of Jewkes, but had a notion he'd entered the hall. A gathering of some sort was about to take place, he realized, and there was a general movement of men in one direction. Yet he satisfied himself that Jewkes was not among them, and made his way back to the main doors. If the man caught sight of him, his plan would fail before it had begun. And a thought struck him: that his journey to Dorset had not gone unnoticed. If Oxenham could follow him down here, so could others . . . but with an effort, he dismissed the notion. Surely he was the last person Jewkes would expect to see?

His eyes sweeping the hall for the last time, he ventured out into the sunlight and looked about, but there was no sign of his quarry. He crossed the street and stood beneath an overhang. To his left where West Street petered out, lay the ruins of what had been part of the old town wall. Children were playing, climbing on the stones; idly he turned away . . . and then, he saw his man.

Quickly he averted his gaze, though he was sure Jewkes hadn't noticed him. He stood perhaps thirty yards off, and seemed to be sniffing the air – as he had done more than a week ago, on the jetty at Salisbury house. He wore different clothes, but there was little doubt it was he; in the shadows, Marbeck waited. And when the man finally moved off and rounded the corner of the main square, he followed. It was only a short walk, however, and his face clouded: Jewkes was entering what looked like a stable. If his horse was there, he would be gone before Marbeck got Cobb saddled . . .

He paused, thinking on what Mary had said. There was no knowing whether Jewkes was on his way to Quiney's manor, or whether he had been there already and was returning to London. By the time Marbeck had ascertained his direction it could be too late. Following him in daylight would be unwise, and would mean leaving Mary alone. Swift action was called for; that and a measure of luck.

He straightened himself, placed a hand on his sword-hilt

and strode to the stable. He passed under the low threshold into the interior, its air heavy with the smell of hay and animals . . . and there was Jewkes coming towards him, leading a fine roan horse. Both men stopped short, but Marbeck's reactions were quicker.

'Jewkes . . . or is it Master Goodenough?'

Silence; in the dim interior, horses shifted and snorted.

'Simon Jewkes?' Marbeck persisted.

Still the man said nothing; the tip of his tongue emerged to wet his lips, then: 'You mistake – my name's Combes.'

'I think not.' Emboldened, Marbeck took a step forward. With some force, it struck him that one clue to the mystery that had racked him for the past nine days was standing before him: a thin-faced, round-shouldered man who dressed like a wealthy merchant, but had the eyes and demeanour of a cutpurse. Moreover, he appeared to be alone.

'I think you're Jewkes, who hired a man called Solomon Tye to work for you,' he said. And when the other bristled, he went on: 'I also think you've been poking your fingers where you shouldn't . . . and when I came looking at the Black Horse, you cracked me on the head. And more—'

'I suggest you look behind you,' Jewkes said harshly.

Marbeck froze. Was it a footfall he'd heard, or a sound from the street? He looked the man in the eye and bluffed.

'I care not who's behind me,' he said. 'I mean to swear out a warrant against you for assault, have you arrested and—' Then he broke off, and whirled about. There had been no noise; the only sign was a glint in Jewkes's eyes, but it was enough.

Two men stood inside the stable entrance, and one glance was all Marbeck needed. As hired ruffians went, they were a cut above the average: alert and muscular. They were dressed as huntsmen, in brown fustian; one had a long knife at his belt, while the other held a small caliver which he levelled at Marbeck. There was a click as he cocked it.

'You were saying?'

Marbeck turned back to Jewkes, who was regarding him with controlled anger. Despite his haughty manner, he was a wharf-weasel at heart – though compared to him, Marbeck thought, his old informant Peter Mayne was a gentleman. He

made no answer, whereupon the other spoke in a tone of contempt
tinged with amusement.

'I regret I can't spare the time to continue our conversation,'
he said. 'Instead, I'll leave you in the company of my friends
. . . now, will you kindly move yourself?'

Marbeck looked round, as the hired men advanced and
motioned him to stand aside. He backed to the nearest stall,
whereupon Jewkes led his thoroughbred mount past them. As
he went, he couldn't resist a smirk at Marbeck: cold eyes
mocking him, signalling his fate. At the entrance he paused,
reins in hand, to speak low to one of his followers. Then he
mounted, and without looking back rode away. Marbeck
watched him disappear, then eyed his captors.

'I don't think you'll use that,' he said, with a nod at the
weapon. 'The noise would bring half the town running . . .'

'We go outside,' said the man holding the caliver, a well-
built fellow with a strong London accent. 'And I don't need
to use it, for this one will be behind you.' Whereupon the
other man – a gaunt, hatchet-faced individual – pulled out his
hunting-knife and moved forward. Pressing the point to the
base of Marbeck's spine, he clapped him on the shoulder and
gave him a shove.

His face blank, Marbeck walked to the door and out into
the sunlight, the two men at his back. He glanced about, but
made no resistance as they steered him briskly away from the
busy square, along a quieter street and finally out to the riverside,
where he'd walked but an hour ago. This time, however, he was
marched upriver for a hundred yards or more, to a bridge.
After crossing the Frome they then followed a road which led
roughly northwards through fields, before turning aside to a
wood. Soon they were among the trees, hidden from the road
and far enough from the town. They stopped, and the one with
the knife backed off. Standing in dappled sunlight Marbeck
steeled himself, weighing his chances.

'Kneel,' the well-built man ordered.

'Do you know, I don't think I will,' Marbeck said.

'On your knees, you whoreson devil!' the other growled.
He was the angry one: more dangerous perhaps, but also less
controlled, and hence the weaker . . . Marbeck paused, then
turned boldly to him.

'Are you a gambler?' he asked conversationally. 'I'll wager a half-angel you can't spike me before I get my poniard out . . .'

'Stop.' The one with the caliver, though still calm, was losing patience. 'Force him to his knees,' he said, with a glance at his companion.

The other hesitated, but only briefly. Glowering at Marbeck, with the knife held forward he stepped close and lifted his free hand – then yelped as, with a movement so fast that both men barely saw it, Marbeck grabbed his arm and twisted it. At the same moment something appeared in his other hand: a tailor's bodkin; and a second later, it was embedded up to its handle in the hatchet-faced man's neck.

After that, things slowed down somewhat. In horror the man with the caliver stared as a thin stream of blood shot from his companion's artery, splashing his hunting-coat. The long knife dropped to the forest floor, followed by the victim himself who sat down with a thud, eyes bulging. Shakily he put a hand to his neck, gripped the bodkin and pulled it out – which only made the blood spurt further.

The other man however, was recovering his wits. With an oath he pointed his caliver at Marbeck – but he was far too late. The weapon was seized by its barrel and torn from his grasp, as the side of Marbeck's closed fist thudded hard against his mouth. He reeled back, his own fists flailing, but that too was fruitless: a sword flashed in the sunlight, and its point was at his neck.

'Why don't you kneel instead?' Marbeck breathed.

FOURTEEN

It took a very few minutes for the man Marbeck had stabbed to lose consciousness. Soon he was a pale figure lying flat on the ground, eyes closed. While his fellow, silent and chastened, knelt at Marbeck's mercy.

'Jewkes,' Marbeck said briskly. 'Where's he gone – to Abbotsbury or to London?'

The man was breathing hard, eyes down. He wavered, whereupon Marbeck thought to give him a jab of encouragement. His sword-arm twitched, and he got his answer.

'To London . . . we awaited him here. I never go to Abbotsbury . . .'

'Sir Edward Quiney: what's he to Jewkes? Or should I say, what's Jewkes to him?'

But there was no answer; the man's gaze strayed to his dying companion, then dropped.

'You know what this is, don't you?' Marbeck bent close to his ear, making him flinch. 'This is your death. In a while you'll be lying alongside your friend. Then I'll cover you both with branches and grass, and none will know you're here until foxes mangle your corpses – or until somebody notices the smell. That's the fate you had in mind for me, was it not?'

There was a shudder; sweat stood out on the man's brow and trickled down his face. 'Get it done, then,' he said savagely. 'And the devil take you!'

'No, you misunderstand,' Marbeck said patiently. 'It won't be a quick death. I work for the Crown, learned a few tricks in the Marshalsea. I mean to get everything I want first, bit by bit . . . You see?' And with that he raised his tailor's bodkin, now removed from the hand of the dying man, and held it in front of his victim's eyes.

'By God . . . who are you?' the other demanded, with a baleful look. But all he got was a gentle prod with the bodkin.

'Quiney and Jewkes,' Marbeck said flatly. 'Tell me about

them, or I'll start work in earnest.' For emphasis he jabbed the point in the fellow's arm.

He jerked, and let out an oath. 'You don't know what you're doing, friend!' he spat. 'Jewkes isn't the one to fear . . . you're throwing your life away—'

'Signing my own death warrant?' Marbeck broke in. 'I've already been told that, by a man named Buck, in Weymouth. Know him too, do you?'

'I know the name . . . but it matters not.' The other gave a groan, of sheer exasperation. 'You're dealing with powerful men,' he said harshly. 'They can have you hanged, for any crime they choose to think up . . .'

'Piracy, for example?' Marbeck brought his face close again. 'Perhaps I've been asking the wrong questions . . . Will you speak of the Sea Locusts instead? What of Swann – and Reuben Beck?'

He straightened up and waited. At first there was no reaction, then finally his victim sighed. 'You'd better pray they never find you,' he said wearily. 'If they do, they'll ship you to Barbary. You'll be chained to an oar, and to the bench of an open galley on the high seas, shitting where you toil, your only diet vinegar and biscuit . . . you wouldn't last a month.'

Slowly Marbeck nodded. 'I've heard such tales . . . but they're not my concern. I need to know about Jewkes, and I'm asking for the last time: what's he to Quiney?'

A moment followed, then a sigh. 'Haven't you guessed?' the kneeling man said at last, with a bitter edge to his voice. 'He's *nothing* to Quiney – that's the nub of it!'

Marbeck stared at him . . . and understood. 'You mean he's the face,' he said, piecing it together as he spoke. 'The shield, for the man who never gets a drop on him when blood spills. The errand-boy . . . who dresses like a gentleman, but in the end is just a lackey.'

And when no answer came, because none was needed, he exhaled and lowered his sword. The other gave a start, and looked up.

'So,' Marbeck said at last. 'The question remains, what am I to do with you?'

*   *   *

In the afternoon, he and Mary Kellett sat in the chamber at the Ship and talked: not about her miserable life at the house of John Buck but about Sir Edward Quiney, who had fathered her on a servant, kept her as a scullion and finally cast her out. She told Marbeck too of the sea captains who sometimes came at night, like Gideon Swann, the man from Weymouth. And servants sometimes spoke darkly of another who was known as El Mirlo, meaning 'the Blackbird' in the Spanish tongue. Jewkes also came at various times, to the great manor house on the hills above Abbotsbury. By the time their talk was finished, Marbeck had learned all he needed to know.

Mary looked like a different person, dressed in the clothes Marbeck had given her. The shoes she was very taken with, though they would take the most getting used to. She had eaten dinner, and was now eager to leave Dorchester. But when he told her what he had decided, her face fell.

'You're not coming with me?'

'I cannot,' Marbeck said. 'There are things I must do – but you'll be safe. I'll find a carrier, a reliable man, and pay him to take you to Cranborne manor. I'll give you a letter to show to the steward, or whoever is in charge. When he reads it, he should let you stay there until he hears from his master. His master's an important man, who'll find a place for you. You have my word on this . . . if that's enough.'

'It is enough,' she said, after a moment. 'And it pains me that I can never repay you.'

'But you have,' he said at once. 'You've told me a great deal that's of use . . .' Then as she didn't understand, he added: 'To do with Buck, I mean. In time he may be brought to justice. Would that ease your heart somewhat?'

To that, she merely nodded. 'Will I never see you after this, Master Blunt?'

'Who can say?' Marbeck told her, summoning a smile. 'Never is a long time.' Whereupon he left her once again, and went out to make some purchases.

In the town, as he moved through the afternoon crowd, his manner grew brisk. A few hours ago he had left Jewkes's henchmen in the wood, one dying, the other very much alive. But he had no fear on the latter's count: in the end, the man had been so relieved to have his life spared he would have assented to anything. As it was, disarmed and subdued, he swore to obey Marbeck's order: to take his friend's body and leave the county, never to return. He'd agreed to this because, by the end, he was convinced that Marbeck was some kind of messenger for the Privy Council, with real powers – and more, because Marbeck hinted that the Council's eyes were on Sir Edward Quiney, whose days were numbered. On that understanding they had parted, with Marbeck satisfied that the man would not run to Jewkes: he'd allowed him to think that Jewkes too was now under scrutiny.

Now, however, he faced his most difficult task, that would stretch him to his limits. After taking time to think before returning to Mary, he'd abandoned his notion of going to Quiney's manor. The man had never seen Marbeck, but still the risk of failure was too great. Hence Marbeck had a different strategy in mind: to get Quiney to come to him. Since the man rarely left his home, the only way he could do that was to pose as someone as important as Quiney himself. And the man he had invented was Marcus Janes, unscrupulous merchant and venturer, newly returned from a sojourn in France.

To become Janes, Marbeck had work to do. His horse would serve, as would his good sword, but he needed fine clothes, jewels and other trappings. This would be difficult; the purse he had from Oxenham turned out to contain less money than he expected, and he had to see Mary on her way to Cranborne. But he had a few ideas, among them to scour the fripperers' stalls again and find the best garb available, the sort passed to servants by their masters and sold on. Then he would find a jeweller who made convincing fakes, and finally he would visit a barber and have his hair and beard styled. Thinking on barbers gave him another idea; unappealing as the notion was, there was one man who could aid him: Thomas Woollard. He would do so because Marbeck would give him a bleak choice: help him, or feel the weight of Levinus Monk's wrath, when the spymaster learned that Woollard had acted against the interests of the Crown.

Having formed his resolve, he spent the rest of the day fitting himself out, returning to the inn in the evening. His last task had been to approach a carrier who made regular trips to

Blandford and Salisbury, and pay him to convey his young sister to Cranborne manor. Receiving a payment in advance, with the prospect of a tip at the end, the man readily agreed; he was leaving the following morning. So by nightfall it was settled, and after a supper Marbeck left Mary in her chamber, while he retired to the taproom and called for the strongest ale.

Here, however, he flagged, as the events of the last two days caught up with him: two men dead by his hand, one of them a fellow-intelligencer. Other dark thoughts welled up, too; at one point he found himself clenching his fists, occasioning looks from other drinkers. Thereafter, knowing he had drunk more than was good for him, he cast caution aside and drank even more . . . with the end result that when dawn broke, he awoke to find himself in a strange room, lying on a greasy pallet with a blowsy trull snoring beside him. Sitting up too quickly, his head throbbing, he fell back and slept for another hour, before at last staggering to his feet. Stark naked, he swayed once, and found his hostess's eyes on him.

'We agreed six pence, sir,' the doxy said, covering her own modesty with the sheet. 'I got half out of you last night . . . I'll have the rest now.' When Marbeck merely blinked, however, she gave a sigh and relented. 'Oh, well-a-day . . . since you did naught but sleep and grunt like a boar, we'll say another penny for the bed. Will that suit?'

An hour later he stood on the east road out of Dorchester beside the riverbank, to see Mary Kellett off on her journey.

Sitting beside the carrier in her new clothes, she looked what she was: a slim girl of eleven years, but one who had been cruelly used, and had ceased to be a child. In the end, as they parted she found no words, merely allowed the tall carrier to lift her onto the bench, where she sat staring ahead. But when the man at last cracked his long whip and sent it snaking over the heads of the horses, Marbeck saw her shoulders droop.

He watched the wagon pull away, his thoughts already turning to business. Together with the letter to the steward at Cranborne, he had given Mary another, marked urgently for Lord Cecil himself. It contained a hasty report he had compiled the evening before; he could only hope that the steward saw fit to send it promptly to his master in London.

By midmorning he had paid the inn's reckoning and left the town, riding out on the southward road towards the Downs. The sun had disappeared, and clouds scudded in from the west, but he barely noticed. Sitting high in the saddle with a haughty air, richly dressed and clean-shaven, he prepared to take on his role as Marcus Janes.

The rain began after he had crossed the Downs and was walking Cobb through the tiny village of Upwey. Forced to shelter in a barn to protect his new clothes, he waited for the shower to pass, then rode on through Broadwey and downhill towards the coast. By the time Melcombe came into view the afternoon was waning, but he would not wait for nightfall. Instead he dismounted and led the horse into the town. When last here, he'd been Giles Blunt: black-clad and bearded. Now he was bejewelled, dressed in russet-and-gold silk and beardless. With the effect of those changes and his new manner, he felt confident enough. Soon he was passing through rain-washed streets to the house close to the sea, and knocking on Woollard's door. It opened, the man appeared, and almost jumped off his feet.

'Good Christ!' He drew back, peering through his spectacles. 'What in heaven's name do you want?'

'Best if I come in, isn't it?' Marbeck said.

'No! You've brought me troubles enough . . .'

'Not as bad as others I could bring,' Marbeck said. 'Will you admit me, or do I make a coil here on the doorstep?'

Woollard cursed audibly, but went back into the house leaving the door ajar. In a moment Marbeck was safely inside, following the man into his parlour.

'Well?' Angrily the barber-surgeon faced him. 'Haven't I done enough for you, or is there another corpse to shift?'

Without invitation, Marbeck sank wearily onto a stool. The ride from Dorchester was only eight miles, but he was still recovering from his drinking bout of the night before. Forgetting about Marcus Janes, he pulled out a kerchief and wiped the grime of the road from his face.

'I've no choice but to ask you to aid me further, Woollard,' he said finally. 'It will mean stepping aside from your cosy life and working for me . . . or rather for Cecil, in the end. I can't promise reward, or even thanks. But you still know right from wrong, I believe. As I believe you'll step up to the mark when you have to.'

'The what?' Woollard's face fell: suddenly, he looked a haggard old man. 'You don't mean that . . . and in any case, I'd be no use! To the devil with Cecil – and with you too!'

'That's what I expected you to say,' Marbeck replied. He looked round the man's chamber: at his flasks and instruments, his books and wall-charts of anatomy. 'But I've set a course, and I need you. Or are you content to let the Sea Locusts thrive, carrying children like Mary Kellett to the slave-marts of Algiers?'

At that Woollard swallowed audibly. 'You're not serious, are you? I've told you of those people, as I've told you I'm known to them . . .' He stared, his fear plain to see. 'Do you wish to cause my demise, as you did that of the poor wretch you ran through with your sword?'

'Not if I can help it,' Marbeck said. He turned as the door opened, and there stood a plain woman who had to be Woollard's servant. For a moment he wondered why it wasn't she who'd answered the door, then remembered she was deaf.

'Leave us,' Woollard said loudly. 'All's well.' But as the woman started to go, he called her back. 'Place the sign on the door – I'm not to be troubled.' She went out, whereupon he found Marbeck's gaze upon him.

'See now, this won't do . . . I've too much to lose,' he began in an exasperated tone. 'People here rely on me. I'm not suited for danger any more . . .'

'You live with it daily, do you not?' Marbeck eyed him without expression. 'You said you've been useful to these people, the Sea Locusts. They let you practise, but they could rein you in any time they choose.'

'Precisely so,' Woollard retorted. 'And I've no intention of offending them. I was hard pressed enough to get the body of your friend away without attracting attention—'

'Indeed,' Marbeck said. 'But you've already shot your bolt there. The man was Thomas Oxenham, one of Cecil's intelligencers. Once he hears of it he'll have you brought to London, tied to a horse. I might even be the one who has to convey you.'

'What do you mean?' Aghast, Woollard stared at him. 'I saved your neck . . . allowed you to get clear – and that's how you'd repay me?' When Marbeck made no reply, he backed to his chair and slumped down in it.

'So . . . nothing's changed in sixteen years,' he said bitterly. 'Men like you are as they always were: as unscrupulous as those you work against . . .'

'I think not,' Marbeck said abruptly. 'For the man I mean to snare is the one who runs the Sea Locusts. He's Sir Edward Quiney. Odd you didn't mention his name when we spoke before.'

Now the fear in Woollard's eyes increased. Marbeck allowed the words to sink in, then added: 'I won't ask more of you than you can accomplish. But I need to devise a means to meet with Quiney, alone if that's possible—'

'It isn't!' Woollard snapped. 'He's never alone, nor would he meet with someone he doesn't know.'

'He'd see you, though, would he not?'

The other's mouth fell open.

'Were you to send an urgent message, telling him that he was in danger, for instance?' Marbeck spoke calmly. 'That you'd received word of a body of men, say – sent by order of the High Court of the Admiralty – who were coming to arrest him—'

'He'd never believe that!' Woollard shook his head fiercely. 'He's well informed – were it true, he'd have known of it sooner. More, he'd suspect me of exactly the sort of double-dealing you're proposing!'

'Double-dealing?' Suddenly, Marbeck felt inclined to laugh. 'Forgive me, but who is it owns corsair ships, equips them to sail off and snatch slaves, and carry them to Barbary? Who's likely in league with a fleet of Spanish renegades, and whose influence is felt in London, thanks to his grubby right arm: a villain called Jewkes. And who's the man who gives his bastard daughter to a jackal like John Buck, to sell as he pleases . . .'

'Enough!' In agitation, Woollard threw up a hand as if to ward off such thoughts. 'Damn you . . . you've no right!' Suddenly he was on his feet, pointing a finger at Marbeck. 'I served the Crown loyally – came within an inch of my life doing it, and nearly lost my sanity too! I'll not be judged . . .' Almost shaking, he broke off and sat down again.

'I know,' Marbeck said gently. 'I feel the same, some days.'

Woollard's eyes were closed, his breathing rapid, until by some means he mastered himself and opened then again.

'Do this one thing for me,' Marbeck said. 'You know it's right. It may be my last act, since I got Mary Kellett away from Weymouth and sent her to a place of safety.'

Woollard gave a start. 'You took her from John Buck?'

Briefly, Marbeck nodded.

'And you weren't followed?'

'Perhaps I was. But I'm here now – and if you care to know more, I'll flesh out the details. Are you willing to listen?'

There was a moment's silence, before the barber-surgeon heaved a sigh. 'There's a man in Melcombe – an astrologer, whom I always thought a charlatan,' he said at last. 'He told me my death would come in on horseback, with the rain . . . is it you who brings it?'

Marbeck had no answer.

FIFTEEN

The two of them talked, as they had two nights ago in the same room, though to very different purpose. Woollard told his servant to bring a cold supper but ate little himself. A gloom was upon him; and Marbeck's plan, after he'd outlined it, was soon the object of his scorn. The notion of sending a message to a man like Sir Edward Quiney, from a stranger who wished to do business with him, was doomed from the outset. Moreover, Quiney would force whoever brought the message to remain under his roof until he'd got to the bottom of it.

'He trusts no one, not even his captains,' Woollard said. 'They work together because the rewards are so great, they'd be fools to do otherwise. More, the captains themselves are rivals who detest each other, and Reuben Beck – "el Mirlo" – deals harshly with any man who doesn't knuckle under to him.'

'What of Swann?' Marbeck asked. 'Do his sons not sail with him?'

'The older one did, so I heard. But even he had no stomach for the trade . . . deals in contraband wines instead.'

'And so thwarts the customs,' Marbeck said drily, letting his thoughts drift. 'Do you know who will hold the Great Farm soon, take handsome fees in import duties? No less a man than Lord Cecil himself, I hear – another token of King James's gratitude, for services rendered.'

'Well, at least that's something in your favour,' Woollard growled. 'If you were to accomplish the unlikely feat of spoiling the Swanns' trade, you'd reap a reward from your master.'

'I doubt it,' Marbeck said. 'Cecil takes the services of his intelligencers for granted nowadays.' He frowned. 'But see now, what of their father, Gideon Swann?'

'A rogue, though the less poisonous of the two. Lost an arm in a fight at sea, and drinks himself so senseless each night, his crew must put him to bed. That's one reason his sons won't sail with him, I think . . .' Woollard shook his head. 'The man you should fear is the master of the *Amity*, which lies offshore . . .' He gave a snort. 'The word means "friendship", yet I can think of few names less apt for a ship of doom, captained by someone you'd not wish to meet. I speak of Beck, of course: one who truly enjoys his work. Takes his pick of the women they capture, they say, and uses them at sea worse than they'll be used in Barbary . . .' Seeing Marbeck's expression, he paused. 'I know how your mind moves. It's more than likely Mary Kellett would be in his hands by now, if you hadn't stolen her away. Can you imagine what a man like that would do to you, if he knew? Or perhaps he knows already – have you thought on that?'

For Marbeck however, a scheme was taking shape: one that he would probably regret later, but that quickened his pulse. 'The *Amity* is still here?' he said. 'You said she lies offshore – I assumed Beck had left . . .'

'He's here yet – as is Swann's ship, the *Lion's Whelp*,' Woollard answered. 'The lights of both vessels can be seen, out in the bay. Everyone in Weymouth knows they're the Sea Locusts, though none would dare admit it. They've been taking on water, making repairs and readying for another voyage. Though it can't be long before they sail . . .' He frowned at Marbeck. 'I hope you're not thinking of—'

'Going out there? Hardly – I get seasick crossing the Channel.'

Woollard gave a sickly smile. 'That's unfortunate.'

'But if I could get one of them to come ashore,' Marbeck added thoughtfully, 'use him as bait, to entice Quiney . . .'

'Unlikely,' Woollard said, his face grave again. 'They seldom leave their ships.'

'They might if one was sinking, wouldn't they?'

The other looked impatient. 'Now you grow reckless.'

'Could it not be done? There are guns at Portland Castle, facing the bay . . .'

But Woollard shook his head firmly. 'The garrison wouldn't fire on an English vessel, whatever you might accuse them of.'

Now, Marbeck was starting to get annoyed. 'Then what's to be done?' he demanded. 'Should Beck and Swann be allowed to sail off on another of their ventures, while we simply wish them "God speed"?'

'That's what people here do. The Sea Locusts bring business to the towns, and their paymaster Quiney has always rewarded those who play his game. Those who wouldn't . . .' Woollard shrugged.

'By the Christ!' Marbeck stood up, frustration getting the better of him, and took a turn about the table. 'There must be a weak point,' he insisted. 'Someone who can be bought . . . or made to fear something worse than what Quiney or his captains could do.'

'That would be difficult,' Woollard remarked drily.

'What of that wooden-faced rogue who sits on his backside in the Customs House? If I threatened him with the rope . . .'

'Too much to lose – Quiney bought him off years back, I'd wager.'

'The Swann brothers, then? They're young, they think they have a future. If I put the fear of God into them – or rather, the fear of a pirate's death at Execution Dock . . .'

At that Woollard put on a different expression: not one of approval, but at least of doubt. 'The older boy, Jack – he'd slit your throat before he'd bargain with you,' he said. 'But the younger one, Henry, has a girl he wants to marry.'

Marbeck frowned. He recalled his meeting with the two brothers on Chesil Beach: their hostility, as well as their unease. He recalled too the younger one's anger when he spoke of Mary Kellett. Moving to his chair, he sat down again.

'There's a chance, isn't there?' he said finally. When Woollard made no reply, he added: 'If I can convince the boy a noose is closing around the Sea Locusts – around Quiney too – and he has the means of saving his father's neck, or see him face a watery gallows at Wapping? Or, what if Marcus Janes isn't a man chasing profits, but a messenger of the Privy Council? Better still, an official of the High Court of Admiralty?'

Woollard thought for a moment. 'There's one thing, and perhaps one only, that might entice Gideon Swann ashore,' he allowed: 'the prospect of a royal pardon. I've a suspicion the man's tired. He's a widower who sees himself growing old, with no berth to fall back to. He's been steeped in the vile trade too long, and now he drinks to dull the guilt . . .' He eyed Marbeck grimly. 'But it would be a hard task to convince his sons that the offer was genuine – let alone Swann himself.'

'Unless he agreed to turn King's evidence against his fellow slaver,' Marbeck said. Suddenly he was excited: out of the gloom, a flame of hope flared. 'And against Quiney too . . . but it would be difficult to carry this off alone. An official of the Admiralty would arrive with an escort, servants . . .'

'You don't mean to include me?' Woollard broke in with a start. 'I've told you, I'm well known here . . .'

'You could help me forge documents, at least,' Marbeck persisted. 'You have sealing wax, do you not, and paper of good quality?' Then another thought struck him. 'As for Portland Castle: if I presented myself to the commander as a servant of the Crown, and showed him a written order, would he not supply the escort?'

'I suppose he might,' Woollard said, after a moment. 'But you play with lives here, Giles Blunt: your own, and mine too.' He heaved a sigh of resignation. 'God help us both.'

The following morning, Marbeck left the barber-surgeon's house in a state of excitement tempered with caution. The better for a night's rest under Woollard's roof, he nevertheless felt a burden on his shoulders, with little chance of relieving it any time soon.

He had amended his role: Marcus Janes was now a special envoy of Charles Howard, Earl of Nottingham – the Lord Admiral. In his pocket was a document bearing a convincing-looking seal that had cost both Marbeck and Woollard hours of labour the night before. Addressed to the commander of the garrison at Portland Castle, it requested him to supply Janes with an escort of armed men, to accompany him as and when directed, on warrant from the High Court of Admiralty. Thus equipped, and with a new purpose in his stride, he took Cobb out of Woollard's tiny lean-to and rode out along the coastal path to Portland.

The day was fair, the grass lush after the night's rain. Below and to his left, a few fishing boats were moving. Soon he had passed Sandsfoot Castle and reached the end of the peninsula, from where a narrow ribbon of land led out to the Isle of

Portland. Chesil Beach was over to his right, with the English Channel stretching away to the horizon. But his eyes were fixed on the low fortification ahead, now visible where the land widened again: Portland Castle, built upon the rocky coast facing the bay. A few minutes later he was presenting himself at the gates and showing his papers to a sentry. And a short while after that he was in a chamber of the castle, facing a grizzled captain seated behind a table untidy with charts and dockets, who gave his name as Niles.

'The Lord Admiral sent you?' He eyed Marbeck with frank scepticism. 'I thought he'd forgotten our very existence here . . . why the sudden interest?'

So Marbeck took a breath, and span his tale. The Privy Council had learned of corsair activity by two vessels owned and fitted out by a wealthy venturer close to Weymouth. The ships had been running contraband, as well as abducting people and selling them into slavery, and the Lord Howard was keen to arrest them if chance arose, which it appeared to have done . . .

'Wealthy venturer?' Niles echoed. 'Who might that be?' And when Marbeck told him, the frown deepened. 'Quiney! But he's the biggest landowner hereabouts . . . he supplies us with grain.'

'As he supplies slaves to Barbary,' Marbeck said flatly. 'English men, women – and children. His captains sell them in the slave markets in Algiers and Tunis.'

The other frowned. 'Do you have evidence of this?'

'I have the testimony of a freed captive, and no doubt others will be found,' Marbeck said. He had no wish to elaborate, for he knew this man could make difficulties. To his relief, however, Captain Niles's mind was running in a different direction.

'Well, here's a turnabout,' he said thoughtfully. 'You're not the first to level charges of villainy against Quiney's vessels. Though none has dared point the finger at Sir Edward himself.' He peered again at Marbeck's forged paper. 'You name only one of the captains: Gideon Swann. What of the other?'

'The other's . . .' Marbeck broke off, realizing that what he was saying would not be news to Captain Niles. Likely the man knew more of these people than he did. 'I think you know who I speak of,' he resumed. 'Swann and Beck – the Sea Locusts.'

'Oh yes . . . I've heard of them.' Niles regarded him for a long moment from under his spiky eyebrows. 'There's a name that's been feared for years, though rarely spoken aloud – all along the coast from Portsmouth to Plymouth . . . but again I ask – why now?'

'They've strayed too far,' Marbeck told him, thinking fast. 'Attacked and looted Spanish vessels, in violation of the new law – which makes them pirates. Now that Lords Howard and Cecil are conducting peace negotiations, an example must be made: a goodwill gesture to the King of Spain.'

Niles looked down again, fingering the paper. Marbeck could only hope that the seal looked real enough. The text – full of long words and Latin phrases dreamed up by Woollard and himself – should pass muster, he thought. Assuming a haughty air he allowed impatience to show. 'Come, Captain,' he said, 'time grows short, and I have plans. I hope to entice Gideon Swann ashore – perhaps this very night. If he lands at Newton's Cove, we can take him . . .'

'We?' Niles raised his brows.

'Myself, and a small company of your best soldiers, if you will – as many as you can spare. Well armed, of course . . .'

'And if we did manage to capture the man, without loss of life – what then?'

'I would ask you to hold him here, until arrangements can be made to take him to London,' Marbeck replied. Though he was far from confident on that score: even if his scheme succeeded, he was uncertain what Monk's reaction would be when he made his report, let alone what the Lord Secretary would say. As for forging the Lord Admiral's seal . . . it was a felony. Standing stiffly, facing a plain man like Niles who appeared a stranger to deception, he steeled himself for disappointment.

'You're a courageous man, Janes,' the captain said at last.

Marbeck said nothing.

'Whatever strategy you have for getting a man like Swann to come ashore, I'd applaud you for it – if it works,' he added. 'My part's somewhat easier, if my men have only to take him prisoner and clap him in a dungeon.' He leaned back, and let out a sigh. 'But at the first hint of his capture, the other vessel will be gone, out of our reach. The Lord Admiral may hate pirates, but he has no ships near. And as for Quiney, he's beyond your warrant.'

'I understand that,' Marbeck said. 'If I get a message to you later, could you have a troop ready? A corporal perhaps, and say, four or five men . . .'

'Three men,' Niles said. 'And there'll be no corporal: I'll command them myself.'

Hiding his relief, Marbeck nodded his agreement.

He was over one hurdle, even if it was perhaps the least of them. And late that same afternoon, as he prepared to move his plan forward, Woollard proved to be another.

'I humoured you last night,' the barber-surgeon said. 'But in the light of day, I've decided you're off your head. I won't say you should be in Bedlam: it's not a place to which I'd condemn any man.'

They were outdoors walking the sandy, upper part of the beach; Marbeck led Cobb, ready saddled. Having learned from Woollard where the Swann brothers lived, he was eager to confront them, but the other man was on edge. 'You're putting your head in a maw,' he protested. 'What if they disbelieve you? There are a hundred ways you can disappear, and no one would ever know you'd been here, let alone find your body. From what you've told me the Swanns got a good look at you at Chesil – do you not think they'll recognize you?'

'Of course they will,' Marbeck said. 'I'll have to bluff . . . when they see how stark the choice is, I believe they'll comply.'

'Even if they will, what makes you think the father would follow?' Woollard demanded. 'He'd suspect he was putting his own neck in the noose.'

'Then I'll have to be at my most persuasive,' Marbeck said briskly. 'Now – the message to Captain Niles at Portland. Can you have it delivered when I ask?'

'Yes . . .' Seeing that he could not dissuade him, the other sighed. 'There's a boy runs errands for me, who knows how to hold his tongue. He also knows the coast path. He can get it there within an hour.'

'Good.' Marbeck filled his lungs with sea air, and looked up at the gulls wheeling. 'Then you've done your part, and I'm in your debt.' Facing Woollard, he lowered his voice.

'None shall know of your service save my masters, when the time comes . . .'

'*If* it comes,' Woollard muttered. 'And as for knowing I've aided you: I've told you, they probably do already.' And with that he walked off towards the town. Marbeck watched him go, a hunched figure in his black gown, and a feeling of unease stole over him. But forcing it aside, he turned his thoughts elsewhere.

He led Cobb off the stony beach, mounted up and shook the reins. And a short while later he was riding out of Melcombe once again, over the bridge into Weymouth. Dogs barked and skittered away as he clattered onto the cobbles, heads turned as people paused from their quayside tasks, but he paid no attention. Turning to his right he rode to the edge of the little town, to a handful of mean cottages that clustered at the bend of the river, where it bent away northwards. Soon, still in the saddle, he reined in outside an open door and, reaching down, rapped loudly with the hilt of his poniard. Here was the home of the Swann family, or those that lived: the mother was dead, the father on his ship. When a figure appeared, Marbeck sheathed the dagger and straightened up.

'Master Swann!' He looked down his nose at the younger boy, who started in alarm. 'My name's Janes, envoy of the High Court of the Admiralty. I have a choice for you: find your brother and bring him to me, or I'll arrest you and have you clapped up on Portland Castle. So – what will it be?'

SIXTEEN

As evening drew in, Henry Swann sat on a sea chest in the downstairs room of his father's house and threw Marbeck a look of hate. Finally, after the last of several silences, he spoke up. 'He'll never believe you . . . he smells treachery everywhere.'

Marbeck waited. He had spelled out the position, clearly and simply. And though the young man had at first been defiant, the sight of the written warrant had shaken him. When Marbeck also told him that ships of the King's navy would soon be setting out in pursuit of the *Amity* and the *Lion's Whelp*, he struggled to hide his fear.

'Anyways, Father pays no mind to what me and Jack say,' he blustered. 'He'll sail soon. He never comes ashore when he's about to sail.'

'I think you sell yourself short, Henry,' Marbeck said. 'A little persuasion is all that's needed. What of the pardon: is that not what he secretly wishes?'

'How do you know what he wishes?' the boy retorted angrily. 'You don't know him – you don't know anything of us!'

'You forget what happened last Sabbath,' Marbeck broke in. 'You thought I was snooping, and you were right. I found one of your kegs of Madeira . . .' He paused. 'But you know that already, having spoken with your friend Buck.'

'He's no friend of mine, or Jack's!' the other threw back. 'He's a varlet who . . .' He stopped himself, whereupon Marbeck finished for him.

'A varlet who pandered Mary Kellett – used her like a beast,' he said sharply. 'But he also owns the boat and gives you orders, doesn't he? And he's a man you wouldn't cross even if your life depended on it . . . only now you see, it does.'

The boy gave a start. 'What do you mean?'

'You still don't understand?' Marbeck raised his eyebrows. 'Evading customs fees is a felony, which strikes at the very heart of government. You steal from the Lord Secretary himself

. . . Lord Cecil, who has the farm on imported wines. Do you truly think he would let a pair of wretches like you and your brother humiliate him, and go free?'

Henry stared. 'By the Christ,' he muttered, 'I wish . . .'

'What do you wish – that whoever caught me at Hope Cove had ended my life, instead of merely giving me a keepsake?' Letting his own anger show, Marbeck lifted his sewn-up ear lobe, which made the boy flinch. 'Were you one of those?' he demanded, placing his hand on his sword. 'Then perhaps I should settle the score now, and deal with your brother instead—'

'No, I wasn't!' The boy was on his feet suddenly. 'You should ask Buck about that . . .'

'I did,' Marbeck snapped. 'And make no mistake, he'll pay in time. But what about you – do you think they'll let you walk away with merely a whipping and a branding? I know a justice who'll send you to the Dorchester gibbet and laugh while he does it. As for your brother, who sailed on the *Lion's Whelp* . . .' He shook his head. 'Along with your father, he'll face the gallows at Execution Dock, where his body will dangle until three tides have washed over it—'

'You're lying!' Henry shouted. Near to tears, he struggled to master himself. 'Jack knew you were an Admiralty man!' he cried. 'I thought you were one of Beck's . . .'

'What?' Marbeck eyed him. 'What of Beck? Speak up!'

The boy was looking wretched now. 'He's spied on us before. He don't like what we do . . . says it's not our proper work . . .'

'You mean enslavement,' Marbeck said sharply. 'That's outside my warrant, as it happens. But once it's bruited far and wide, I believe there will be kinfolk of the stolen ones who'll want vengeance for what's been done. In short, they'll come looking for Beck and for your father . . . and if they feel half as much rage as I do, they'll coat him in tar and watch him burn. I've seen a human torch, Henry . . . it's not a sight you forget.'

The boy gazed at him in horror; and when Marbeck merely stared back he slumped down on the chest. Outside the sun was low, and gulls were flying down the estuary for the night. Eyes downcast, he swallowed audibly.

'You swear it's true, about the royal pardon?' he asked in

a woeful tone. 'If my father testifies against Beck, he'll go free?'

'Well, not quite,' Marbeck said. 'He has to testify against his master too, the owner of the vessels.'

But at that, Henry's anguish deepened. 'No . . . don't ask that of him,' he mumbled. 'You can't . . .'

'I can and I do,' Marbeck replied.

A moment passed, before the boy looked up again. 'It was you stole Mary Kellett away from Buck, wasn't it?'

'I didn't steal her, I freed her,' Marbeck said shortly. 'She's safe now.'

'But you're not,' the other said at once. 'He'll kill you . . . or Beck will. She was worth a lot to them.'

'I can imagine,' Marbeck broke in. 'And I don't think you liked the notion any more than I did. But pray, don't concern yourself about me – what of your father and brother?'

Henry hesitated, but it was clear that his mind was made up; having believed Marbeck's testimony, what other choice had he? Shakily, he gave a nod. 'I'll get a message to Father tonight,' he said. 'As for Jack . . .' He winced. 'Likely he'll use his fists on me, just for talking to you. But if Father agrees to your terms, he'll follow.' He frowned. 'The pardon's for all of us, you say – Father, Jack and me?'

Marbeck indicated assent, but another thought struck the boy. 'See now, I can't swear to what'll happen, in the matter of Sir—' he began, before cutting himself off abruptly.

'You mean Sir Edward Quiney – whose involvement is no longer a secret,' Marbeck said in a conversational tone. 'His time too may be shorter than he thinks. But for now, the fate of your family lies in your hands – I'd advise you not to fail.'

Defeated, the boy sagged. 'Where will you be, then?' he asked finally. 'To await their answer?'

'Melcombe beach, at the town end,' Marbeck replied. 'I'll walk out there once in every hour, from noon tomorrow – after nightfall too. Whoever comes, if he's a stranger to me, let him make a sign, like this.' Lifting his hand, palm upwards, Marbeck rotated it. 'Will that serve?'

But the other could barely manage a nod. With heavy heart, he stared at the floor.

* * *

After that, there followed a night and a day of inaction that pushed even Marbeck's patience to its limits. But for Thomas Woollard, the wait was intolerable.

It was a working day and the man had patients to attend to, which at least kept him occupied. Every hour, as he had told Henry Swann, Marbeck walked on the beach and waited, but nobody arrived to give him a sign. The rest of the time he stayed out of sight in the barber-surgeon's house, writing up a detailed report for his masters. He believed Henry would carry out what was agreed: for a contrabander, he thought, the boy was short on guile as well as ruthlessness. His brother constituted a more serious threat; but if their father saw an opportunity to change his future, Marbeck thought he would take it. Even Woollard had admitted that possibility, while remaining convinced that the whole scheme was doomed. And that evening, he gave vent to his frustration.

'Can you even be certain of your Captain Niles?' he demanded. 'The man's an unknown quantity. Some of those war veterans are out-and-out rogues . . . he might even be close with Swann and Beck himself.'

'It's possible,' Marbeck allowed. They sat in Woollard's parlour again, the barber-surgeon nursing a jug of claret for comfort. 'But I sent a report, which should have reached Cranborne by now.'

'But any assistance that came – *if* it came – would be too late,' Woollard grumbled. 'You've set your stall out here for all to see . . . heaven knows what they're plotting.'

'You mean Buck, Beck or the Swanns?'

'Any of them! I've told you their reach is long. None here dares stand against them. As for Quiney . . .' The surgeon raised his hands, and let them fall helplessly. 'He could arraign you for slander, or swear out a warrant for any offence he cares to name. He can buy witnesses aplenty to testify against you.'

'Might I ask a favour of you?' Marbeck said coolly. 'Will you drop the subject, and let me fret for both of us?'

With a sigh, the surgeon turned away and took a drink. The evening was closing in, and after a while he got up to light candles. When his servant appeared to ask if he needed anything he sent her to bed, then found a book and tried to read it. But within the hour, when Marbeck had been out again and returned empty-handed, he threw it down with an oath. 'How long do you propose to give them?' he asked.

Marbeck was gazing at the table, letting his mind roam over events. But having asked himself that very question, he gave his answer. 'If there's no word by morning, I may have to cut my losses and leave,' he admitted.

'At last, some prudence,' the other grunted, with a glance at the window. 'That's another night's sleep you've cost me . . .' Sensing Marbeck's impatience, he paused. 'The boy that I know . . . even if you receive the message you want, I fear to send him along the coast path at night.'

'Yes.' Marbeck nodded. 'We'll leave him out of it. If word comes I'll ride to Niles myself; it's not far from the castle to Newton's Cove.'

Relieved, Woollard took a gulp of claret. 'You do know that every cottage on that cove houses either a friend of Gideon Swann, or at the least someone who wouldn't dare speak against him?' he said gloomily. 'It could be you who finds yourself in a trap; three or four soldiers, however well armed, might not be enough . . .'

'By the heavens, Woollard!' Marbeck exclaimed. 'I've sworn to keep you out, haven't I? If it comes to the worst I'll confess I held you hostage. You tried to warn them, but I threatened you with this.' He tapped his sword-hilt. 'Beyond that, you said you could bluff. God knows you're never short of words . . .'

He trailed off: Woollard's face was haggard, and there was shame in his eyes. When Marbeck opened his mouth again, however, the other stayed him.

'No . . . say nothing further,' he muttered. 'Do your work, I'll fashion a tale for myself.' He glanced at the window again. 'It's about time you took another turn outside, isn't it?'

Marbeck hesitated, then gave a nod and went out.

The air was still warm when he walked the path out to the beach, for the eighth or ninth time; he had almost lost count. But the evening light was gone, with a breeze coming in from the south-west. He walked a few yards towards the shoreline, the noise of the surf rising. But a few nights ago, Oxenham had come at him out of the dark . . . He stopped, breathing deeply, his face to the sky . . . until a voice made him whirl round.

'You're Janes?'

Hand on sword, Marbeck peered at the figure, barely visible in the gloom. 'I am.' He took a step forward, and the other did the same – but even before he made out the features, he thought he recognized the voice.

'And you are Jack Swann?'

The young man stopped, looked him up and down and gave a snort. 'I was right about you, back on Chesil,' he said in a surly tone. 'Combed your hair and took your beard off, have you? Why, you think it makes you a better man?'

'The message,' Marbeck said mildly. 'I've waited long enough – what's it to be?'

'Aye, the bargain . . .' The other drew a long breath. 'You were mighty lucky you found Henry home, and not me. I'd have taken a closer look at that warrant, and if I thought it was fake, you'd not be standing here now.'

'I've no time for your bombast,' Marbeck said, summoning an officious tone. 'My warrant bears the Lord Admiral's seal. Troops stand ready to aid me. You strike at me, you'll feel the full measure of the law – though since I'd have the right to act in my defence, I doubt you'd live that long.'

At that, the youth swore an oath. 'If I wasn't here at the behest of another,' he began, 'I'd let you try!'

'Gideon Swann,' Marbeck snapped. 'What's his answer – does he accept my terms or not?'

The other glowered. 'He might,' he said finally. 'He'll parley anyway – only not at Newton's Cove. He'd be somewhat closed in there, he says. He'll meet you tonight, at Chesil. You and no one else.'

Marbeck hesitated, his mind working. The beach was exposed, and some distance from any habitation; it would be difficult for Niles and his men to conceal themselves . . .

'Does that make difficulties?' Swann took another step forward. Stuck in his belt was an old pistol, and another, curious-looking weapon: like a narrow billhook with a curve at the end. Catching Marbeck's glance, he smiled. 'Like my blade, do you?' he said lightly. 'It's Italian. They call it a *roncola.*'

'How quaint,' Marbeck sniffed.

'It took a man's arm off once.'

'Not your father's, I hope?'

'You whoreson . . .' The youth tensed, as if ready to draw the weapon there and then. 'One-armed or not, Gideon Swann could butcher a cur like you!'

'Chesil Beach,' Marbeck broke in. 'It'll have to serve. I'll be there at midnight, with a torch. But if I'm to come alone I demand similar terms – I'll expect to see you and your father, and none else.'

A moment passed. Jack Swann's face was filled with anger and suspicion, and Marbeck was in little doubt that he had some strategy in mind. But then, he was planning a little surprise of his own.

'Then what will happen?' the youth wanted to know. 'Father won't stand for being treated like a captive . . . he'd fight to the death.'

'There's no need for that,' Marbeck said. 'I've a written statement prepared; all you and he have to do is put your names to it – and be ready to appear as witnesses later.' He put on a look of contempt. 'That is, if you can write your names. Otherwise, a cross is the usual procedure. I'd have to witness it.'

'I can write – and read!' the other retorted. 'And I'll be taking a close look at that statement you speak of, before either of us put our names to it, and at your warrant too.'

'My pleasure,' Marbeck said. 'Now, hadn't you better be on your way? I'm a busy man . . .' He paused, and glanced out to the bay. 'I take it the *Lion's Whelp* is at anchor out there. Will you send a longboat round Portland Isle, or . . .'

'What does it matter to you?' Swann's eyes narrowed. 'Just be there, like you've said.' Whereupon with a final look at Marbeck he turned about and disappeared into the dusk. His footsteps crunched on the shingle, then ceased.

Marbeck stood motionless, hearing the swell of the surf: the tide was incoming. Then he too left the beach, to tell Woollard that things were at last in motion. He would take Cobb out and ride to Portland to arrange a welcoming party – and set eyes, at last, on one of the Sea Locusts.

After that he would be obliged to place his trust in the reliability of Captain Niles, the credulity of Gideon Swann . . . and as always, in luck.

SEVENTEEN

Midnight had passed; Marbeck had no means of telling the hour, but he was certain of it. And as yet there had been no sign of a boat.

Cloaked against the night chill, he sat on his haunches and peered out to sea. Half a dozen yards away the surf pounded and hissed . . . the tide was up, and the breeze too. His torch, stuck in a cairn of pebbles, flickered so wildly he feared it would blow out. Away from its light, some distance behind him, Captain Niles and his soldiers huddled in a tight group. They had waited for more than an hour already, and though he could neither see nor hear them he sensed their restlessness. In fact he was uncomfortable about their presence: on taking the news to Niles earlier that night, he'd found the man somewhat cool in his response, though willing to honour his promise. Try as he might, Marbeck was forced to the grim conclusion that, whatever happened on Chesil Beach, he might be thrown upon his own resources.

Pushing the thought aside, once again he went over the procedure they had agreed. When Swann's boat appeared, Marbeck would show himself and hail them. Having made certain that only the two men, father and son, were present, he would draw them to the torch to show the document he and Woollard had prepared. Since he half-expected that the Swanns would spring some trap of their own, he would be ready for the worst. But at his signal Niles would close in with one of his soldiers, while the other two skirted around behind. Trouble might arise if, for caution's sake, Swann brought more men with him – in which case, Niles had made clear, his priority was the well-being of his own people: he was unwilling to engage in a pitched battle in the dark.

With the breeze in his face, Marbeck's eyes swept the great expanse of water. Out at sea, he could make out the distant light of a vessel riding at anchor. It had been there as long as he had, but whether it was Swann's ship or another he didn't know. Nor, not being a seaman, did he know whether the man had had time enough to sail his vessel round Portland Bill to its western side. Not that it mattered, for the choice of Chesil Beach had been Swann's – and Marbeck was determined to make him a prisoner. He also cherished a notion that, if held at the Crown's pleasure, Swann might be used as a bargaining tool to force Reuben Beck to talk terms. Here on a wild beach in the dark, however, that possibility seemed remote. A man like Beck would simply weigh anchor and sail away, leaving the other Sea Locust to his fate. Yet Marbeck's abiding hope was that with Swann forced to testify, Sir Edward Quiney might face justice . . . In fact, he realized, just now he cared more about that than about anything else.

A yawn was coming on; shifting position, he closed his eyes and stretched himself. His body was stiff, the hurts of recent days still tender. Slowly he straightened up . . . then froze.

Seemingly come from nowhere, a light was bobbing on the sea, barely a dozen paces from the shore. In its faint glow he saw the outline of a small boat, and the gleaming shafts of oars. Swiftly he turned towards where Niles waited, and heard a low whistle: the man had seen it and was ready. So throwing off his cloak, Marbeck strode forward, pebbles crunching underfoot.

'Over here!' he called. 'Come ashore and show yourselves!'

There was no answer from the incoming boat. He watched it materialize: a dinghy, clinker-built, rope buffers hanging over its sides. There were two figures, one erect in the bows, the other active behind him, shipping his oars. The forward figure was narrow-shouldered, bare-headed and motionless. Keenly Marbeck's eyes swept the water, either side of the boat and beyond, but there was no sign of another. Soon the little craft was beached, grating on the shingle, and at once the forward figure sprang into life. With an alacrity that took Marbeck by surprise he leaped from the dinghy and waded ashore, waist-deep in foaming surf. A light swayed crazily: he was carrying a lantern. Soon he was in the shallows, a surprisingly tall man in shirt and knee-breeches . . . and now there was no mistake. The hand with the lantern was above his head, but where the right arm should have been there was but an empty half-sleeve. Standing rigid, Marbeck waited for Gideon Swann to approach. So intent was his gaze, he paid little attention to Jack Swann, who was also in the water, heaving the boat onto the shore. Then at last he was face to face with his quarry.

The man was wheezing: Marbeck heard the rasp in his throat. He was heavily bearded, an old-fashioned lace collar about his neck. Bringing the lantern forward, he peered into Marbeck's face, then an oath flew from his mouth like a small explosion.

'Where's this pardon?'

Marbeck breathed in, but did not reply immediately. From the corner of his eye, he watched the younger Swann drop a rope onto the shingle and anchor it with large stones. Finally he said: 'It's by the torch . . . will you come closer?'

'Nay – this light will serve,' the older man grunted. Marbeck could see his eyes now: wary and hard as granite. His face was deep-lined, crosshatched with tiny scars, the mouth turned down in a permanent grimace.

'I have quill and inkhorn there,' Marbeck persisted. 'I need your signature.'

'So I heard,' Swann muttered. And when his son came up to stand beside him and glower at Marbeck, he added: 'I also heard you've had hard words with my boys, throwing your weight about. That's a dangerous thing to do . . . Being a stranger hereabouts, you mightn't know it.'

Marbeck glanced at Jack Swann, who was armed as before with a pistol and his billhook. His father wore an old cutlass at his belt, but no other weapon. Choosing another tack, he went on the offensive.

'You're in no position to throw out barbs, Swann,' he said flatly. 'If you fail to satisfy my warrant, the Lord Admiral's sworn to send a fleet to hunt you, even to the high seas. He's a loathing for pirates . . . You know how that'll end.'

But the other man seemed unfazed. Marbeck smelled his breath now, and recalled Woollard's words about his dulling his senses with drink. He gave a sniff, and said: 'Or are you so afraid of Quiney, you set your own life at naught?'

'Afraid?' Swann echoed. Beside him his son bristled, but held his peace; clearly he was under orders to do so. 'Why

yes . . . I'm afraid, my friend.' He thrust his face forward and
a lop-sided grin appeared, revealing the stumps of a few teeth.
'That's how I've lived long; too long, some would say. But
they're not here, and I am – as are you, for now.'

Marbeck steeled himself. Only yards away the surf thundered . . . he couldn't hear Niles and his soldiers, but hoped
they were closing in. Meanwhile, the air of menace directed
at him from both Swanns, father and son, would have made
most men quail. His hand strayed unbidden to his sword, and
only with an effort could he stay it.

'I grow tired of this,' he said finally. 'Are you willing to
take my offer? Turn King's evidence against your fellow
Reuben Beck, and against the owner of your vessels . . .'

'Who?'

Without warning, Swann lowered the lantern so that his face
was in darkness. Deliberately he set it on the pebbles, and
took a side-step. The light would be visible out at sea . . .
warning bells clanged in Marbeck's head, but he stood his
ground. 'The captain of the *Amity:* the devil you sail with,'
he snapped. 'As a prize, I wager he's worth more than you
are. They'll spend a fortune chasing him, and in the end he'll
hang at Wapping. Do you want the same fate?'

Swann made no reply. His head was cocked, as was his
son's. Both had tensed visibly; involuntarily, Marbeck grasped
his sword-hilt. 'I've already spelled out the terms,' he said
harshly. 'You've a chance to alter your life's course, come
ashore and spend what days remain to you as a free man. Or
do you mean to die like a brigand with—'

But he broke off, and his heart sank; for in that moment he
knew he had failed. There was noise from behind: footsteps
clattering on the pebbles, and Niles's voice rang out.

'Hold! You men are arrested in the King's name – give up
your weapons!'

As if for emphasis, the crash of a large wave followed –
and at once both Gideon and Jack Swann sprang apart, hands
going to their belts. Marbeck groaned: the fight which he'd
feared was about to start anyway. Stepping back, he drew his
own sword as figures loomed in the lantern-light. Weapons
were being drawn; *why couldn't they wait for my signal*, he
thought . . .

'Stand still! Carbines are trained on you!' Niles shouted. He stepped forward, a squat figure in cuirass and helmet. One of his men came up and dropped to a knee; he did indeed hold a light caliver, which he levelled at Gideon Swann. And now, the remaining two soldiers came into view.

'Well, what's to be done?' Marbeck demanded, sounding a good deal more confident than he felt. 'You can die where you stand, and few will care. Or you can give yourself up and—'

His last words, however, were drowned by the report of a heavy firearm – but it came from the direction of the sea. Someone cried out . . . Marbeck ducked, his gaze swinging to left and right, even as an answering shot came from Niles's carbineer. And at once, matters were out of control: there was a cry of agony, and he knew that Gideon Swann had been hit. Then, in the lantern's dim light, he saw them: two narrow boats coming in fast, crunching onto the shingle. Figures leaped ashore, splashing through the waves . . . and in seconds, mayhem broke out.

It couldn't be called a battle: it was a vicious brawl. Niles was shouting, sword in hand. Another shot rang out, then another, but it was impossible to know from where, or whether either had found a mark. His soldiers thrashed about in the light of torch and lantern . . . while from the surf, at least a dozen barefoot men ran with savage cries, swords and daggers in hand. One thing was clear, however: Gideon Swann was in a sitting position on the shingle, and beside him his son knelt, bawling at him.

'Damn you! You wouldn't listen . . . Have you lost your nose for betrayal? We're dead meat!'

A curse on his lips, Marbeck moved forward – then checked himself: from his right one of the seamen was bearing down on him, cutlass raised. Crouching, he swung his rapier and parried the man's blow, while his left hand yanked his poniard from its sheath. As their swords clashed, his opponent's weight threatened to throw him off balance. But when the cutlass flew up again, he drew back slightly, then thrust his poniard forward into the sailor's stomach. There was a shriek, and he fell on his back; his blade swept the air, but he was no longer a threat.

Others were, however: whirling round, Marbeck grew aware

of the cacophony of shouts and clashing weapons that had been going on all along. He saw bodies on the shingle: two or three, at least. Niles had vanished, while the Swanns were . . . where?

They too had disappeared; he looked about, but saw no sign of either of them. Jack, he assumed, had raised his father up and was trying to get him away. Sword outstretched, he took a step towards the waves, where the outline of three boats was visible: Swann's, and the new arrivals. They had waited offshore all along, he surmised, without lights. Cursing again he made for the sounds of combat, and stumbled upon two seamen, standing over one of Niles's soldiers. By the time Marbeck drew near the death-stroke had been given: blood spurted as the man's neck was pierced.

But the men saw him and prepared to engage – whereupon a recklessness came upon him: a mixture of rage and regret that left no room for self-preservation. Noise filled his ears: shouts and cries, the clang of weapons, the roar of the surf. A blade sliced towards him which he was hard-pressed to dodge, but it gave him a chance: a powerful thrust and his poniard found its target, sending his assailant reeling away. At the same time he lunged at the second man, who was a yard behind. It was a cruel move – one he rarely used, but it served: he felt the sword-point quiver as it sank into his assailant's throat. The man choked but managed a last jab with his cutlass, which caught Marbeck's arm.

Yet he felt no pain: only a tug as his sleeve was torn. The next moment cold rage took over: slashing to left and right he drove his opponent back, watched him topple over, yet kept on. The man was whimpering, blood everywhere, then suddenly he went limp. Panting, Marbeck stepped back, and veered aside as pebbles crunched behind him. Breathlessly he flung himself round . . . and stopped dead.

'El Mirlo don't like what's done here.'

A figure stood before him, lightly built and alert in every muscle. He wore a good coat trimmed with copper lace, while his hair hung to his shoulders, bound in plaits. He also wore a necklace of what looked like little blackened sticks . . . until with a shock, Marbeck recalled the grisly trophy hanging from a beam in the King's Arms, and saw what they were:

human forefingers, a dozen or more, threaded on a cord. Then he met the man's glittering eyes, and knew at once whom he faced.

'You see the tokens,' Reuben Beck said, in a voice that grated like a rusty lock. 'They were the lucky ones . . . others gave up their choicest parts: they decorate a bulkhead on the *Amity*.' He gave a chuckle, then spat . . . and abruptly a pistol appeared, to be thrust in Marbeck's face.

'Who art thou?' he demanded.

Marbeck returned his gaze, but gave no answer.

'You're the last to fall – did ye not know it?'

His mouth dry, Marbeck glanced swiftly about and realized that the fighting had ceased. There were groans from the wounded and dying . . . sprawled bodies were visible, on the edge of the torchlight. Then one of the newly arrived sailors walked into view, bare feet slapping on the pebbles.

'Do we get Swann?' he said, moving close to Beck. 'The son, I mean . . . the old man's dead.'

There was a pause before, without taking eyes off Marbeck, the captain nodded – then spoke in Spanish. '*El Mirlo permito.*'

The seaman disappeared, and a moment later Marbeck heard a cry of pain: Jack Swann was about to suffer some terrible fate. He eyed his captor, realizing that he still held his sword and poniard.

'Let those fall,' Beck said, seemingly a step ahead of him. Marbeck drew a breath and dropped his weapons on to the shingle. Without looking down, the other kicked his rapier away. 'A question was asked,' he said in his curious speech, with its vaguely Mediterranean accent. 'Who art thou?'

'Janes,' Marbeck said. 'Envoy of the Lord Admiral . . .'

'You lie.'

Without rancour Beck smiled, as if he'd expected it. 'El Mirlo thinks you serve another master. But the master of the *Lion's Whelp* heeded you, and not the warnings of his crew. He was weak . . . his men knew it, and cleaved to me. Now he's paid, and they'll choose another from amongst their number, so their trade may continue.'

'Trade?' From somewhere, Marbeck found his anger: a source of strength. Breathing steadily, he threw a baleful look at his enemy. 'I know about that,' he said. 'As I know who fits you out, and takes the bulk of the proceeds. Do you think it could stay a secret for ever? Word has already gone—'

A painful blow silenced him, a crack on the side of his head from the barrel of Beck's pistol. The man moved so quickly, even Marbeck was caught unawares. His temple throbbing, he swayed slightly, but kept his balance.

'El Mirlo's prize is short,' the man said softly. 'He expected more captives. Now there's only the other Swann boy, but he will be found. Which leaves you . . . a lucky man.'

Keeping expression from his face, Marbeck stared back at him. Outside his field of vision things were in motion: he heard the voices of Beck's men, those who survived . . . or rather, as he had now learned, they were Swann's own men who had mutinied against him. *The weaker of the two . . .* Woollard's phrase flew into his mind, even as grim awareness swept over him: Niles's men were dead or dying, as was Gideon Swann, while his son was a prisoner. Niles himself had either fled, or was also dead. Marbeck was indeed the last . . . was that what Beck meant, by calling him *a lucky man*? Then the penny dropped.

'You mean to make me a slave,' he said. And when his only reply was another throaty laugh, he added: 'Well, I won't let that happen. I'd prefer to die on English soil. A doomed patriot, if you like.'

A frown appeared on Beck's brow. 'That would be a pity,' he replied. 'You fought well . . . you're strong. Fetch a good price in the Bedestan.' He glanced at Marbeck's clothes, and his brow cleared. 'A handsome dandy,' he said. 'El Mirlo can barter with that. Painted and decked as a maid, you'd fetch an even higher price, from men of certain tastes.'

Marbeck's teeth were set tight. He was struggling to form some strategy, however desperate, when there came a shout: looking aside, he saw the sailors readying their boats. Already some had climbed aboard; matches flared as lanterns were lit. The bodies of their dead comrades, he realized, were simply being left behind. Another man was scavenging, collecting up weapons. Someone else appeared, grasped the handle of Gideon Swann's lantern which was still on the shingle, and took that away; now only the flickering light of Marbeck's torch remained.

Then came a commotion, as a figure was manhandled towards the water. Jack Swann, tightly bound, was about to leave England for a life of slavery. Marbeck watched as he was forced to the nearest boat, head bowed in misery; his precious Italian blade had been taken from him. Turning his gaze back to Reuben Beck, Marbeck would have spoken – but the man wagged his pistol, its muzzle an inch from his eyes.

'El Mirlo knows you don't mean it,' he said.

For a moment Marbeck didn't understand; then he did. Beck was referring to his wish to die on English soil . . . and the implication was obvious. He would be offered a choice: submit to being taken away, or die a slow death.

'You see it.' Beck nodded, his tarred pigtails wobbling. 'Are you ready to go, or to perish here like a fool?'

Suddenly, Marbeck felt oddly calm. For some bizarre reason, the figure of Machiavelli from *The Jew of Malta* flew to mind, leering at the audience, speaking with glee of power and strength. But he had faced impossible odds before, as he had faced death, and it had yet to lay hands on him. Was it to find him here on a wild beach in Dorset, where none would know of his passing save for his killer and a broken-down barber-surgeon in Melcombe? A while ago he might have laughed at the notion, but now . . .

Then his torch blew out, and both he and the surviving Sea Locust were plunged into darkness.

EIGHTEEN

Marbeck was running. Sliding on loose stones, falling and scrambling up again, he ran: away from the sea in pitch darkness, in the direction of the great bank of pebbles that fringed the beach. At his back the noise of the surf grew fainter; then he heard a distant report, and dropped flat. The pistol ball whistled past, but it was wide: they were firing blind. He got up again, and when a second shot came, trusted to luck and kept running. Hearing no sound of a ball he slowed his pace, his breath coming in short bursts. Then abruptly the shingle rose beneath his feet, and he began clambering up the steep slope. Stones rolled away under his shoes, he lost his balance but managed to claw his way up. Then the wind hit him, and he fell forward; he was on the crest of the barrier. A moment later he was sliding down the other side on his rump – to land with a shock in cold water.

He was sitting in the ditch beyond the Chesil bank, submerged to his waist. Gasping for breath, he began to get up – then started as a voice called out from only yards away.

'Who's that? Speak – I have a sword!'

'Niles?' Marbeck stared into blackness. 'It's me – Janes.'

There was a moment, then an oath flew out of the dark. 'By God! I'd like to run you through as well!'

With much splashing, the man waded towards him. As Marbeck straightened up a spark was struck, a flame appeared and Niles was there, holding his tinderbox.

'Were you followed?' he demanded.

But Marbeck blinked, for the commander of Portland Castle was a sorry sight. His helmet was gone, and one side of his face, from the hairline downwards, was streaked with blood. His steel cuirass was dented from blows received, his leather jerkin scarred and slashed.

'I don't know.' Bending, Marbeck drew several long breaths. In the feeble light he saw blood on his own sleeve, and for the first time felt pain. Seeing the other was in no mood to

wait he told him what had happened, which prompted a stream
of curses. 'I've lost my entire escort, thanks to you! Meanwhile,
those devils have got away. I chased one of them, he was
skulking in the rear – ran like a rabbit, but I caught him on
the bank. Come and look.'

Holding his tinderbox up, Niles took a few paces in the
water. Marbeck followed . . . then stopped at the sight of a
blooded corpse, lying half in the ditch.

'It's Henry Swann,' he said.

Niles gave a start, and suddenly the flame in his hand shook.
'Good Christ . . . he's just a boy.'

'His father's dead,' Marbeck said tiredly. 'The other son's
been taken away by Beck.'

Niles cursed again, then swayed suddenly and slipped into
the water. The flame went out, prompting a groan.

'Can you stand up?' In the dark, Marbeck groped towards
him, almost falling over in the process. 'My horse is tethered
by the path. If we can get to it—'

'Damn you to hell!' Niles gave vent to his rage, born of
pain and despair. 'I should have held you at Portland . . .
trusted my suspicions. What was all this, some private feud
with the Sea Locusts? You're no Admiralty man – and I'll wager
that warrant's a forgery, you vile bastard!'

The man's rant ceased, giving way to a grunt of pain. He
forced himself to his knees, then to his feet. Marbeck reached
out a hand, but when it touched Niles's arm it was immediately
grasped and held in a fierce grip. At the same time, he heard
the scrape of a poniard being unsheathed.

'I'm unarmed,' Marbeck said. 'You hold the cards: you can
either spike me, or I'll help you to my mount, provided we
can find him. Then I'll get you to Portland—'

'No!' Niles cried. 'I'll not face them . . . not yet. In the
morning, perhaps . . .' He sighed, racked with shame. 'I'm
unfit to command! If I face a court martial it's no less than I
deserve . . . Jesu, why didn't I die along with them?'

Marbeck said nothing, and after a moment his arm was
released. Knee-deep in water, the two men stood in silence:
survivors, but brothers only in shame.

'Tomorrow, then,' Marbeck said at last. 'Meanwhile I can
take you to a barber-surgeon in Melcombe. He's a friend,

and . . .' He paused, having made a quick decision. 'And he was once an intelligencer like me,' he added. 'He served Walsingham, as I serve Lord Cecil. You were right: the warrant was forged, and my name's not Janes – it's Marbeck. I came here seeking answers, and found myself up against a posse of slavers. Now a lot of men are dead because of me – so you're not alone in your remorse.'

Niles was silent, his breathing loud in the darkness. Marbeck was suddenly aware of the clammy coldness of his wet clothes, and somehow it brought him to his senses. He had almost lost his life – but while he lived, he could act . . .

'A barber-surgeon?' The captain's voice was subdued. 'And you say he too is an intelligencer?'

'He was. I trust him . . . and you need a healing-man quickly.'

Another moment passed, then another sigh came out of the gloom. 'I'll lean on you,' Niles muttered. 'Let's get out of this whoreson ditch.'

But the night was not done with them yet.

Blooded and exhausted, Niles seated on Cobb with Marbeck leading, the two made a slow journey back to Weymouth, descended the steep hill and crossed the bridge into Melcombe. The town was silent, with barely a light anywhere. They skirted the quay and neared Woollard's house, whereupon Niles said he would get down. His pride gone along with his anger, he allowed Marbeck to help him. Soon they were at the door, with a light showing from within – but at once Marbeck knew something was wrong.

'What is it?' Niles demanded, sensing his unease. Leaning on the door-frame, he reached for his poniard. 'Take this . . . or do you want my sword?'

With a shake of his head Marbeck took the poniard, then lifted the latch. The door was unlocked; he pushed it open, but nobody appeared. As he entered the dark hallway there came a sound from the parlour, and at once he knew what it was: a woman weeping desperately. In a moment he had thrown the inner door wide, and stopped on the threshold.

In the candlelit room Woollard lay sprawled on the floor, his lifeless eyes staring upwards. Beside him, cradling his head, knelt his servant in floods of tears. At sight of Marbeck she looked up sharply, then gave a cry of despair. 'I couldn't save him!' she wailed. 'My poor master . . .'

A chill swept over Marbeck. He dropped the poniard, took a step and dropped to his knees beside her.

'When . . .?' he began, then remembered the woman was deaf.

'Couldn't do it . . .' She shook her head helplessly. 'Too much bleeding . . . even with what he taught me, I couldn't.'

Now he saw wads of linen, soaked with blood. Blood covered Woollard's shirt, the servant's skirts and hands. She had tried . . . Marbeck put a hand about her thin shoulder, which prompted a jerk of alarm. But she turned to him, her face filled with anguish. 'It was Buck,' she said.

His pulse leaped. 'Buck . . . you're certain?' He repeated the words, mouthing them emphatically, and she nodded.

'John Buck . . . slew him with a sword. Like the devils on the church wall, smiling while they stab with their forks . . . I thought he'd kill me too, but he went away.'

There was a sound from behind; Niles was standing in the doorway. He took in the situation, and flagged visibly.

'John Buck's killed him,' Marbeck said.

The other leaned against the door. The servant bowed her head, weeping afresh. After a moment Marbeck withdrew his arm and stood up. He turned to Niles, who caught his expression and frowned.

'Can you fend for yourself?' Marbeck asked.

Niles hesitated. His gaze went to the woman. She looked up and gave a start. 'You must sit down,' she said after a moment. 'I can do what is needed.' Slowly she too got to her feet, her cheeks wet with tears, and faced Marbeck. 'He would have helped,' she said. 'And so will I.'

She meant Woollard. And when neither man spoke, she added: 'Rest . . . take whatever you need. They can do no more to me . . . my life was here, and it's over.'

Marbeck looked at Niles, who managed a nod. Clumsily he unbuckled his belt and handed it over, sword, scabbard and all. 'I'll return to Portland tomorrow,' he murmured. 'If you come back . . .'

But Woollard's servant came and stood between them. After peering at Niles's scalp wound she turned to Marbeck, saw his bloodstained sleeve and took hold of his arm. He stiffened, but allowed her to lift it.

'It will bleed more,' she said. 'I can stitch you – both of you. You're weak . . . you need food and rest. Now is not the time to seek revenge.'

They stared at her, a slip of a woman, defiant in her grief; then Niles dropped his gaze. 'She shames us all.'

Marbeck took her hand, and let his eyes speak. Whereupon she gestured to them both to sit, and quickly became busy.

In the morning a sea mist had rolled in, shrouding Melcombe and Weymouth. It dulled the sounds from the harbour, as it muffled the church bells; it was the Sabbath, the thirteenth day since Marbeck had got up from his sickbed in the Three Cups in Botolph Lane and gone to the theatre with Levinus Monk. Today he arose from a pallet in the chamber he had shared with Niles, leaving him sleeping. Stripped of cuirass and jerkin, his head bandaged, the soldier lay like a dead man.

Stiffly he descended the stairs and entered the parlour, to find the room transformed. Woollard's body was gone, as was the pile of bloody rags. The floor had been scrubbed, the instruments washed and put back in their places. The woman had been up all night, he guessed. He started to go out, whereupon she appeared in the hallway. She looked tired but alert, in fresh clothes and a clean apron. Lost for words, he threw her a look of gratitude. But when he started to make signs, she shook her head.

'There are people who will come to my aid. You cannot stay here . . . nor should you.'

'What's your name?' he asked, speaking distinctly.

'Marjorie Howarth. And I know who you are, and what you wish to do – my master told me.' Biting her lip, she added: 'He was more than a master . . . I think you know that.'

'I caused his death,' Marbeck said. 'He foresaw it . . .'

'Don't speak like that . . . not now.' She touched his arm, the one without stitches or bandage. 'Go to your task. I'll watch over the captain until he's on his feet.'

She was right; there was little Marbeck could do, he thought, apart from help to deal with Woollard's body. Meanwhile, his murderer was free. 'I'm in your debt, more than I can repay,' he said, but she didn't hear.

'Avenge my master – bring those people to justice.'

'Yes.' Meeting her eye, he placed his hands on her shoulders. 'I'll do all that I can.'

She nodded and stepped aside. By the doorway where he had left it was Niles's sword-belt, with the poniard back in its sheath. Taking it up, Marbeck turned from Marjorie Howarth and went out of the door without looking back. In a short time he had saddled Cobb and was walking him out of Woollard's lean-to. Then he was mounted, guiding the horse through the swirling clouds of vapour.

Determinedly, he pushed his grief aside; there would be time for that later . . . more than enough. Without looking about at the town, he spoke low to Cobb as the horse picked his way from Maiden Street to the quayside, and finally across the bridge to Weymouth. Once again they seemed to pass through an unseen barrier; even the vapour seemed thicker here. Without checking his pace Marbeck rode beside the harbour, past people who started at the sight of him looming out of the mist. Having reached the opening to Hope Cove he dismounted, led Cobb a few paces and tethered him to a chain. Then he was at the door of the Bucks' house, where he stopped; it was wide open, and the place was empty.

He knew it even before he went inside. The house looked as he last remembered it, when he had spirited Mary Kellett away, leaving Sarah Buck bound and gagged in her parlour. Now there was no sign of her or her husband, or even of any hasty departure.

But then, after what had happened, Buck was bound to flee. Woollard had been right: the Sea Locusts and their associates had known of his involvement all along. Buck had been ordered to despatch him – by Sir Edward Quiney, perhaps? Not that it mattered: after what had happened the previous night, Marbeck now saw things differently. Gideon Swann was dead, and Reuben Beck himself had come ashore to see him despatched. The arrival of Niles and his men might have forced the Sea Locusts to change their plans – or more importantly, forced their owner to rethink his. If Quiney believed the Lord Admiral was now aware of his activities, perhaps the man was making certain preparations. But in the meantime, where might Buck have gone – to his master, or further afield?

For a while he stood, sifting ideas and rejecting them, until at last a way forward appeared. The distant clang of a bell reminded him: it was exactly a week since he had entered the Customs House at Melcombe and questioned a man who, if Woollard was right, was also in the pay of Quiney. He would go there now – and this time he would get some answers.

His mouth set tight, he left the empty house and walked back to Cobb. As he stooped to loose the rein, however, he grew aware of a murmur of voices. Looking up, he found himself being watched by an assorted group of Weymouth folk, all of them eying him warily. His gaze swept over them, but when no one spoke he climbed into the saddle and stared down.

'Do you know that Gideon Swann's dead?' he said harshly, his hand on his sword-hilt. And when the only result was a few frightened looks, he added: 'So is his son Henry – and Jack Swann's taken to the Barbary states, to suffer the kind of life his father meted out to others. John Buck's days are numbered too . . . will that serve you for news, on this Sabbath day?'

But there was only a silence; that, and a few dark looks passing between some of the men. With an impatient tug of the rein, Marbeck urged Cobb away towards the bridge.

In Melcombe once again, he dismounted and led the horse along the quayside. The town was quiet, church services still in progress; but as before, the door to the Customs House was ajar. Leaving the horse outside, he assumed a brazen air and walked in to find the same grizzled man seated by his table. Seeing no one else present, Marbeck closed the door and drew its heavy bolt across. Then he turned about, and before the other could say a word, strode over to him. Gripping his coat, he yanked him to his feet.

'I bring news,' he said. 'Last time we spoke, you said you'd forgotten who owns the *Amity*. Well, it's Sir Edward Quiney, who also owns the *Lion's Whelp*. The captain of the latter is dead: Gideon Swann, that is. The other is Reuben Beck, who still lives – though not for long if I can help it. Now I've jogged your memory a little, I'd like a proper talk . . . does that sit well with you?'

The other was agog, especially when he met Marbeck's eye and saw someone who meant business. Still, he would have struggled had Marbeck not thrust him backwards into his chair. A poniard appeared swiftly, to be stuck under the man's chin.

'You can't do this to me!' he cried, in mingled fear and outrage. 'I'm not some wharf-monkey, to be manhandled like—'

'Who are you then?' Marbeck demanded. 'One of Quiney's lackeys, the local clerk who tidies up the loose ends?'

The other gulped. 'You look like a man who's lost his reason,' he said hoarsely. 'I'm beholden to the Crown . . . I take customs fees, search ships for seditious books—'

But Marbeck leaned closer, keeping the dagger's point tight against his skin. 'You mean you work for Lord Cecil?'

'Well, in a way I do,' the other retorted. 'And he'll never brook this insult. You will find yourself arrested!'

'But I work for Lord Cecil too,' Marbeck said. 'Do you not see?'

The man stared at him. 'See what?' he snapped. 'Do you mean to tell me we're on the same side, or . . .'

'Oh no . . .' Slowly, Marbeck lowered the dagger. 'Don't make that mistake. In fact, I've a mind to turn you over to the commander of Portland Castle – Captain Niles, that is. He's a friend, you might say . . . and somewhat angry with those who serve Sir Edward Quiney just now. There was a fight on Chesil Beach last night – Gideon Swann was killed, along with one of his sons.'

With that he straightened up and looked down on the customs master, who was badly shaken. 'And I wonder if my Lord Secretary is aware of how you run things down here, so far from London?' Marbeck went on. 'I've an idea he'll be most interested when he hears.'

'Who are you?' the other faltered. 'What do you want?'

'What do I want?' Marbeck held his gaze. 'I want everything you've got. By the time I leave here, you'll have told me all about Sir Edward Quiney . . . but first you can tell me about John Buck. He killed a man last night, someone who'd become a friend of mine. Likely you'll know him: Thomas Woollard, barber-surgeon.'

At that the man jerked backwards with a look of disbelief. 'You're lying. He wouldn't do such . . .'

'I think you know he would, if he thought he had to – or if he were ordered to,' Marbeck replied coolly. 'As I think you know that, like you, Woollard was useful to Quiney's people . . . tending injured men, perhaps, or even disposing of bodies.' He paused. 'I speak of the Sea Locusts: those you said were but a fable; an old Dorset folk tale. But we both know they're two ships, the *Amity* and the *Lion's Whelp*, who deal in a particular kind of bulk cargo: human creatures, to be taken to the Barbary states and sold into slavery.'

A long moment passed. The other man swallowed, then fumbled in his coat and produced a kerchief. Beads of sweat showed on his forehead, and were quickly mopped. 'Slavery's naught to do with me,' he said. 'What happens on the high seas is beyond English law . . .'

'But attacking Spanish vessels, in defiance of the King's proclamation, amounts to piracy,' Marbeck broke in. 'After disposing of their human cargo, I think the Sea Locusts dislike returning to their home port with their holds empty. Hence, a little sea-plunder on the way back doesn't go amiss, does it? To be landed here and brought ashore in secret, avoiding duties – while you turn a blind eye to the trade.' He allowed himself a wry smile. 'Believe me, Lord Cecil is ruthless when his own interests are at stake.'

Another moment passed; then the other heaved a sigh. 'I understand you,' he said, struggling to master himself. Marbeck merely waited – and was unsurprised when the offer came.

'I can get you two hundred crowns by tonight . . . that, and a promise of another two hundred to follow. Plus a pension for life, paid wherever you choose. Now, what say you?'

To the man's dismay, however, Marbeck appeared to relax. He even sheathed the poniard, glancing idly at the window. The streets were filling up, as the people of Melcombe emerged from their churches.

'My thanks,' he said. 'You've confirmed what I needed to know. But I still wonder where John Buck is. My thoughts stray towards Quiney's manor at Abbotsbury – what say *you*?'

NINETEEN

In the early afternoon, Marbeck rode along the cliff path above Weymouth bay, then followed the narrow spit of land to the Isle of Portland. The mist had lifted, and the sea was a bright steel-blue. But his eyes were downcast, his thoughts bleak. The final part of what had become a terrible mission lay ahead . . . and he knew it might even be his last.

He had been back to Woollard's house, and found that Niles had already left. He learned this from Marjorie Howarth, who also told him that her master's body lay in a nearby church. Many had cause to be grateful to the barber-surgeon, she said, and he would receive a proper funeral and burial. She was pale but calm, and spoke of leaving Melcombe soon after. Marbeck offered her money, but it was refused. Instead, she had filled a leather flask with her late master's claret and given it to him as a token. Then with few words, they had parted.

At Portland Castle he dismounted and spoke to the sentry, who sent him to the commander's quarters. Here he found Niles seated with one of his subordinates. When Marbeck appeared he looked up sharply, his face taut. A new bandage was about his head, another around his hand. The two exchanged looks, before Niles turned to his fellow, a young ensign, and gave a brief order. The man got up, threw Marbeck a curious glance and went out, leaving them alone.

'You aided me last night,' Niles said. 'Yet I'll not thank you. Your actions have cost me dear . . . if my men knew the extent of it, I'd wager you wouldn't leave here alive.'

His gaze was frank, the eyes clear. 'I came to return your sword-belt,' Marbeck said quietly. 'And to tell you John Buck's fled – to Quiney's manor, I think.'

The other frowned. 'How do you know that?'

'I found out this morning, along with other intelligence. Would you like to hear it?'

After a moment Niles nodded, and gestured him to a stool. So Marbeck sat and recounted what he had learned. By the end of his time with the customs master, he related, the man had become frightened enough to tell a great deal: enough, perhaps, to have Sir Edward Quiney arraigned for piracy along with Reuben Beck. But news of the fight on the beach, together with Swann's death, would have reached Quiney immediately. The man would move swiftly to protect himself, including silencing those he saw as a threat. Buck had served as a hired assassin in the past; if ordered to deal with Woollard, he would then have run straight back to his paymaster.

He finished his account and waited. Niles had taken in the information without expression, but now another frown appeared. 'I could send to my commander and ask for orders,' he said, 'but it would take too long. If Quiney knows I escaped he'll think he's under threat, and hence he may flee. So I will act now – this very night.'

Marbeck sat up abruptly.

'It's a ten-mile march to Abbotsbury.' Niles stood up, and took a few paces. 'I know Quiney's manor. It has easy access to the sea, but we can block that. I'll take twenty men; it leaves too small a force to man this castle, which could mean my losing my post. But just now, that isn't my chief concern.'

'No . . . the destruction of the Sea Locusts is,' Marbeck said quietly. 'And I'm asking leave to accompany you. I can fight.'

'I don't doubt that,' Niles replied. He thought for a moment, then: 'You may come as a volunteer, for reasons of your own. I'll deny all knowledge of your purpose if you wish, as I'll forget the name you gave me last night. You can be Marcus Janes again, if you prefer.'

They eyed each other; few words were needed. 'I'll give no other name, for the present,' Marbeck said.

'Very well . . . then I'll take my sword back, and have you outfitted from the armoury. We'll march as soon as it's dark, take positions about the house and enter it at dawn. Now, I have despatches to write. A rider will leave within the hour.'

'For where?' Marbeck asked quickly. 'I have a report in my saddle-bag, addressed to Salisbury House in London.'

'Give it to me, and I'll see it gets there,' Niles said. 'Meanwhile you can stay here, rest and eat. Will you call my ensign back?'

In relief, Marbeck nodded and got to his feet. Despite the heaviness of his heart, as he went to the door he felt a faint stirring: if not of hope, then of possibilities.

And when night fell at last, he was ready.

It had been a tense wait in Portland Castle, though he had tried to keep himself occupied. He had shed Marcus Janes's garish clothes and attired himself in his customary black. He wore a plain but serviceable sword supplied by the castle's armourer, and had seen Cobb fed and rested. His despatch to Cecil was sent, and he was free to think on the matter in hand – though in this, he knew he had strayed far from his territory.

He was no longer Marbeck the intelligencer; at best he had become a self-appointed Crown officer, at worst a private citizen bent on revenge. Like Niles, he no longer cared about the consequences; but as far as the previous night's debacle was concerned, it was impossible to forget it. It was impossible, because a party of Niles's men had already been out to Chesil Beach to bring back their dead comrades. A few stunned onlookers had gathered, staring at the bodies, which had been stripped of clothing as well as weapons. The corpses of seamen from Swann's crew were also brought in, and thrown into a common grave. Gideon Swann's body, along with that of his younger son, had been taken to Weymouth to be dealt with by the townspeople. Otherwise, there was no trace of the Sea Locusts. And when dusk fell, no ships' lights were visible out in the bay; Reuben Beck had escaped, and was beyond reach.

As a result a mood of gloom hung over Portland Castle, which by nightfall had changed to anger. Niles's men seethed with resentment – partly at their commander, who had escaped and left his men behind, dead or dying as they were. Though his pursuit of one he believed to be a raider was understood, it would be a long time before he was forgiven. Marbeck saw it, as he saw the man's reasons for the march. Niles was acting in lieu of a knight-marshal, making an arrest he would later have to justify; Sir Edward Quiney was no common criminal, but a powerful man.

Marbeck, however, no longer felt bound by any constraint. The events of the past weeks had crystallized into a desire to avenge people: Woollard, Mary Kellett . . . even Oxenham in a way. Above all, he burned with the desire to confront John Buck, and to hear him beg for his life.

Finally, it was time. As darkness fell the troop assembled, moving out of the castle gates onto the rocky foreshore. They were all mounted: Niles's best men, well armed. Their captain wore his battered cuirass; Marbeck had refused the offer of armour, and wore only his padded doublet. The company carried no torches, but would rely on the half-moon and starlight to guide them along the coast road. When they reached Quiney's manor, on the hills above Abbotsbury, they would secure the path to Chesil Beach and surround the house. Then at Niles's order, they would advance from all sides. If the gates were locked they would be forced open; after that, Niles was relying on his subordinates to maintain discipline. There would be no killing or looting, he ordered – and Sir Edward Quiney must be taken alive and unharmed. So at last they left Portland and passed in file along the narrow isthmus, with the sea on either side. On reaching the mainland they turned west: a line of riders, barely visible in the dark.

They rode in silence, walking the horses, with Marbeck in the rear. His presence had been explained by their captain: he was a Crown messenger, here to witness events and report back to the Admiralty court. He was soon ignored, the soldiers banding into a tight column. As he followed them he felt their strength of purpose, and wondered whether Niles's orders would be followed: in their place, he thought, anger might well have overruled him. But he settled down to his ride, Cobb keeping pace with the dim outline of the horse in front. And in this way, when perhaps two hours had elapsed, they neared their destination and halted.

What followed would be the most difficult part: the final wait before the dawn attack. The troop dismounted, a picket line was set up and men detailed to guard the horses. Others descended the grassy slopes to Chesil Beach to take positions. Finally the remaining force of about a dozen gathered together, and Marbeck was able to approach Niles. He was recognized in the gloom, and waved forward.

'Over there,' Niles said, pointing. 'Do you see?'

Following his arm, Marbeck peered into the distance. Half a mile away, on a hilltop, a faint light was visible.

'Quiney's manor is walled, the house in the shape of a great I. Stables and other buildings are also inside the walls, as I remember. There's a two-storey gatehouse, no doubt with a watchman.' Niles turned to his ensign, who stood near. 'Take your force round to the right, then spread out, twenty paces from the walls. My cohort will come up on the left and complete the encirclement.'

'I can place a marksman near the gatehouse,' the young man said. 'What about the road?'

'One man concealed on either side of the gates,' the captain began – then suddenly he gave a snort. 'But it's not an army we face, is it? It's Sir Edward Quiney, his family and servants . . . even if some are sure to be armed.'

'As Buck will be, if he's there,' Marbeck put in.

Niles looked away. 'I thought I might leave him to you. I can't be everywhere.'

After that there was silence. Niles's men sat, squatted or stood about, some shifting restlessly; dawn was still some hours away. Then came a minor stir, and a soldier hurried through the company to halt before his commander, somewhat out of breath.

'They've caught a man down on the beach, sir,' he said. 'One of Quiney's servants, the corporal thinks. He was guarding a boat. They're bringing him up now.'

All heads turned towards the path, which sloped away through gorse and coarse grass to Chesil. Marbeck heard no sound save the distant rattle of surf on pebbles. The company waited, until finally voices could be heard. Niles and his men formed a rough semicircle as three figures appeared. Two were soldiers, while the other, being marched between them, was a man in plain garb. He was thrust forward roughly, to fall at Niles's feet in terror.

'Mercy, sir!' he cried. 'I was but minding the skiff, and getting ready for a bit of fishing when the tide comes in . . . believe me, I've done no harm to anyone!'

'You serve Sir Edward Quiney?' Niles enquired briskly.

'I do, sir. I'm an Abbotsbury man . . . I catch rats and trap coneys, nothing more—'

'Where's your master?'

'Sir Edward? He's . . . he's at home, far as I know . . .'

The man nodded quickly, avoiding the captain's gaze. Niles regarded him for a moment, then spoke to his ensign. 'There's hardly a tree hereabouts,' he said casually. 'But could you rig up a tripod, high enough to hoist this rat-catcher off the ground by his wrists?'

'With ease, sir,' the lieutenant said, straight-faced.

The prisoner gulped, and a moan slipped from his mouth. 'Jesu, master! I beg, ask what you will of me—'

'I did ask,' Niles said. 'But I think you lied. You wouldn't want to do that – not to me.'

He waited until the man found courage to look up. 'Then, I beg pardon . . .' He swallowed, and dropped his gaze. 'Sir Edward has gone away, is what I meant to say.'

There was a stir from the soldiers. 'Gone where?' Niles demanded. 'Speak the truth, or I'll have you taken to Portland Castle and put in chains!'

The servant started to shake. 'I know not where he is, sir – I swear it. There was a fearful coil here this morning . . . Lady Quiney went away in the coach with her daughter and her maids. The master sent riders off with messages, one by boat too. Then this afternoon Sir Edward himself took a boat, and was rowed out to sea with his servants. That's all I know . . . I swear to you!'

'John Buck – is he in the house?' Marbeck asked sharply, staring down at the quaking prisoner. When nobody challenged his right to speak, he added: 'I have powers to interrogate you too, so it's best you tell me.'

The man was nodding again. 'Buck came here Saturday, after dark. Rowed himself up from Wyke, by Weymouth. His wife was with him too – the master was displeased, I heard. I've been on the beach since sunset, so I know not if they're still at the house . . .' He threw a scared look at Niles. 'Indeed, master, I know not if anyone is there now. There's no need for arms – you may enter freely and see for yourself.'

'My thanks, but I'll decide how best to proceed,' the captain said coldly.

For a while nobody spoke. Soldiers shifted impatiently, while the ensign looked pointedly at Niles. Finally the captain drew a breath and said: 'We won't wait until dawn. Give the order to mount – we ride in now.'

There was a collective sigh of relief, and at once the soldiers began to move. Marbeck was about to go too, when he heard the captain say: 'It looks as if there may be no one to fight. I know that'll be a disappointment to you.'

'Do you mind if I search the house anyway?' Marbeck asked. 'I'd like something to take back to my masters, however trivial.' And when the other gave a nod, he went to find Cobb.

But he walked heavily, for what he felt was more than disappointment. Too often, in recent years, he had watched powerful men escape justice. Somehow the prime movers of plots and stratagems always managed to avoid capture, leaving lesser figures to pay the price. He'd seen it happen the year before, when the money-lender Augusto Spinola had vanished after financing a plot to put a Catholic monarch on the English throne. Now Sir Edward Quiney, who owned the Sea Locusts and profited by them, was gone to sea.

Once mounted, however, he forced such thoughts aside: he was eager to get to the manor and search every corner of it. Restlessly he waited while the troop got horsed and ready, until finally the order came to move. Thereafter, following a path through long grass, the party moved swiftly towards the distant light, the ground rising steadily. After a while the path petered out and they were riding through cleared land with an uninterrupted view of the manor. Soon the gatehouse rose ahead of them, with the shape of house and outbuildings beyond. Marbeck was in front now, a little way behind Niles . . . and as one, they halted.

The gates stood wide open, and the courtyard beyond appeared deserted.

'I can take half a dozen men and ride around the walls,' the ensign said, reining in close by. 'Just to make certain.'

'Do that,' Niles murmured, his disappointment plain to see. Having waited for the ensign to ride off, he turned to Marbeck. 'I won't give you orders, but if you come upon anything I should know about, inform me at once.'

Marbeck said nothing; and after calling out an order, the captain shook his reins and rode forward, under the arch of the gatehouse. No lights burned anywhere, and no one appeared. Soon the entire company had passed inside, and there was a mêlée as men dismounted. Torches were lit, and Niles, followed by others, was soon striding towards an imposing flight of steps leading into the house itself.

Marbeck walked Cobb slowly through the gateway, then halted and remained in the saddle, taking his bearings. He saw a light at an upper window, and guessed it was the one seen from a distance. He also guessed that on entering the chamber, they would find it empty. Was the entire manor deserted? It seemed bizarre that, whatever Sir Edward Quiney had learned or even suspected, he would simply abandon his country seat, servants and all, and flee headlong. Men like him, in Marbeck's experience, usually stood upon their rank and status, demanding explanations for the intrusion. But then, this man's crimes were dark . . . dark enough, perhaps, to suspect he might struggle to find support anywhere.

After a while he dismounted, let Cobb's reins trail and walked towards what appeared to be the stables. Other soldiers were moving about, opening doors. The stables were closed and bolted, but Marbeck opened the door and was greeted by the snicker of horses. Finding a lantern, he struck a flame and lit it . . . and found two nags in their stalls, seemingly hungry and glad to see him.

There was a footfall behind; he turned to see the ensign looking in. 'We've found something of interest,' he said.

Marbeck stiffened. 'You've found John Buck?'

'No, but we've found his wife. Will you come and see?'

'I will,' Marbeck said at once . . . then he caught the man's expression, and stiffened.

'That's right,' the ensign said. 'She's dead.'

TWENTY

Sarah Buck had been strangled, her body clumsily concealed in a wash-house. And by the time morning broke, the extent of the disorder at Sir Edward Quiney's manor was clear. The knight had fled, taking his family and favoured servants with him, and left the rest to their fate.

Those that remained, afraid to come out when Niles's troop arrived, were found hiding in various places and brought out to the courtyard. They were mainly older servants, those with nowhere to go: a dozen at most, frightened and distraught. Having searched the entire manor, Niles was satisfied they were all that was left of Quiney's household; Marbeck, however, was not.

It was only instinct on his part, yet the feeling was strong. With the rest of Niles's force, he stood in the walled yard as the sun rose above the Downs, surveying the unhappy group. There was no danger; nor, it transpired, had there been all along. The soldiers were bitter, their captain subdued. Marbeck knew the man's frustration matched his own; and at the first opportunity he drew near to him and spoke.

'I believe Buck's still here.'

Impatiently, Niles faced him. 'We've scoured every corner. The only hiding place could be a priest's hole. The manor's old, so I suppose it's possible.'

'Do I have your leave to poke about?'

'If you must. I'm taking my men out soon . . .' The captain sighed. 'There's nothing I can do here. We've looked for contraband, but there isn't any. Then, Quiney would never be foolish enough to hide it under his own roof.'

'What will happen to these people?'

'The servants?' Niles gave a shrug. 'They've done nothing wrong that I know of . . . they'll have to fadge for themselves.'

Marbeck looked them over: a cowed and humble assembly. When asked about John Buck, they had claimed he was gone;

as for Sarah Buck, none knew anything of her death. The Bucks were not members of the household, they said, and were not welcome when they'd arrived two days ago. The master had refused to see Buck, for some reason. Most of this information was obtained from Quiney's cook, a wizened man too old to run anywhere, and willing enough to talk about his master now that he'd fled.

Sarah Buck's body, swathed in linen, was now tied to a horse and would be conveyed to Weymouth where, it seemed, she had relatives. Niles was about to mount his horse, but at sight of Marbeck's face he frowned slightly. 'I cannot delay,' he said. 'Nor can I spare men for any further searching, which will likely prove fruitless.'

'If I find Buck hiding . . .' Marbeck began – but Niles placed his foot in the stirrup and heaved himself into the saddle.

'I didn't hear you,' he said.

A moment passed; their eyes met, and finally the captain leaned down and stuck out his bandaged hand. 'I'll say farewell to you here and now . . . Master Janes,' he said quietly. 'Don't grip me too hard.'

Marbeck hesitated, then took his hand. 'You have my thanks.'

'And you have mine, for what they're worth,' the captain replied. They loosed hands, and he straightened up. Then looking ahead, he shook the reins and led his company out through the gate. Marbeck watched them go, then glanced at the servants, who were already melting away.

Drawing a breath, he walked to the centre of the courtyard and stood still. He scanned the house and outbuildings; if there were a priest's hiding-hole, it could be almost anywhere. But Niles and his men had searched the house thoroughly . . . Then his gaze fell on the wash-house at the corner of the yard, where Sarah Buck's body had been found. On impulse, he walked towards it. It was low and solidly built, with a postern gate nearby leading to the gardens where the washer-woman would spread out her linen.

The door was ajar, so he entered the building and stood motionless. There was no sound save for a distant murmur of voices from the house, and birds cheeping on the roof. He looked round, at a huge buck-tub raised on bricks, and a few empty wash-baskets stacked beside the fireplace. The fireplace itself was large, though no fire had been lit in it for some time. He peered into it and around it, but saw only a solid chimney-breast. Finally he drew his poniard and knocked on the brickwork, satisfying himself there was no hollow space behind. He even put his ear to it, but heard nothing. Then he stood back, his eyes sweeping walls and ceiling. They were whitewashed, with a small window giving a meagre light. The roof-space was bare, with nothing between beams and thatch. He had seen hiding-holes in many places, a relic of the days, still recent, when priests travelled the land giving mass in the homes of Papist families, in constant fear of arrest. But a wash-house was an unusual location . . . In frustration he pushed the column of baskets aside – and froze.

It was nothing much: just a patch of wall by the corner that looked slightly different to the rest. He stared at it, stepped forward and kicked it – and his pulse leaped. Immediately he reached for his sword, but being unfamiliar, the army weapon caught in the scabbard. He barely had time to get it clear before a wooden panel crashed outwards. A figure loomed up – and at last, he was face to face with John Buck.

'You?' Buck's expression was one of amazement. 'By the Christ . . .'

'Drop to your knees,' Marbeck said, raising his sword.

But the other stared, and slowly shook his head. 'I won't.'

'You will – or we'll finish it here.'

A moment passed, then Buck gave a sigh. 'Aye . . . mayhap we'd better.'

'As you wish,' Marbeck replied. His sword-point was levelled at Buck's chest, which was half-exposed: the man wore only a loose shirt and breeches. His face was dirty, and dust fell from his clothing as, with an unhurried movement, he stepped forward until Marbeck's blade was touching him.

'Well now – can't you do it?' he breathed.

'Believe me, I can,' Marbeck told him. 'But first, I want you to know you'll die because of Mary Kellett, and the other women and girls you wronged. She's safe, by the way . . .'

'I care nothing about that,' Buck growled.

'Nor for your wife either, I see.'

The other's mouth tightened. 'That's none of your affair.'

'But I mean to make you remorseful,' Marbeck replied. 'For I don't propose to make it a quick death.'

Buck was glowering now. 'I should have finished you a while back. But no matter: yours won't be a quick death, either.'

Outside, the courtyard was silent; even the birds on the roof had grown quiet. His eyes fixed on Buck's, Marbeck readied himself for any movement. 'I almost forgot,' he added. 'It's for Woollard too . . . he was a friend.'

But at that Buck smiled broadly: the man was drawing Marbeck, trying to make him angry. In his anger he could act hastily, and Buck would be ready. As when he had first seen him, the man had no weapon but his large, calloused hands.

'I think we're done,' Marbeck said finally. 'If you won't kneel . . .' But he was cut off – for at once Buck's hand shot up, to grip the blade of his sword. Grinning savagely, he squeezed it, forcing it aside; blood ran through his fingers, but he gave no sound of pain. Marbeck felt the blade slice through the man's palm . . . and knew that his life lay in the balance.

Still smiling, and believing that since Marbeck wore no poniard, he was at his mercy, Buck raised his other hand and put it to Marbeck's throat. It would remain there until he had squeezed the life out of him; there was a split second to act, yet Marbeck felt calm: calm, and a quiet rage. His hand flew to his pocket, the tailor's bodkin appeared, and was jabbed hard into Buck's wrist.

The man hissed with pain, yet still held on to Marbeck's sword. His hand dripped blood . . . but his grip weakened slightly: it was barely noticeable, but it was enough. With all his strength Marbeck yanked his sword from the man's fist, wrenched himself away and dropped into a fencer's crouch.

And now at last, Buck saw his looming death.

Their eyes locked, and Marbeck had enough time to register the man's fear before dealing the fatal blow. It was a *stoccata*: a straight lunge to the heart. The rapier entered between the ribs, causing blood to well out. Yet he continued to drive forward using his body weight, while Buck went rigid, both hands now clasping Marbeck's sword. This time, however, it didn't work: the blade cleaved muscle and tissue, then stopped as it struck bone: the back of Buck's ribcage. Breathing hard, he let go of the hilt and stepped back.

For what seemed a long moment, Buck remained upright with the sword protruding from his chest. He kept hold of it, as if trying desperately to pull it free, but his strength was failing; suddenly he let go, and with a gasp slumped to the floor. He looked down, watching his life's blood run into the floor of packed earth. Finally he raised his eyes and looked at Marbeck, but made no sound. A sickly pall spread slowly over his face, and his eyelids drooped; then he toppled to one side and lay still.

Marbeck stood for a while, feeling the clamminess of cold sweat on his body. Then he turned about, pushed the door wide and stepped out into the courtyard. It was bathed in sunlight, and some distance away the servants stood watching. Marbeck barely gave them a second glance. Instead he crossed to the stables, where Cobb was still saddled. Then he got himself mounted, and without looking back rode out of the yard, through the gatehouse and on to the road.

Within the hour he had skirted the southern edge of the Downs, and reached the Roman road at Upwey. There at last he turned northwards to Dorchester, and began his long journey back to London.

TWENTY-ONE

I t took him four days to reach the city, for he was in no hurry. Later, he would barely remember what towns he had stayed in en route: Shaftesbury, Andover once again, while on the third night, with his purse empty, he had bedded down in a barn near Wokingham. At last, on a cloudy afternoon, he rode through Ludgate and by St Paul's into Knightrider Street; London crowded and stinking, the air heavy with the promise of a thunderstorm. Leading Cobb by Candlewick Street, East Cheap and Tower Street he made his way to Hart Lane where, having nowhere else to go just now, he found the house of Meriel Walden's sister. To his relief, Meriel was at home; but at sight of Marbeck standing in the cloud-dark street, she tensed in alarm.

'Your pardon,' he said. 'I came seeking a place to sleep . . . if the house is full, I'll move on.'

She stared at him: at his dirty, bloodstained clothes, his unkempt hair and stubble of new beard, and at his ear where stitches showed through pale scars. Beside him Cobb stood with head drooping, horse and rider alike the image of exhaustion. Finally she said: 'You may have my bed. I'll share my sister's chamber . . . her husband's away.'

He murmured his gratitude, and said he would find a stable for the horse. But before he could go she stayed him. 'They came here, looking for you.'

Blearily he met her gaze. 'Who did?'

'I didn't know the first one: a dandyish fellow, red-faced. A fortnight back, perhaps . . . he was agitated, eager to know where you'd gone. But of course, I could tell him nothing.'

Oxenham . . . Marbeck let out a sigh. 'You said "they"?'

'The other was here a week ago, the same man who came for you when you were fevered, at the Three Cups: a dry stick, and bad-tempered. He wouldn't believe I didn't know anything. He even threatened me. He said if you ever turned up I was to send word to him at once. He gave me a location . . . a letter-drop, I suppose.'

'Your pardon again,' Marbeck said. 'I'll go to him and explain.' He sagged, lowering his eyes. 'I'd best go now . . .'

'That's madness,' Meriel broke in. 'You look like a beggar. You need food and rest – and clean clothes.'

'That's what he said,' Marbeck replied vaguely. Before him swam a picture of Levinus Monk standing by his bedside, telling him to rouse himself . . . how long ago was it? He raised his eyes and saw a look of grave concern on Meriel's face. But it disappeared, to be replaced by a wry expression.

'See to your horse – he needs rest even more than you do.'

With a nod, he led Cobb away. As he turned out of Hart Lane there was a bright flash, followed by a deafening clap of thunder; and within seconds the rain was falling in torrents.

In the night, having slept exhaustedly for some hours, he awoke from troubled dreams. As so often, he forgot where he was; then as the room began to take shape he remembered. A rush light burned, illuminating Meriel's tiny chamber: a press, pegs for clothes, and the bed, narrow and unyielding; he slept better on hard surfaces. The rain had stopped, though water still dripped from the thatch. After a while he sat up, leaned back against the wall and allowed himself to think. For there was little doubt in his mind; he had known it for days, perhaps weeks: his days as a Crown intelligencer were probably over. He might even find himself arrested; Monk had made it clear that he had little patience with a man like him.

Lying in the semi-darkness, he found his mind drifting back to Dorset. Faces rose up: first Mary Kellett's, pinched and pale; then those of Oxenham, Woollard, Gideon and Henry Swann . . . and finally John Buck, slumping down before him, covered in blood. A bleak thought occurred to him: all at once the long gallery at his father's house in Lancashire sprang to his mind, with its portraits of long-dead ancestors. Now he could have his own collection: the faces of those he had killed or seen killed, ranged along a wall . . . He drew breath through his teeth, closing his eyes.

Then the door opened, and Meriel came in.

He looked round sharply, but she was facing away from him, closing the door. Then she turned about, and stood still. Neither of them spoke; he could hear her breathing rapidly in the small room. At last, he drew back the coverlet and sat up.

'Are you certain of this?'

'No . . . far from certain.' She looked down at him, then put a hand to her neck, to the laces of her night-gown. 'But I've waited long enough.'

And when he stood up, she came forward and put the other hand to his face.

The next morning, in borrowed clothes, Marbeck walked through puddled streets, all the way to Temple Stairs to look for Matthew Herle. Finding that the man was out doing business, he sat on the steps to wait. Just now, the thought of waiting all day didn't trouble him, even when the watermen who came and went started to cast disapproving looks his way, and then to ask him what he wanted. But when he responded with a cold smile, they grew wary and let him be. Finally, after perhaps an hour had passed, he saw the square-shouldered Herle bringing his boat smartly towards the stairs. He had two passengers; he saw Marbeck, but gave no sign of recognition. The moment the couple had come ashore, however, he gestured to the skiff. In silence, Marbeck stepped into it and sat down.

'I'll take you eastwards, straight away,' the boatman said, as soon as they were on the water. 'Those were Monk's orders, if I saw you again.'

'Where is he?' Marbeck asked. 'Not Castle Lane?'

'No – we're going to the Tower.'

After that nothing was said, though Marbeck's mind became busy. For a moment he entertained the absurd notion that as the son of a knight he was about to be imprisoned in the most prestigious gaol in England, reserved for the highest. Then he wondered if Levinus Monk had been promoted to some higher office, or whether the man was in chamber with Lord Cecil himself . . . whereupon he suddenly remembered the treaty talks, at Somerset House. It was a matter of consternation to think he could have forgotten them.

'The peace negotiations with the Spanish,' he ventured. 'Are they still in train?'

Bending hard to his oars, Herle glanced up. 'They are –
progressing well, I hear.'

It was a relief, more than Marbeck expected. He would have
asked more, but the waterman was looking darkly at him.

'I've no desire to talk,' he said.

So Marbeck turned away to stare at the rain-swollen Thames,
and at the boats that drifted by, or crossed the water before
and behind them. On the Southwark shore, some were drawn
up at the Paris Garden Stairs. He thought of John Miller,
bringing trulls across to Salisbury House. He even smiled at
the thought that with his master in residence, the man's sideline
had likely been spoiled. Then he looked ahead, until the bridge
loomed, and beyond it the forbidding bulk of the Tower of
London.

Herle dropped him at the stairs, then pushed his skiff away
without a word. On Tower Wharf he was challenged by a
guard in royal livery, but when he mentioned Levinus Monk's
name he was admitted through the postern. Skirting the inner
courtyard, he was directed past the Mint, his gloom deepening
with every step. Officials walked by and servants hurried about,
there was bustle but there was order. Finally he found himself
at a door, and entered a lantern-lit chamber . . . only to stop
short.

It wasn't Monk who stood facing him: it was Solomon Tye.

Stunned, Marbeck looked him up and down . . . and as on
the last occasion they had met, his hand wandered towards his
sword-hilt.

'You won't need that,' Tye said. 'I'm not your enemy.'

Marbeck said nothing.

'And I ask pardon for attacking you that day, at the Black
Horse. I had to convince – as I had to kick you, when we
were interrupted.'

Slowly, very slowly, Marbeck started to relax; as if from a
fog the truth began to emerge, leaving him drained even of
anger. When the other man pointed to a bench, he sat down
without a word. A cup appeared, and was offered to him.

'It's just ale,' Tye said. 'Wine won't do . . . you'll need a
clear head.'

So Marbeck took it and drank. Finally, since something
needed to be said, he asked where Levinus Monk was.

'He's called elsewhere. And before you ask, he knew nothing of my mission until recently. Or he wouldn't have told you to watch me, when you both saw me at the Fortune.'

'Jewkes . . .' Marbeck began, but the other shook his head. 'In good time. First, will you give me your intelligence? I already have a report you sent from Portland. It arrived by courier two days ago.'

'*You* have it?' Marbeck was finding his voice. 'And I thought you were a turncoat, paid to wreck the treaty talks.'

'That's how it had to look,' Tye said briskly. 'But as you know, no real harm was done. Now, tell me your tale.'

'No real harm?' Marbeck echoed. Then he checked himself: first, information. He took another pull of the ale, which was watered but good. He faced Tye, who was now seated too, and began.

It took some time, for he was still in no hurry. Leaving nothing out, he gave an account of events from his leaving Salisbury House to his return to London. Tye, alert and somewhat impatient, stopped him at times and asked for clarification. But by the end of the story his manner had changed to one of satisfaction, almost of jubilation. Having told all he could, Marbeck eyed him coldly.

'You've been working for Cecil, all along,' he said.

Tye gave a shrug. 'You know how things are.'

'Indeed I do . . .' Marbeck raised his cup and drained it in one. 'Yet His Lordship seldom fails to trip me. I've been the mark, have I? Were you the setter?'

Tye gave a half-smile; the tricks of gaming-house gangs were familiar to both of them. 'I was merely the verser,' he replied. 'Cecil set up the game.'

'Of course he did.' Marbeck's anger rose, but he managed to subdue it; when all was said and done, this man wasn't the cause of his ills. And suddenly, Tye was on his feet.

'The details you've uncovered are vital,' he said. 'We weren't sure where Quiney is, now we know he's at sea. No matter – he can wait. We've had him watched . . .'

'For how long?' Marbeck broke in, frowning.

'Since the spring, when Cecil began to suspect him.'

'Suspect him of what? Running contraband?'

'Oh no, nothing so trivial as that.' Tye's mouth flattened

into a thin line. 'And you may hear some of it now, Marbeck, for you and I might be about to work together . . . if you've no objection?'

It was becoming a lot to take in. Matching the other's expression, Marbeck said: 'I'd like a few answers first – if *you've* no objection?'

The other raised an eyebrow, inviting him to continue.

'Monk . . .' Marbeck spoke the name with some distaste. 'What's his position, or should I ask who has control, you or he?'

Tye hesitated. 'Let's say he's been eased aside for the present . . . given less challenging duties.'

'Whereas, you . . .'

'As you surmised, I take orders from my Lord Secretary.'

'To what end?'

'To the end of ensuring that nothing inhibits the success of the talks at Somerset House. Which, thanks partly to you, nothing will. They are now, in his lordship's words, "entered into the bowels of the treaty". They even have a name for it: the Treaty of London. It brings peace after eighteen years of war: a triumph for our King, and for the Privy Council . . .'

'The sabotage,' Marbeck broke in curtly. 'The false accusation against de Tassis, the shot at Somerset House, the needle device . . .'

'Mostly my work,' Tye replied. 'A balance had to be struck between making the attempts look real, and allowing the talks to proceed. Cecil's diplomacy saw to the rest . . .' A frown appeared. 'But the shot fired at the ambassador – that wasn't me. I wouldn't have missed.'

Marbeck blinked. 'Someone else was trying—'

'To stir things up – of course. And with what you've told me, we know who it was. A man who served a different master entirely . . . not because he wished to, but because he was given no choice. The same one who tried to kill you too – because he had no choice.'

Thomas Oxenham. Marbeck lowered his gaze and sighed.

Tye shrugged. 'Who else could have missed the ambassador at that range, and hit a servant instead? The poor fool was never meant for this sort of work – and it was bad judgement on Monk's part to take the man into his service as soon as he appeared. As you may imagine, Lord Cecil is displeased.'

But Marbeck barely listened. In his mind's eye he saw Oxenham, blooded and dying on the table in Thomas Woollard's house in Melcombe, spilling his terrible tale with his last breath. The man had failed in one task, then followed Marbeck all the way to Dorset only to fail again. The *djinn*, as told to him by Fahz the three-fingered, had turned out to be one of promise only, with little substance.

'So . . . at the same time as you feigned to be attempting to wreck the talks, others were doing the same in earnest,' he said after a moment. 'Those of our enemies who wish the war to continue . . . Las Langostas – and allied to them, partners in savagery, are the Sea Locusts.'

But hearing his words, Tye grew uneasy. 'That's a matter beyond me. We must leave it to Cecil, and the Lord Admiral. Your business, and mine, lies closer to home.'

All at once, however, Marbeck was greedy for answers. 'What of Richard Gurran?' he said. 'The carpenter of the *Amity*?'

'Poisoned, after he'd done what he was paid to do,' Tye replied. 'I knew him of old . . . but it was too great a risk, leaving a witness. And he was an evil cove, like all the crew of that benighted vessel. Though like you, he must have had an iron constitution: he should have died at sea, not lived long enough to be taken ashore at his home port.'

In silence Marbeck took in the news, recalling the man's body being lifted on to the quay at Weymouth. Tye watched him, then said: 'You were right about most things. Cecil knows you too well . . . he knew you'd be unable to resist the trail, once it was laid out for you. As he made it uncomfortable enough at Salisbury House for you to be eager to leave.'

'After I'd got a good look at Simon Jewkes. And had my curiosity teased, as a cutpurse teases his victim.'

'Indeed . . .' Tye put on a smile. 'If it's any consolation I've a purse here for you, to cover expenses. Thirty crowns . . .'

'Blood money?'

Tye shrugged again, his smile fading. But despite all that had happened, Marbeck couldn't find it in himself to be angry with him. Had things gone another way, back in that dingy chamber at the Black Horse, he might have wounded or even killed the man. Then, so much seemed to have been left to chance in this whole affair, he was almost dumbstruck by it.

'My Lord Secretary has played a very dangerous game indeed,' he said finally.

'He believed he had to,' Tye said.

They were both silent for a while, until Marbeck asked again about Simon Jewkes. And this time, the other grew animated.

'Now we come to the nub of it. Those who watched Quiney's movements had a hard task, for the man never left his home county, hadn't done so in years. Hence we were at pains to find out who did the spadework in London . . . the one who dirtied his hands on Sir Edward's behalf. And the man flitted between here and Dorset so often, it had to be Jewkes – as you too surmised.'

'In which case,' Marbeck said with a frown, 'why didn't you simply pick him up and put him to the question? He would have named Quiney as his master.'

But when Tye hesitated again, a new thought sprang up. 'You mean – Quiney wasn't the driving force?'

Tye didn't answer – but already, his words had served to put the last fragment in place.

'The desire wasn't to spoil the treaty, but to delay it,' Marbeck said, piecing it together as he spoke. 'The scheme was hatched by someone who wanted war with Spain to continue, because the profits were too great. Someone at a high level, who still had vessels out at sea, and wanted to reap the rewards in secret while he could . . . and who asked Quiney to arrange it. Someone who knew the man, and what he would stoop to . . .'

He paused, both shocked and fascinated by the brazen act of betrayal. Tye was looking uncomfortable, but Marbeck was in no mood to mince words. 'I mean one who had to remain untouched,' he persisted, his temper rising. Suddenly, he found himself on his feet. 'Because this man sits on the very body that negotiates with the Spanish . . . a man like the Lord Admiral himself—'

'Enough!' Tye raised a hand sharply. 'I haven't said a name, and nor must you. It's a matter for our masters.'

Marbeck stared at him, his mind in a whirl. He had been used, been sent to within an inch of his life, merely to confirm Cecil's suspicions: that the real culprit was on the Privy Council itself . . . He looked away, struggling with his anger.

'I believe his lordship will speak to you, about such aspects of the matter,' Tye said after a moment. He spoke without rancour, as if he understood Marbeck's feelings. 'You can back away if you wish, for your part is done now – aside from one thing. I said you and I might work together, for I had a notion you might like to be part of what I intend to do – this very night.'

He waited, but Marbeck shook his head. 'I'm done with guessing.'

The other eyed him. 'Isn't it obvious? I mean to arrest Simon Jewkes.'

And when Marbeck merely stared, he added: 'I know where he is – in fact just now, I'm the only one who does. The poor man still thinks I work for him, and I have a desire to see his face when I tell him otherwise – don't you?'

TWENTY-TWO

It was on the Thames, of course, but not in London. Whether word of Quiney's flight from his manor at Abbotsbury had reached Simon Jewkes, or whether other intelligence had, the man was too clever not to know that a net was closing about him. According to Tye, he had taken the long ferry to Gravesend and was waiting for a ship to get him out of England. But since none were leaving for several days, there was time to act.

'And if I know the man,' Tye said, 'he'll be at the end of his tether, fearing the worst – which we're about to deliver.'

It was evening, many hours after their conversation in the private room in the Tower. The distance to Gravesend was twenty miles along the Dover road, but since midday they had already covered most of it. They rode hard: Marbeck on Cobb, Tye on a swift jennet. Jewkes would be watching all boats, he said, so their best weapon was surprise. Whether or not he had men with him Tye was uncertain, but he was confident the two of them could deal with him. Jewkes would admit no one but Tye; Marbeck would be his unwelcome guest.

The town was busy, then Gravesend always was. Ships rode at anchor in the broad estuary, while longboats plied between them and the shore. Close to the beach the round fortress rose, with the old church on the hill above. Lights showed and the inns were busy, as the two intelligencers walked their mounts through the streets to a row of cottages on the southern edge of the town. As they reined in, Marbeck turned to his companion.

'Is he still Master Goodenough, or is he Combes? That was his name in Dorchester, before his friends took me off for a walk.'

'I don't know,' Tye replied. 'But if he's at home, he'll admit me.'

They dismounted, stretching their limbs, and drank from their leather flasks. Then Tye pointed to a house, and without further word they walked towards it. Marbeck loosened his sword, but Tye put out a warning hand; people were looking curiously at them. A passer-by approached, sensed trouble and hurried past.

Tye went to the door and knocked, while Marbeck stood back. It opened and he stepped inside, only to emerge within seconds, his face taut. 'He's not there. Gone down to the harbour . . . he goes several times day, his landlord says.' He muttered an oath. 'If we both go, he'll recognize you.'

'But he thinks I'm dead,' Marbeck said. 'At least, I hope he does.'

'True . . .' Tye considered. 'Perhaps we can use that?'

Taking up the reins, they led the horses away. Twilight was drawing in as they made their way back through the town and down to the waterside. They found a drinking trough and watered the mounts, while scanning the shore carefully. Boats were tied up, people of all ages about. A tilt-boat from London was moored for the night, her stern-lantern burning. For Marbeck, weeks flew back to when he had searched Dorchester's guildhall, before finding his quarry standing in the street . . .

'By God, I see him,' he breathed.

Tye stiffened, following his gaze, then showed his relief. Together they observed the man, familiar to both: round-shouldered, his slim form padded out with an expensive-looking doublet, a cloak over one shoulder. He was standing apart from passers-by – and he was alone.

'Can it be this easy?' Marbeck murmured.

'Why should it not?' Tye said. 'He's all but unknown here. He may be fretting, but for the present he thinks he's safe. I'll go down – follow when you see me place an arm about him.'

Marbeck watched Tye walk off, sauntering as if taking the evening air. He moved leisurely between booths and barrows, making for the shoreline. Here and there seamen and boatmen stood, talking and smoking. Finally he came up swiftly behind the figure of Simon Jewkes, and stopped as if greeting a friend. Marbeck couldn't hear what was said, but he saw the man jerk round as if struck. He waited until Tye drew the man away – then his arm came up to rest on Jewkes's shoulder; where-upon at once Marbeck left the horses and strode forward.

He reached the shore, where dogs ran about. Tye and Jewkes were moving off together, towards the jetty where the London tilt-boat was moored. Soon they were stepping on to the boards – and Marbeck understood. With a sense of triumph, he gained the jetty and hurried along it. Hearing his approach, Jewkes span round . . . and gaped.

'Did I mention that I'd brought a companion?' Tye said.

Jewkes went rigid, his hands working nervously. He glanced round, looked into Tye's face . . . and gulped. And he realized something else: that Tye and Marbeck were blocking his exit from the jetty.

'I . . . I cannot swim!'

For a moment Marbeck though Tye would laugh aloud; then he thought he would instead. But with an effort, hand on sword, he threw his fellow-intelligencer a glance and said: 'That could be unfortunate, could it not?'

'Indeed so . . .' Tye's grip on the man's shoulder tightened. 'I wouldn't want you to slip and fall off,' he said quietly. 'That's what used to happen to some of your victims on the London quays, as I recall.'

'I recall that too,' Marbeck said. 'As I recall being marched out of Dorchester into a wood, to be slaughtered and buried . . . only as you see, matters took a different turn.'

Jewkes was breathing fast. For a moment he looked as if he might call out, or even make a run for it. But when Tye put his free hand to his belt, he flinched.

'That's right,' Tye said, patting the hilt of his poniard. 'I should follow orders and take you to London for questioning – but if I have to, I'll finish you here.'

'Or I might,' Marbeck put in. 'I'm thinking of that bump on the head I got at the Black Horse, not to mention having a caliver levelled at me in a wood by the Frome . . .'

'What do you want?'

Jewkes snapped the words out, his face twitching. His eyes roved the town and its harbour, but no help was near. His tongue emerged to wet his lips, as Marbeck remembered in the stable at Dorchester.

'See now, whatever you are – Admiralty men, Crown officers – it matters not,' Jewkes said quickly. 'Your wage is nothing: I can pay you tenfold – a hundredfold. You can take ship together, leave England. I know people who'll heap riches upon you, beyond the stuff of dreams! You can live in a grand house, in perpetual summer – keep servants, women . . .'

But he broke off, his eyes filled with alarm. Marbeck was staring hard at him . . . and unbidden, his hand went to his pocket to reappear with something small, which he jabbed sharply into the man's side. Jewkes gasped, and shuddered from head to foot.

'Do you mean a harem?' Marbeck said softly.

The man blinked, but was silent.

'Was that what Quiney promised you, for loyal service? The chance to live like a lord, keep slaves and deal in stolen booty? Rub shoulders with the pashas of Algiers and Tunis? Have the pick of fair women . . . as young as you like?'

Marbeck had moved forward, bringing his face close to Jewkes. He smelled musk perfume . . . and he smelled fear. The man was trembling, at which both Marbeck and Tye shared a moment of satisfaction. And something else passed between them too: something dark and unspoken.

'I don't think I can bear the thought,' Tye said at last. 'Having to spend the night guarding this toad, then the long ride back to London, hearing him whimper and wheedle . . . can you?'

'I'm not sure I can,' Marbeck answered. 'A tedious notion . . .' He raised his eyebrows. 'But then, what's to be done?'

'It's a conundrum, isn't it?' Tye said, still holding on to Jewkes's shoulder. The eyes of the two intelligencers met, letting the thought hang in the air. Dusk was falling, and people had drifted away from the waterside. Far across the river, the lights of Tilbury glowed faintly.

'This town was burned once, did you know that?' Tye remarked casually. 'Centuries back, in the time of the French wars.' Then he signalled with his eyes: whoever had the right, he seemed to say, he would assume the task.

Gently, Marbeck lowered his bodkin and stowed it in his pocket. He looked away, heard the scrape of iron on leather as Tye drew out his poniard, the heavy thud as its hilt fell with some force upon Simon Jewkes's head. There was a faint moan, a rustle of fine silk, and then a loud splash as the man toppled from the end of the jetty into deep water.

From thirty yards away, a pair of boatmen glanced in their direction, pipes in mouths. But seeing only two men on the jetty, seemingly taking the air, they turned away and resumed their conversation.

EPILOGUE

On a warm day in August, Marbeck emerged from a stone-flagged tiring room into bright sunlight, naked but for a scanty loincloth, and stepped to the edge of the King's bath. The pool, the largest and finest one, reserved for those of noble birth, was almost empty this afternoon. But in any case, there could be no mistaking the man he had come a long way to see. His poor crooked frame, pale as bleached linen, was immersed in the soothing mineral waters up to his neck. He sat motionless in one of the stone alcoves, legs stretched out, apparently oblivious to his surroundings. But Marbeck knew better. Unhurriedly, he walked to the corner steps and descended into the blue-green water to his waist. Wading slowly, sending ripples across the pool, he approached the other man and eased himself down beside him.

'I first came here as a boy,' Lord Cecil said, without turning his head. 'My late father had great faith in the curative power of the baths. But the vapour gave me a severe headache. Now I've learned to time my immersions better.'

Marbeck inclined his head and waited.

'I hear you've been at Dover . . . a pleasant sojourn?'

'It was quiet, my lord,' Marbeck answered. 'I took a little time to rest, and to ponder my future.'

Cecil made no answer, merely shifted his position. Carefully Marbeck refrained from looking at his hunched body, his pigeon legs. Other nobles took the waters often, here in the town of Bath; even Queen Elizabeth had tried them. But it surprised him that Cecil, ever conscious of his deformity, had called him to this place. None but the man's wife and closest body-servant, it was assumed, had ever seen him unclothed. Perhaps that accounted for the absence of other bathers: glancing round, Marbeck saw only a handful of other men, and from the way they regarded him he guessed all were employed by the Lord Secretary.

'You'll have heard that the negotiations are over and done,'

Cecil said suddenly. 'The Constable of Castile has put his seal on behalf of King Philip, and we are now at peace with Spain.'

'It's a matter for rejoicing,' Marbeck said.

'Quite so,' Cecil agreed. 'Given the lengths some people went to, to spoil it.'

At last he turned to face Marbeck, who received something of a shock: the strain in the man's face was alarming. Cecil was forty-one years old, but had the careworn looks of a man ten years older. 'I've seen the reports . . . in fact I've only had time to read them all in the past week,' he went on, holding Marbeck's gaze. 'Much has turned out as I hoped . . . while some things have turned out otherwise.'

'You mean Thomas Oxenham, my lord?' Marbeck drew a breath. 'I fear the memory will live with me always. That's the chief reason I went to Dover, to keep my promise to seek out his father. The old man wept, but in the end he was calm. I was at pains to embroider his son's death, paint him a hero . . . which he was in a way, if a reluctant one.'

'One who faced rejection from my service, and went on a desperate mission to redeem himself,' the Lord Secretary said drily. 'But you are right: in the end, he laid bare the extent of the threat that stretches across Europe. I've passed the intelligence he gave you to the Count de Tassis, who will report it to his king. Those Spanish locusts may find themselves facing retribution from many quarters.'

Marbeck was silent. The acts of Las Langostas, including their bold plan to send Oxenham to assassinate the Spanish ambassador, still had the power to surprise him. But the fact that El Roble, as he now chose to call himself, harboured sufficient grudge against Marbeck to want him killed too, was less of a surprise now. Emboldened by the frankness his master was showing towards him, he spoke of it.

'The former spymaster, Juan Roble,' he said. 'With regard to me, it's a personal matter . . . I believe its cause lies in what I did to his mistress, the Comtesse de Paiva, four years ago.'

'Nothing to do with breaking his circle of intelligencers, then?' Cecil raised an eyebrow. 'The ones who went by the names of fruits, as I remember?'

'That too, my lord,' Marbeck replied. 'A man like that could not forgive such a slight. But I laid hands on his mistress, which he can never forget. Nor will he, I expect.'

Neither spoke for a while. The tepid water lapped Marbeck's chest, its heady vapour filling his nostrils. He stifled a sneeze, but at the other's next words, turned quickly.

'The girl you sent to Cranborne . . . Mary something? She is hard-working and well liked, my steward says. They've given her a place in the kitchens. She may even serve as a lady's maid, in time.'

'I'm sure she's grateful, my lord,' Marbeck said. 'She's courageous. It's partly through her that I found out what I did. She was cruelly used in Weymouth . . .'

'Yes, yes,' Cecil broke in. 'I've read the reports.' He was frowning; Marbeck waited, then heard him say: 'The death of the man you knew as Woollard was unfortunate.'

'Unfortunate?' Quickly Marbeck looked away; where the Lord Secretary was concerned, showing one's feelings was pointless.

'Indeed . . . He was once a loyal and useful servant of the Crown. He served my father, as he served Walsingham, but the poor man lost his mind, you know.'

Marbeck breathed in and held his peace – whereupon abruptly, Cecil changed the subject. 'I thought you might be interested to hear of a plan of my own,' he said. 'One being hatched as we speak. In short, Marbeck, I've offered the Sea Locusts a full pardon.'

Marbeck froze, his face blank.

'More particularly, the pardon is offered to Sir Edward Quiney,' Cecil went on, regarding him without expression. 'The man could of course sail to Barbary or wherever he chose, and live the life of any despot – but his wife would loathe the notion. Do you know anything of the Lady Quiney?'

With an effort, Marbeck murmured that he did not.

'She's of a somewhat delicate constitution, as indeed is Sir Edward himself,' Cecil went on. 'Neither could bear to live in a hot clime – the south of England's quite warm enough for them. Moreover, Quiney hates the sea, and I imagine he's sick of it by now. A message will reach him soon, when one of our ships encounters his, that if he lands on the Dorset coast and turns King's evidence against his captains he may be spared. He'd merely have to serve a few weeks in the Tower, to allay hostile opinion.'

Marbeck eyed his master, then saw the glint in the other's eye. 'The Dorset coast?' he echoed.

'Where he will be received with due formality, as befits one of his rank and station . . . except for one thing.' At last, Cecil allowed himself a wry smile. 'The offer is made by the Court of Common Law. The coast between high- and low-water mark is subject to such law . . . hence, once Quiney steps ashore he is on English soil. However, we'll arrange matters so that our party isn't ready to receive him until high tide . . . Do you begin to follow?'

'I'm not sure that I do, my lord,' Marbeck said quietly; the man was playing him as he used to, like a fish on the line.

'Then let me enlighten you. You may not know of a curious anomaly in English law: that when the tide is in, the water comes under the jurisdiction of the High Court of Admiralty. Hence, my offer of a pardon can be overruled. In short Quiney will be arrested for piracy, by order of the Lord Admiral. It's a little scheme His Lordship and I have concocted between us.'

A moment passed; lying beside his spymaster in the water, Marbeck almost smiled at the ingenuity of it. 'You are modest, my lord,' he said at last. 'I venture to suggest that it's you who concocted the scheme, whereupon the Lord Admiral readily agreed to it.' And when Cecil offered no denial, he added: 'I also believe that the usual punishment for piracy – the gallows at Execution Dock – might be appropriate for the Sea Locusts, but not for Sir Edward. In which case . . .'

'Now you overreach yourself, Marbeck,' the other said. 'It's out of my hands . . . the Admiralty court will try him, and decide the best course.'

Marbeck lay back; he felt slightly giddy, as if a weight had been lifted from his shoulders. There was no denying now that the reign of the Sea Locusts was over. He saw it, let out a sigh, then sneezed.

'Have a care,' Cecil said. 'You aren't used to these waters. They play tricks with a man's senses – and his sensibilities too.'

'My thanks for your concern, my lord,' Marbeck replied.

Another moment passed – until Cecil caught him unawares. 'Is it true what Gifford has been saying?' he enquired suddenly. 'That you stole his paramour off him?'

With a start, Marbeck sat up. Some distance away, His Lordship's guards sat up too. But seeing the expression of unconcern on their master's face, they relaxed.

'I fear you may be the butt of one of Gifford's jests, my lord,' Marbeck replied stiffly. 'Mistress Walden is a friend to us both . . . but any liaison between herself and Gifford ended some time ago.'

'Well, I'm relieved to hear that,' Cecil said. 'As I was also relieved to hear that you have ceased to dally with Celia, the widow of Sir Richard Scroop.'

Now, Marbeck was well and truly caught; what was about to follow, or how he was supposed to react, he had no idea. The truth was, he had thought little of Celia in recent times: once his secret paramour, she was now all but a recluse in her house at Chelsea. Even she had finally grown tired of his ways: his turning up unannounced, only to disappear again for weeks or months . . .

'I fear Lady Scroop wants more than I can give her, my lord,' he said finally. 'A new husband perhaps, before she grows too old . . .'

'It's understandable,' the Lord Secretary said smoothly. Then having startled Marbeck as he intended to, he turned deliberately to face him.

'Tye told me how you voiced suspicions that Sir Edward Quiney didn't act alone, but at the private request of a member of the King's own council. Someone who might have profited, had the treaty been postponed.'

Marbeck blinked; suddenly, the water seemed somewhat chilly.

'You'll know that many benefited from outfitting vessels, and sending them to sea under the protection of letters of marque and reprisal,' the Lord Secretary continued, rather quickly. 'I did so myself, as did the Lord Admiral and others – a simple business venture. Though of course, as soon as His Majesty made it known that he would cancel such arrangements and sue for peace with Spain, we ceased the practice.'

He stopped then; and seeing he was expecting some reply, Marbeck spoke carefully. 'That's common knowledge, my lord.'

'Yet you suspected some may have flouted the law, and permitted their ships to continue waylaying Spanish vessels on the high seas.'

The change in his tone was startling. Having played the benign spymaster placating a loyal intelligencer, he was suddenly the ruthless statesman: the man who signed death warrants without a second thought. Marbeck, however, knew both sides of the man; keeping expression from his face, he waited. The silence continued until he could hardly bear it, then:

'As I thought: you won't lie to me,' Cecil said at last. 'There are few men of whom I can say that with any certainty. You lie in my service of course, as do others. Some loathe it, but do so because they must: like my steward at Salisbury House, whom you upset some months ago. Poor Langton's never forgotten it – I fear he'll never forgive you. Nor will my boatman, for ruining his arrangement with the trulls of Paris Garden. Regrettably I've had to let him go, and his son too.'

In silence, Marbeck looked away.

'You see, there's nothing I don't know,' the spymaster added. 'And if there is, I make certain that I learn of it sooner or later.'

Another silence followed, even longer. Then at last, mastering himself as best he could, Marbeck eyed him.

'My suspicions were as you describe them, my lord,' he said. 'Though I've kept them to myself, apart from that day in the Tower when I voiced them to Solomon Tye.'

'I'm relieved to hear that,' Cecil replied. 'It would be rash indeed to accuse a man of such high status of committing treason.'

'I know it,' Marbeck said.

'Good . . . but are you also aware that in assisting Tye despatch a man in cold blood as he did – against my orders, I might add – you are an accessory to murder?'

Marbeck swallowed; it could have been the heady vapour that was making his mouth dry, but he doubted it. In his mind's eye he saw the look on Tye's face, in the moment before he knocked Simon Jewkes on the head . . . and now all became clear. It was a considered act, with the intention not only of removing a man who could testify against one of high status, as Cecil had put it, but to implicate Marbeck in the deed too. Hence, Cecil had a cast-iron hold over him – and more, all traces of the Lord Admiral's indirect involvement in the affairs of the Sea Locusts could be suppressed. He turned to Cecil, but had no words.

'Perhaps you should return to London now,' the Lord Secretary suggested, after a moment. 'To Mistress Walden, I mean. And to whatever other tasks may come your way, in time.'

Whereupon the man put on a look Marbeck knew well – the same look he used to employ when ringing the little bell that stood on his desk. The audience was over. And as if by some design, a shadow appeared over the King's bath just then: a single cloud, blocking the sun.

Together they waited for it to pass. Marbeck kept his eyes on it: he had been summoned here for neither explanations nor thanks, but to receive a stark warning. When sunlight flooded down again he looked at Lord Cecil, but the man's eyes were closed, his face serene; the benign spymaster was back.

Without a word, Marbeck rose and waded towards the steps. He emerged dripping from the pool, and glanced round to see the Lord Secretary motionless, lying like a plucked chicken in the water.